3—

# UNRAVELED

# UNRAVELED

kate jarvik birch

Entangled Publishing, LLC
2614 South Timberline Road
Suite 105, PMB 159
Fort Collins, CO 80525

Entangled Teen is an imprint of Entangled Publishing, LLC.

Visit our website at www.entangledpublishing.com.

Edited by Heather Howland
Cover design by Kelley York and Heather Howland
Interior design by Heather Howland

ISBN  978-1-63375-913-8
Ebook ISBN  978-1-63375-914-5

Manufactured in the United States of America

First Edition April 2018

10  9  8  7  6  5  4  3  2  1

entangled teen
an imprint of Entangled Publishing LLC

*To all the freedom fighters.*
*You know who you are.*

# One

*I* owed Missy my freedom.

And tonight, I'd repay her.

I grabbed Penn's hand in the dark. Above us, a hint of the moon's glow crept over the fortresslike wall of the warehouse. It wasn't enough light to read the expression on his face, but if we ended up dead before morning came, at least I'd have the memory of his fingers twined through mine.

What a waste it would be to come so close to happiness. So close. But at least I could savor this moment: the press of his leg against me, the warmth of his hand in mine, the taste of his mouth still on my lips. I could draw courage from it. He'd always been a part of my strength. After all, it was his love that showed me we were equal…that this heart of mine was every bit as human as the one that beat in his chest.

"I have a bad feeling about this," Penn said, his voice a soft breeze near my ear. His grip on my hand tightened. "Why don't you let me go in with them? You wait out here. If something goes wrong, it'll be easier for you to get away."

No. I needed to get in there. The Liberationists had a good lead that the other pets who'd been ripped from their homes or dumped at kennels by their owners in the upheaval over the NuPet scandal were in danger of being killed. If the intel was to be believed, we'd find them hidden inside.

I trusted the Liberationists. Markus, Ian, Jane, Dave… all of them. Of course I did. After all, they were the ones who'd saved Penn and me when NuPet's men were closing in on us. Without them, I'd be just another girl in this warehouse in need of rescue, or worse. And Penn? I hated to think what his father would do to him for stealing me away again, for betraying his father the way he had, all to keep me safe. Even if it got him killed, Penn would come with me to the ends of the earth.

I'd love him for the rest of my life.

I took a deep breath, tucking that love into a safe corner of my heart so I could focus. "She's my friend." The last word stuck in my throat and I shifted away from him, readying myself to stand, to run, to fight. If Missy was inside, I was going to be the one to go in and get her. "I can't push this off onto someone else, not after what she did for me."

Penn nodded silently, his warm brown eyes telling me he understood. We'd already been through this debate. He knew my conditions. He knew my priorities. Number one: rescue Missy. I couldn't even begin to think about anything else until that happened. This was my fight, and Missy was my responsibility.

I couldn't turn my back on her now, not after she'd helped me escape from Canada. Not after she managed to hide us both in the black market so I could get all the way back to Penn. And certainly not after she sacrificed herself when NuPet's men came.

She was all I'd thought about for the past nine days. Missy was the closest thing I would ever have to a sister, and I'd allowed them to take her in my place. I'd let them mistake her for me. As we'd hunkered down in the Liberationists' headquarters after the raid, I played our last moments together over and over in my mind, her final words whispering past my ear in a perpetual loop.

"If anyone can fix this thing, it's you."

And maybe I had begun to believe her.

Markus must have, too. It was the reason he and the Liberationists had tracked me down. Why he'd rescued me from falling back into the hands of the congressman. And I was grateful to him for that, even if I wasn't sure how much of an asset I could be.

I shifted, anxiety prickling in my chest. The brick wall of the warehouse was cool and thick at my back, completely unwilling to share any of the secrets that lay behind it. If I could only look through it, like glass, and know whether I'd find Missy there.

In front of us, Markus crouched next to Ian, his second-in-command. Other than their coloring, they looked like they could be brothers: the same fit, compact bodies, the same almond-shaped eyes, and strong jaws. I didn't know their exact ages, but they couldn't have been more than ten years older than me.

Honestly, it still shocked me that there were male pets in the world—not that NuPet had created them, just that they had existed all this time without my knowing. There was so much NuPet had kept from us. Our ignorance gave them power.

Now, the secret was out. Pets like Markus and Ian craved the same freedom we did. That need boiled in them. I could see it simmering in Markus now, amping up his already intense demeanor like he might erupt from it at any second.

He turned around, and the group of us drew in a collective breath, waiting for his signal. We'd rehearsed the plan at least twenty times. The side door would be open. The informant had told us that much. Ian would hold the door, making sure we each made it inside.

Ian met my eye. The corners of his mouth curved up ever so slightly, and he nodded. It wasn't a large gesture, but it felt as reassuring as a hug, as calming as if he'd placed his solid hands on my shoulders and looked into my eyes, telling me that he believed in me.

Markus and Ian had kept Penn and me involved in their planning, treating us like we were one of them from the moment we'd arrived. Penn was a natural. He joked that all the time he'd spent watching crime dramas had been like years of free training, but it didn't come easily for me. For days my head had ached with the newness of it. How could there be so many words I didn't know? Intel, floaters, moles, informants, leaks, bona fides, covers... I felt like I was fresh out of the kennel again, when everything was unfamiliar and overwhelming.

They couldn't slow the pace to wait for me to catch up, so I did my best to take it all in. There were phone calls to intercept and whispered conversations to record in back rooms and alleys. They rolled out maps of the warehouse for us to familiarize ourselves with. But even though I knew I needed this information, I couldn't concentrate. I kept going back to what the reporter, Ms. Westly, had told us before the men from NuPet broke down the door and took Missy.

"They aren't going to recondition the pets. They're going to kill them."

*Kill them.* Those words echoed in my ears along with Missy's.

None of the girls had shown up at the kennel yet for NuPet's promised "reconditioning" program—Markus was 100 percent confident about that. He had eyes stationed inside and out of the NuPet facilities. But it wasn't until the tip came in the night after I arrived that he learned about NuPet's plans to dispose of the girls outside the kennel grounds.

The tip had been accompanied by a grainy cell phone photo of at least fifty girls huddled together in the middle of the warehouse—*this* warehouse—each shackled around the ankle to a long chain winding around their feet like a giant snake.

Fifty girls. It didn't seem like that many, not compared to how many there were still out there in other parts of the country, but to me it looked like a thousand. I had searched their faces for Missy's, but the photo was too grainy. Any of them could have been her. And in a way, they all were. Each blurry face ripped at my heart.

The warehouse was the perfect location. It sat in the middle of an old industrial complex on the edge of town, one of a dozen identical buildings. All of them were vacant now, free from prying eyes. Large cracks crisscrossed the blacktop surrounding the building, a map of jagged lines that had sprouted feathery grasses and lacy weeds, as wild as the fields and woods growing behind Penn's house in Connecticut. It was the kind of place that disappeared in plain sight. It was old, useless, a place you forgot about the moment you passed it.

On the other side of the parking lot, a few of NuPet's black SUVs were parked beside a group of trees that blocked their view from the road, and next to them sat a large white trailer. This was how they'd gotten the girls here, I was sure of it. They'd have packed them inside and unloaded them like packages at one of the warehouse's large dock doors.

Heat flared behind my eyes, and I blinked back the thought.

With the smallest wave of his hand, Markus brought the group of us to our feet.

It was time.

"Are you ready for this?" Penn whispered, giving my hand one final squeeze.

"Yes." I swallowed down the lump in my throat. "Let's get those girls."

Ian darted forward, twisting the rusted handle of the small back door. It creaked open and Markus gave a clear nod. Behind me, our head of intelligence, Jane, sighed in relief. Her intel was good—at least so far.

Jane was a regular citizen and one of the few women who'd volunteered for this mission. Even though Markus and Ian were pets, like me, I felt more of a connection to Jane. Her presence calmed me. There was a boldness in her personality that reminded me a little bit of Missy, and that endeared her to me from the moment we met.

As the person responsible for gathering intelligence, it would have been fine for her to stay at headquarters, but she wasn't the kind of person to sit back and watch other people do a job she could do herself.

It was something I related to.

Ian propped open the door with his body, and we slipped past him into the darkness. A blast of hot air, thick with dust and the musty smell of old paper, struck my face as I ducked in. It was obvious no one had been inside this space for a very long time. It was too dark to see very far into the room, but in the small amount of light the open door allowed, I could make out a stack of old, disintegrating brown boxes leaning against some cracked wooden pallets.

Markus stopped a few feet inside, and the rest of us drew to a halt behind him.

"Don't use your lights," he whispered. "The goggles are bulky, I know, but you'll get used to them soon enough."

I pulled on the goggles that dangled around my neck. We'd been able to try on a pair like them earlier, but the room we'd tested them in at the house hadn't been very dark, and I hadn't gotten a real idea of what it would be like to wear them.

Markus was right. I could see, but not in any way I

ever had before. More like the world had been washed in green. In front of me, the boxes I'd noticed when we first entered solidified. They weren't brown anymore; instead, they were an eerie emerald color.

"We'll split up in the hall," Markus said. "You know your routes."

The six of us nodded. The maps Markus had shown us had this room listed as an office, but from the looks of things, it had been used most recently as a dumping ground for trash. Past the door, I could already imagine the line the hallway made running along the back of the building. It led to what the map labeled "conference rooms and offices."

We picked our way through the debris littering the ground. Penn and I were supposed to go right, curving through an old lunch area that would lead out into the main chamber of the warehouse while the others looped around the other way. They would split up once more, so that by the time we all entered the warehouse, we would be spaced far enough apart that at least one of our groups would have a good path to where the girls were being held, no matter where they were in the room.

Markus and Ian stopped short in front of us, and I thudded into the back of Penn.

The group stood perfectly still. Silent. Was someone out in the hall? Had we been spotted?

My stomach clenched, but my feet stayed planted solidly on the ground. I wasn't stupid enough to run. I'd follow the protocol they'd set up, even if it got me killed. Nine days' worth of training wasn't much, but I was good at following instructions. Sixteen years learning to be an obedient pet for the rich and powerful had made me a perfect student.

"What's going on?" Dave asked, pressing close behind me.

Dave was the equipment man, responsible for the night-vision goggles we wore, the stun guns we had strapped at our sides, the bolt cutters and saws and masks that a few of them carried secured in bags on their backs. He knew about every kind of gadget, but he didn't exactly look like the kind of person you wanted to have next to you in a fight. He wasn't strong like the other men. His long, wiry limbs always seemed to confuse him, as if they were even longer than he remembered. It was hard to see what Jane saw in him, but it had been clear to me when I saw them together that they were an item, even if no one else had mentioned it.

"There's a little hiccup," Markus said, pointing over his shoulder.

The hallway behind him, the one we had all seen so clearly on the maps, looked totally different. It continued only about twelve more feet to the left before it ran into a wall. I couldn't tell what the wall was made out of, but it looked solid.

"When did this happen?" Jane asked. She folded her arms and glared at the wall. The annoyance in her voice was plain. She'd helped Markus formulate the rescue. The two of them had spent hours in front of the warehouse maps.

"Well, we can't go through it," Markus said. "That much is clear. It's thick. Cinder block probably."

I frowned, peering closer at the wall. "That brick

looks newer than everything else," I said. "Doesn't it?"

"Of course it does. It's not on the maps." Dave scoffed. "I've probably got something that can cut through it." He reached for his bag.

"Not without making way too much noise," Markus said. "There's no way we're making a hole in this thing."

"So we lose routes one and two?" Jane asked. "That makes this whole thing impossible."

Markus pursed his lips. "Not necessarily."

Jane gaped at him. "There's not another entrance besides the one at the front of the building," she said. "They've got it covered. You saw their guys."

"We're all going to have to use route three. We'll spread out once we get inside the warehouse floor." Markus sighed. "Look, it's not like the place is going to be entirely empty. There should be plenty of cover. We'll make it work."

"That's the dumbest thing I've ever heard," Jane hissed.

"So we just drop the plan?" Dave asked. "Come on, Jane." He snaked his arm past me and squeezed her arm above the elbow. I'd seen him touch her this way before, when no one else was looking. "Those girls are counting on us."

"I don't know. I think Jane's got a point," Penn said. "We shouldn't risk it."

Dave glared at Penn. "Stop being a wimp." He dropped Jane's arm and hitched his pack up on his back. "We've got this. If you can't roll with the punches, get out of here. You two are just slowing us down anyway."

Penn stiffened beside me.

"Please, Markus—" Jane started.

"No." He shook his head. "Come on, guys. It's just a little change in plans. We'll make it work. Who knows if we'll get another tip like this. We can't risk losing them."

His face locked in a look of resolution. Through my goggles, the green glow seemed to radiate from inside him, his determination shining as bright as a neon sign.

No one argued. Markus was our leader. We'd do what he asked, even if not everyone was happy about it.

Still grumbling, Jane turned, leading the group down the one remaining hallway toward the small lunchroom where Penn and I had planned to travel alone. We scuttled past old office chairs and filing cabinets, squeezing by an old desk that blocked most of the passageway.

Around the corner, the space opened up into the small cafeteria. A half dozen tables were pushed against the far wall next to an old refrigerator with its door flung open. Inside its gaping black mouth, the remnants of a few old bottles and jars smiled back like rotten teeth.

Markus paused in front of the swinging door that separated this room from the warehouse beyond. He raised his finger to his mouth and leaned closer.

Was that...sound coming through the door?

Silence engulfed us, but then more sounds seeped into the room, even clearer this time: the unmistakable low mumble of voices, humming, murmuring from inside the warehouse.

Penn grabbed my hand and gripped it tightly. I squeezed back, hoping he knew I understood. Hoping the press of my fingers could say everything my mouth couldn't. *The girls are here! Missy's here! And we're going to get her back!*

Markus gestured toward the door, and Dave crept forward to stand next to Jane. We were ready. In mere seconds, we'd fan out across the warehouse. The girls wouldn't be far away. From the picture we'd seen, the chain binding them was tethered to a large metal support beam in the center of the warehouse.

NuPet had two guards stationed near the front door and another one seated near the girls, but this late at night, we were hoping fatigue would slow their reflexes. There were enough of us to get the job done, but we'd have to hit our marks quickly. We couldn't afford to have any of the guards calling for backup.

Markus and Ian would have to travel the farthest. The hallway they were supposed to come out of originally had been only a dozen feet away from the entrance. Now, they'd have to sneak across the whole length of the warehouse to overpower the guards by the door.

Jane and Dave wouldn't have to travel much farther than we'd originally planned. From the lunchroom door, they'd have a pretty clear line to the single guard positioned by the girls. Penn and I would follow closely behind, ready to cut the chains and herd the girls back out the way we'd come.

Slowly, Markus cracked the door open. The sound of shuffling and murmuring grew louder, amplified by the cavernous space. The clank of chains echoed against the walls as we slid out into the open.

The room was gigantic. Even with the night-vision goggles, I couldn't see to the other side. The green glow from the lenses was only a haze in front of me, lighting a few stray items close enough to reach. But beyond that, the darkness swallowed everything whole.

And the sound… The mumble and shift and clank we'd heard before grew, filling my whole head. Was it bouncing off the cement? Because it sounded like it was coming at me from every direction.

A few feet inside the space, Markus froze, and a chill shot up my spine.

The others must have sensed it, too.

"Markus?" Jane whispered.

He reached for the flashlight on his belt, and in an instant, a beam of light sliced through the darkness, arching across the warehouse, tracing a yellow band over the walls. Across the room, the base of a steel beam came into view. Only the bottom five feet of it showed in the dark; the rest disappeared into the blackness above. But it was all we needed to see.

"No!" Jane gasped from behind me.

I ripped the goggles from my eyes. They must have been impairing my vision. I must have seen it wrong.

Markus swung the flashlight back in the other direction, and behind me, someone gasped. It couldn't be…

I stumbled back, unable to breathe. Unable to process the sight in front of me. Or rather, what *wasn't* in front of me.

The room was empty. There were no chains.

There were no girls.

"Goddamm it!" Markus shouted.

Penn grabbed my waist, pulling me close to him, as if his body could protect me from all the ways this mission had gone wrong. A wave of dread washed over me, and I yanked him back toward the doorway. Back toward safety. In a flurry, the others scattered, too. The flashlight fell from Markus's hand, clattering against the cement floor.

"Leaving so soon?"

From out of the dark, a cruel voice taunted us. It was deep and gravelly and completely unfamiliar.

Ian's eyes went wide. "Fall back!"

But it was too late. A large body blocked the door at our backs.

How had we let this happen? How had we stepped right into a trap?

"It would be rude to leave now," the voice said, "after all the trouble we've gone through to get you here."

The shuffling sounds that had greeted us since we entered the room switched off with a *click*. Without the noise, the silence overpowered everything, punctuated only by the uneven sound of our own feet and the ragged catch of our breath.

High above us, a light flickered on, illuminating a small patch of ground near the front of the room.

Two figures stood in the light cast from the ceiling. One large. One small.

"Missy!" Her name left my mouth like a blow to the gut.

"Ella?" she cried. "No!"

The look of pain and fear on her face was one I'd never seen before. The strong girl from a little more than a week ago was beaten down and bedraggled. What had they done to her? The black circles under her eyes made me wonder if she'd slept even an hour since she'd been taken. Her hair was a tangled mess, and a yellowing bruise streaked up the side of her cheek.

The man who towered over her, clasping her tightly around the arm, was a stranger to me. He was practically a giant, with arms like tree trunks and a neck as wide as Missy's waist. With the flick of his wrist, he could probably fling her across the room like one of Penn's little sister's dolls.

A small smile ticked at the corners of the man's mouth. He pulled Missy closer to his body, lifting the glinting edge of a knife to her throat, and his smile grew.

The grin of a madman.

## Two

*T* hurtled forward. "Let her go!"

Penn grabbed my waist, cinching his arms around me like a straitjacket, but I strained against him.

"Letting her go can be arranged," the man said with a dark laugh. "We're open to negotiations."

He turned toward the door and nodded once. A second later, a row of lights flicked on one by one, moving clockwise around the warehouse. My stomach sank. From their perch on a metal ledge circling the room, a dozen men, dressed in black, trained their weapons on us.

"No one's negotiating!" Markus shouted. The vein in his throat bulged, and he ripped his goggles from his neck, flinging them onto the ground in rage.

The men shifted their rifles, waiting for the cue to fire, but the man holding Missy only chuckled.

"Come now," he said. "Surely we can work something out. My boss is a reasonable man. You know Congressman Kimball?" He looked from Markus to me. "He's famous for striking deals."

I sagged in Penn's arms. How could he do this—take the fight out of me with just the mention of his name?

"Tell your boss to go to hell!" Ian yelled.

The smile slipped from the man's face.

He nodded ever so slightly, and the giant who'd been blocking our doorway stepped into the light. Without hesitating, he raised the butt of his rifle and slammed it down on Ian's head with a *crack*.

Ian slumped to the floor.

"I suggest you listen," the congressman's henchman said. "Our offer isn't going to last long."

He lifted the blade from Missy's throat and ran it lightly over her cheek.

"This is what you're going to do," he said. "First of all, you're going to give us that pet. In exchange, I'll be happy to return this one. When I start counting, your girl has thirty seconds to be in my arms. Got it?"

Penn twitched behind me. Every muscle in his body felt like it was coiling against my back, ready to grab me and carry me away. Anything to keep me safe.

Even from myself.

"The second time runs out, my men start shooting," the man said. "And believe me, each one is a sure shot. I don't know if you've noticed, but there are a dozen of them and only six of you." He eyed Markus. "And before you get cocky, thinking you've got backup outside, let me assure you, they've already been taken care of, so I'd recommend you follow my instructions closely."

My mouth dropped open. *Please tell me they haven't killed everyone.*

Markus didn't waver. "That's all?" he called. "You just want to trade the girls?"

Penn glared at Markus. "She's not yours to trade!"

"My mission, my rules," Markus shot back. "Now shut your mouth before you get us all killed."

The man grinned. "Seems fair enough, doesn't it?"

My gaze traveled back up to the guns surrounding us. They would shoot. There wasn't a doubt in my mind. All those fingers hovering over the triggers... It would take only the tiniest motion, a muscle twitch.

"I'll do it," I called.

Penn's fingers dug into my arms. "No. You won't."

"They'll shoot you," I said, panic tightening my throat. They would shoot, and he would fall, crumpled in front of me. And then they'd take me anyway, only Penn would be dead. And Markus. And Ian. And Jane. And Dave. I wouldn't let their blood be spilled at my feet for nothing. Not when all those Liberationists who'd been waiting outside, eager to help if we needed it, had likely already been killed. I couldn't have this on my conscience, too.

"Just let me go," I said.

"I'm done waiting," the man called. "Time starts now." His voice boomed through the room, and his countdown began. "Thirty. Twenty-nine. Twenty-eight..."

"Ella," Penn whispered. But it wasn't a question or a demand. It was just my name. No solution.

There wasn't time to hold him. There wasn't even time to look him in the eye. If I did, I would hesitate. If I did, time would buckle in on all of us, like an enormous fist, crushing each and every one of us.

"Twenty-seven, twenty-six…" The man's face hardened.

"Get out of here!" Missy yelled. "Don't you dare listen to him!"

"You're trying my patience," the man said. His blade tipped ever so slightly, moving from Missy's cheekbone down toward her mouth. She squeezed her eyes shut, a red line cresting on her pale skin.

Blood welled along the cut, and my own blood surged, burning like fire. I'd never felt panic like this. Or fear. Or loathing. The hot blood in my veins churned and whirled like a tornado. If I'd ever felt hatred before, even for the congressman, it was nothing compared to this. Fury whipped behind my eyes, pushing like a storm inside my ears.

"Don't lay a hand on her!" I screamed, words flying from my mouth like flames.

"Twenty-four…twenty-three…"

The henchman's voice slowed, dripping from his lips like molasses. Time swelled. It pooled like the blood on Missy's face, brimming. And a second later it all spilled forward. A red drop fell down her cheek like a single tear, and I charged, breaking free from Penn's grasp.

Behind me, Penn shouted my name.

In front of me, Missy's eyes opened, growing wide. I wondered if she could see it, too, my transformation into some sort of demon. For a split second, the smallest smile danced across her lips. It lasted only a moment, though, before the noise wiped it away.

I don't know which sound I heard first. They all mixed

together: the grunted command as the congressman's henchman stopped counting and ordered his men to shoot, the sound of guns and the click of metal. The sound of a canister hitting the ground. The rush of gas as it spewed into the air.

And then the screaming.

The men in black dropped their guns, howling, and raised their hands to their eyes. The gas filled the air, a white cloud billowing up toward the ceiling.

Someone plowed into the back of me as I took my first breath of it. I hit the ground, and the poisoned air rushed out of my lungs, but not before the burning stung my throat.

I clawed at my neck. The world pulsed. My eyes burned. The corners of my vision pricked with specks of black. A few yards in front of me, one of the men in black lay sprawled on the ground, bent and broken where he had landed. Had he jumped? Fallen? My brain couldn't fully form the question.

I arched my back. I needed air. Clean air.

I opened my mouth and something covered my head. A sheet maybe. Or a blanket. Or was it water? It seemed impossible, but that's what it felt like, as if my head had been dunked into the cool, clean water of Penn's pond.

I blinked, and suddenly Markus was there, pulling me to my feet. A gas mask covered his face. I lifted my hand to my eyes, and my fingers met the smooth plastic of my own mask.

Markus's mouth opened. *Run!* his lips were saying. *Run!* The mask muffled the sound, and his words sounded miles away, but my body understood.

Tripping over another body in black, I turned, letting Markus pull me back through the swinging door of the lunchroom. Without our night-vision goggles, the blackness was overpowering. My leg struck the sharp corner of a toppled table, but I scrambled forward.

*Wait—*

I tried to jerk out of Markus's grasp and failed. "Penn!"

Where was he? I couldn't remember where he'd been inside the warehouse after the shots went off. Behind me. He'd been behind me. So that meant he must be ahead of me now. I strained to see in the dark. Were there other people in front of me besides Markus? *Please, please let Penn be okay.*

The mask caught my breath and trapped it, funneling it so the winded sound of my wheezing rushed in my ears. Beyond that, other sounds rang out, too: the slap of my feet as I ran down the hallway, the crunch of old papers. The pop of fireworks from somewhere nearby. The churning of the ocean. The roar of a crowd cheering. Or crying. Or screaming. None of the sounds made sense.

Behind me, someone pushed me to move faster. Had it taken this long to work our way through the hallway when we'd arrived? The blackness was slowing us down, disorienting me, turning me around.

And then a door flew open in front of me, and I was shoved into the looming night.

Near the back door, two bodies lay sprawled on the ground where we had crouched less than thirty minutes earlier, waiting for Markus to give us the go-ahead. They lay facedown, but I recognized them right away, dressed in the same dark-gray jackets the rest of us wore.

My fingers fumbled for the edge of my mask, and I tore it off, tossing it at my feet. My stomach churned. I was going to be sick.

"Don't stand there, Ella! Come on."

I raised my head, confused to see Markus in front of me. He clutched his right arm, the sleeve sticky with blood.

"Penn?" I gasped.

"He'll be there," Markus said, grabbing me by the arm and pulling me away from the building. "I promise."

"No! We can't just leave him."

I reeled back, turning toward the building as Jane burst from the door. From behind her, another spray of bullets hit the doorframe.

She charged at us. "Go! Go! Go!"

She and Markus locked eyes for a moment, and he nodded once before he turned on his heel, pulling me with him away from the building. I dug my feet in, but he was too strong.

Behind us, a bomb went off. The explosion rose up through my stomach, pounding at the walls of my chest like a fist beating at a door. The sky flashed white with heat and flames.

*No.*

"Penn!" I screamed. "Missy!"

My legs collapsed, and I hit the ground hard, knocking the air from my lungs.

Markus hoisted me up against his side, dragging me onward. In front of us, only one of the half dozen rescue vans idled. Where was everyone?

"Help me get her," Markus said to Jane. He stared

back at the glow of the burning building. "We've got to get out of here fast."

"I'm sorry," Jane said. "I didn't know what else to do. It was an ambush. They could have killed us all."

Markus shook his head. "We don't have time to talk about this now." He jerked open the door to the van and poked his head in. "How bad is it?"

"Where is she?" Penn demanded from the back seat. "You said you'd get her!"

Penn! He was here. Safe.

I pushed past Markus, scrambling into the car.

"She's fine," he said. "I told you I had it covered."

Penn's face was smudged with dirt, his eyebrows crinkled in what might have been fear or pain. He dropped the towel he was pressing to the side of Dave's head, jumped over the seat, and desperately pulled me to his chest. His arms tightened around me as if now that he had me back, he'd never, ever let me go.

The car doors slammed, and still Penn held me. In the back seat, Jane whispered softly to Dave. The tires skidded on the pavement, and we swerved onto the road.

"Are you okay?" Penn finally asked, holding me at arm's length. His gaze traveled slowly over my face, studying it as if cataloging each small hair, each pore. He knew my face, knew it better than I knew it myself. And now he looked at me as if he were afraid a piece of me had been lost in the warehouse. And maybe a part of me had.

"We just left her there to die." I turned to Markus. "How could you let that happen?"

I could still see Missy's face, the way the knife sliced

into her skin. Maybe it was a good thing that bomb had gone off. If she survived the explosion, I hated to think what they might do to her.

"You think I had anything to do with that?" Markus said. "That had nothing to do with me. I just saved your life!"

"I didn't ask to be saved," I said. "You should have let me go with them."

He snorted, shaking his head.

"How many of us are left? Did anyone else get away?" Ian asked from the front seat. The back of his head was bloody where the rifle had struck him, but amazingly, he was alive. In fact—I looked around the van—the six of us who had gone inside the warehouse had all made it out. But the others…how many of them had died tonight?

Markus glanced back over his shoulder as if he expected to see another van following behind us in the dark. "I didn't get a complete head count of the dead," he said. "For now, we just have to assume this is it." He turned his attention back to Dave. "How is he?"

Jane glanced under the towel pressed against Dave's head. "I think he'll be okay. It doesn't look deep. I think the bullet just grazed him, but I hate to imagine…" Her face contorted. "I'm so sorry!" she said. "I'm so sorry! I almost got us all killed. If it hadn't been for—"

Markus shook his head. "Stop."

"But I can't," she went on. "I just *can't*. I checked that intel. I swear to God. If we hadn't packed that gas canister or those masks—"

"*Stop!*" Markus yelled.

She did, shocked into silence.

Markus took a deep breath. "I'm sorry," he said. "I'm not mad at you. You can't blame yourself like this. Got it? This was not your fault."

"But I—"

"No. I won't hear it from you, understand?" Markus said, his face turning eerily calm. "This wasn't something you did. We were set up. Someone ratted us out."

The skin on the back of my neck prickled. He was right. And I suspected whoever it was wouldn't be satisfied until we were all dead.

# Three

Half an hour later, Ian pulled the van into a nearly empty McDonald's parking lot. The lights were on inside, although the only movement came from a hanging cardboard sign wavering over the counter.

"Why are we stopping here?" Penn asked. "Please don't tell me you're hungry, because I can't stomach this place on a normal day, let alone now."

"We've got to get cleaned up," Ian said. "This place is as good as any."

"Believe me," Markus said, "you don't want these chemicals on your skin. We need to flush our eyes out. If you don't rinse off now, you're going to be in serious pain later."

The thought of clean, cold water made my mouth water. The skin around my eyes felt raw. Each blink brought tears, but instead of washing away the chemicals, they only made my eyes sting more. My lips and throat didn't feel much better. Even the little hairs on my arms stung, so the smallest movement hurt.

"Are you sure about this?" Dave groaned from the back seat. Thanks to Jane and her insistence that he stay still and let her keep pressure on his head, the bleeding had stopped, but his face was still smudged with blood. "You don't think we're going to look totally suspect, all of us coming in bleeding and raw?" he continued. "We don't exactly look like we're in the market for Egg McMuffins."

"What do these guys care?" Ian asked, waving toward the counter.

"What if they call the cops?" Dave asked. "In case you forgot, there was just a very large explosion at a warehouse not too far from here. I'm sure they'd be happy to have a bit of information on that."

"Where else do you suggest we go?" Markus asked.

"Uh…back home?" Dave said, rolling his eyes, as if this was the most obvious answer in the world.

Markus scoffed. "Home?"

"Fine, headquarters…whatever," Dave said.

"Are you an idiot?" Markus asked. "We can't go back. Not now. Somebody in our own circle just sold us out. You want to go back there?"

"But we can't let everyone back at headquarters think that we all just died! Half of us are still alive! They have the right to know."

"As far as I'm concerned, there are no others. Let them think we're dead," Markus said, climbing out of the car and slamming the door behind him.

The rest of us followed slowly, trailing into the

restaurant like a group of zombies.

"Go wash up in the bathrooms," Markus said once we were all gathered under the fluorescent lighting inside the front door. "I'll order a few drinks. We need to wash this stuff out of our systems."

We filed into the bathrooms, not even bothering to stop and look at the signs on the doors. I followed Penn into the room on the right, heading straight to one of the sinks.

"I don't know what the stuff in that canister was," Penn said, peeling off his jacket and draping it across a handrail, "but I'm glad we had it."

I pulled off my jacket, too. The thin white T-shirt I had on underneath clung to my sweaty skin. My skin burned. Even that layer of fabric hadn't protected me.

Penn turned on the water, and I bent over the sink, wishing I could crawl all the way under the stream. Penn watched me as I splashed my face.

"You got it worse than the rest of us," he said. "I think Markus must have been planning to detonate it the moment he saw that monster of my dad's, but I guess there wasn't really any way to let us know." He stepped closer, gently gathering the hair that fell in front of my eyes. "Does it hurt?"

I blinked under the water. I didn't want to tell him how bad it was, that my eyes felt like they'd been set on fire. I rested my head against the cool porcelain. "It stings, but the water is helping."

Penn cupped his hand under the spout, spilling handful after handful of water over the back of my neck. My skin pricked with pain, but the sensation gradually began to fade. He moved on to my arms, and I held still, letting him rinse every inch of bare skin, imagining the water was his fingertips. When he finished the sweet torture, I stood, wiping my face.

A trickle dripped down my spine. "Do you want me to help you now?"

Penn didn't answer. Didn't move.

"What?" I shifted uncomfortably under his unblinking gaze. "It really does feel better. I promise."

His gaze was unsettling, like he was trying to look inside of me. "Why did you do it? Again!"

He turned away from me, running his hands through his hair as he began to pace the tiled floor.

"It was just like before, when those men from NuPet came. You were just going to *leave* with them. Like you don't even matter. Like *we* don't even matter."

He spun around, and the look on his face made a chill creep over my wet skin. It was fragile and imploring, but there was anger in it, too.

I shivered. "You know I don't think that."

"Do I?"

"I thought you did. What else could I do?" I asked. "It's Missy. I owe her. I wish it was just about you and me, but it's not. It's about them, too—the other pets. I can't just forget about them." I sighed. "I *have* to make this right."

Penn's face softened. There he was, the boy I loved. "I know," he said. "I know that. Sometimes I just want to be selfish. I guess I wish you could forget them." He shook his head. "That's awful. I'm sorry."

"It's not awful." I wished I could be selfish, too.

Wished I could let everything but Penn disappear and live a normal life.

Would we ever have that?

He stepped closer to me, lifting his hand almost timidly to my face, as if he was afraid to hurt me. He paused, hovering above my cheek. Finally he lowered his fingers to my lips, softly brushing them over my skin. He held my gaze for a moment, his eyes imploring. They were asking something of me, but I didn't know what, and my not knowing was hurting him. I was sure of it.

He gave his head a little shake and lowered his eyes, stepping to the sink where he hastily splashed water over his arms and face as if he could wash all that neediness away.

*B*ack in the dining room, Ian and Markus sat at a table by the window, staring glumly out at the dark parking lot. Jane and Dave sank down into the booth across from them while Penn and I pulled up a couple of chairs.

"We've got to go back to headquarters," Jane said. "I'm freaking out. I have to know if anyone else is okay."

"No." Markus shook his head. "I said I don't want to hear this, so drop it, okay?"

"Dammit, Markus! I'm serious," Jane said. "I can't live with myself like this, not knowing how many of my friends I might have killed."

"*You* didn't kill anyone," he said.

Jane knotted her hands into fists on the tabletop. "I

might as well have," she choked out. "It was my information. It was my plan."

"It was *our* plan," Markus said. "We did this together."

She scowled. "Don't try to make me feel better. I should have confirmed my sources. Twice. Three times. I know who's responsible."

Markus banged his hand down on the table. "And I know it's not you!"

Behind the counter, the lone worker who'd appeared sometime while Penn and I were in the bathroom turned around to stare at us.

"Keep it down, man," Dave said, waving the cashier's worried look away with an awkward shrug.

Markus glared at him. "You tell me that again, and I'll break your face. I swear to God!"

Dave narrowed his eyes, but he didn't speak.

Markus shoved his hands into his shaggy brown hair and tugged, frustration knotting his face. "Does anyone besides me even understand what happened tonight?" Markus asked. "This isn't just about those bastards killing our friends. This isn't about losing. This isn't about a failed mission. This is about somebody betraying us. A filthy, lying *traitor*. Got it? This wasn't you, Jane. One of our so-called friends looked us in the eye tonight and then sold us out to the enemy."

The group of us stilled. Yes, the fury in Markus's words was frightening, but even more alarming was the thought that what he was saying was true.

"But how do we know?" Penn asked. "NuPet might have found out what our plans were tonight some other way, right?"

Ian and Dave nodded eagerly, but Markus didn't respond. He held Jane's gaze.

She sighed and looked at us.

"Jane?" Dave asked. His voice shook. He sounded worried. "Come on, Jane. You don't really think one of our own guys would do this to us, do you? You know them. We've been together forever."

"It doesn't matter what I think," Jane said. "All that matters now is keeping us safe. The fact is, Markus is right to be cautious, and if that means we have to assume the worst, it's what we have to do."

"But all of our stuff is back at headquarters," Dave complained.

"It doesn't matter."

"Yes, it does," he insisted, red-faced. "What about all our gear? What about the monitoring system? The computers? Shit! I *have* to go back."

"If it's so important to you, go!" Jane snapped. "But you're not endangering the rest of us. I won't let you."

Markus shook his head. "None of us are going back,"

Under the table I squeezed Penn's hand. I needed something to hold onto. Why was it that the second I began to feel grounded in a place or a group of people, something went wrong? I felt like a balloon, drifting untethered through the sky. And as much as I didn't want to be held down, tied and bound, it was frightening to be blown about, like even the littlest gust of wind might send me spinning out of control.

"So if we're not going back, what do we do now?" Dave asked. His face was still splotched and red, but he was obviously trying to keep it together.

"We need to find a place to go," Markus said.

We all stared at one another, and I realized for the first time that I had no idea where these people lived or if they had families. I had just assumed they were like me, which sounded ridiculous now. Maybe Markus and Ian had lives similar to mine, but Jane and Dave were normal people. They could have come from anywhere.

"I hear Fiji's nice this time of year," Penn joked.

Markus snorted, smiling for the first time all night. "Passports might be a little tricky for half of us," he said.

Dave shifted in his chair, his lips pressed into a thin line. "I've got a place."

Jane rolled her eyes. "We're not going back to headquarters!" she teased, leaning into him. Already the tension was easing.

"No, seriously," Dave said, but he didn't smile back at her. "I've got a place. I just need to make a phone call to make sure it's okay."

He reached for his phone, and Markus's face fell. "Our phones."

Dave frowned. "What about 'em?"

"You don't think they're bugged, do you?" Penn asked.

Markus shrugged, looking to Jane for confirmation. She gave her head one small shake.

"So we can't use them anymore?" Dave tossed his phone onto the table. "We might as well be living in the Stone Age. We can't function like this. We might as well admit they've beaten us."

"Give me a couple days," Markus said. "I'll get us more supplies, I promise. If you can find us a place to stay, I'll do the rest."

Dave picked up his phone. He thumbed a large crack running the length of the screen. "Drink up," he said, gesturing to the two large cups sweating in the center of the table. "We've got a bit of a drive ahead of us."

$\mathcal{T}$he morning light was just beginning to illuminate the sides of the fancy buildings in the Upper East Side when Dave pulled up in front of a tall apartment building.

"You guys wait here," he said. "I'm not making any promises about this, but I'll try."

He hopped out of the car, straightened his shirt, and headed for the man at the door. He gestured to the van and shook the man's hand, then walked inside.

"Whose place is this?" Markus asked, staring over his shoulder at Jane, who sat in the back seat.

"How am I supposed to know?"

"Come on," he said. "You guys aren't fooling anyone. We've known for months that you've been messing around."

Jane's face flushed.

"You don't think we really believed you when you both had to 'run errands' at the same time every night, did you?"

"It's nothing serious," she muttered.

Ian laughed. "Hey, calm down. There's no reason to get defensive. Nobody cares."

"Well, that's not entirely true," Markus said. "There's a reason we don't want our people to get involved with each other. Relationships are messy. They can make you do stupid things…distract you."

Jane's eyes widened, and Markus's face softened. "That's not what I meant. I'm not saying your relationship with Dave had anything to do with what happened tonight," he said. "I'm sorry. I didn't mean that. I promise."

"I know." Jane nodded, but she still looked unwell. "You have to believe me, though. I really don't know who lives here. Dave never mentioned anyone in Manhattan. He doesn't really talk about people."

"No kidding," Ian said. "For someone who likes to babble so much, you'd think I would have heard him mention another human in the last two years I've known him, but no. He only talks about his stupid tech stuff."

"He's just passionate," Jane said.

Ian shrugged. "Speak of the devil." He pointed out the window as Dave came striding out the door.

"All right. It's a go." Dave gestured for us to get out. "Grab your stuff and follow me up."

Penn nudged me. "Our stuff? Like we've got suitcases or something."

"He's just trying to be hospitable," I said, climbing out of the van.

He followed after me. "Dave isn't the hospitable type," he grumbled. "And apparently he's not the type that acknowledges when you practically save his life, either. He was heading for the other exit when Markus detonated that gas. If I hadn't grabbed him, he'd have been stuck on the wrong side of the building."

"I'm sure he's grateful," I said.

Penn snorted. For some reason, Dave had rubbed him the wrong way since the day we'd met. Mostly Penn kept his distance from him, which hadn't been difficult to do back at headquarters, but things might be harder here, with all of us trapped inside some little city apartment together.

I stared up at the building, rising higher than any building I'd ever been in before, towering at least thirty stories above us.

The man at the entrance held the door for us, nodding politely as each of us passed. We'd done a fair enough job cleaning the blood and dirt off of us in the McDonald's bathroom, but we still looked like we'd been dragged through hell. Our eyes were all rimmed with red, our hair matted to our foreheads.

Ian hadn't done the best job washing up. Trailing behind him, I could still see a dribble of blood he hadn't gotten off the back of his neck.

If the doorman judged us poorly, he did a good job hiding it.

He nodded to me as I passed. "Enjoy your stay."

*T*he elevator dinged, and we all filed out behind Dave.

He hesitated in front of a door midway down the hall, looking like he wanted to be anywhere but where we all stood. "So…this is my sister's place," he said. "She's not crazy about having everyone here, but…" He shrugged. "Anyway, just don't bug her too much. She'd like to keep her privacy. So, you know, don't, like, snoop around."

Penn nudged me softly in the side, raising one of his eyebrows.

"We won't. We're just grateful for a place to stay," Markus said.

The door opened, and Dave ushered us awkwardly inside. The foyer opened into a living room with a white sectional couch bookended by ornate golden end tables in the shape of lions with bird's heads and wings. The gold-dipped creatures looked as if they'd been plucked straight from the pages of one of the fairy tales Ruby, Penn's little sister, used to read me, then dumped here, frozen, consigned to holding TV remotes and magazines.

The thought of Ruby warmed me. She and Penn were proof that there was a place for me in this world.

The apartment wasn't huge, but it felt purposeful, elegant. Not in a warm way, like Penn's house had been. This room was stylish, but oddly sterile. I couldn't place what it reminded me of, but I didn't like it. The feeling pricked at my memory. And then it hit me; the cold, antiseptic feeling reminded me of the waiting room at the kennel. It was a lifeless place. How could I trust anyone who chose to live like this?

Beyond the couch, a large glass-topped table was flanked by floor-to-ceiling windows that looked out over the city. Sitting at it was a tall, dark-haired woman, dressed in a simple white silk blouse and black pants. Her face was set in an icy scowl as cold and uninviting as her style. Was there anything warm about her?

She was thin like Dave, but their features were nothing alike. "I'm Dave's sister, Vanessa," she said, folding her arms over her chest. "Did he mention that already?"

Dave stood next to her, smiling uncomfortably.

"No, but it's nice to meet you." Jane reached out for her hand. "Thanks so much for having us."

Vanessa glanced at the outstretched hand but didn't make a move to shake it. Instead, she caught Dave's gaze and held it for a moment. "Yes, Dave said there were extenuating circumstances."

"Well…" Jane slowly lowered her hand. "We appreciate it."

Vanessa's gaze traveled briefly over the rest of us, stopping on me. Her eyes widened ever so slightly before she looked back at her brother. "I've got someplace I need to be," she said, standing abruptly. "You'll show them around, I assume?"

Dave nodded. It was clear his sister made him uncomfortable. I hadn't been around enough siblings to know whether this was common or not, but it certainly wasn't how Ruby and Penn had been together. There had been an easy warmth between the two of them. The tension between Dave and his sister was palpable.

She grabbed her purse off the counter in the kitchen and walked out the door without looking back over her shoulder.

"Are you sure this is a good idea?" Markus asked.

"Do you have any better ideas?" Dave glared at the group of us as if he blamed us all for the situation he'd been placed in. "I need some air. I'll be up on the roof if anyone needs me."

And without waiting for an answer, he walked out the door, too, slamming it behind him.

# Four

The hot water poured down over my head and filled the whole room with steam, turning things foggy and ghostly. The sleek white marble shower walls almost disappeared in front of me, so I could imagine I was standing anywhere, a blank field in my imagination, instead of the guest bathroom in this strange apartment.

Even with the hot water drenching me, my skin still crawled. Maybe it was the chemicals I hadn't completely scrubbed away in the sink earlier, or maybe I just couldn't forget the look on Missy's face as she realized one more time that I was leaving her.

If I closed my eyes and just let the heat drown me, maybe I could forget the last few hours. Maybe I could forget the fact that I kept losing people, that wherever I went, pain and loss trailed behind me like a wolf, nipping at my heels, ready to take me down at any second.

The door to the bathroom creaked open, and I froze. Before I'd sneaked into the shower, everyone else had collapsed in various places across the guest room down the hall: the bed, the plush sheepskin rug, the couch by the window.

"I'll try to be quick," I called, hoping whoever it was would leave. All I wanted was to let this hot water pour over me and forget about the rest of them for a while.

The shower curtain slid open a crack and Penn's head poked in. "Can I join you?"

The tension in my body melted away. The sound of his voice was as wonderful and warm as the water. My hand snaked out and wrapped around his wrist, pulling him into the heat.

"Hold on." He laughed. "I can't shower in these clothes."

Begrudgingly, I let go of his arm and watched him peel his shirt over his head. My lips parted, unable to contain my smile. Even after all we'd been through today, the simple act of watching him undress filled me with joy.

It still startled me that I could share this sort of intimacy with him. Sometimes it overwhelmed me. It wasn't that long ago that I'd heard him play his guitar for the first time and the differences between us had fallen away. The music connected us, made me realize that we'd spoken the same language all along. It whispered through our veins.

For a moment, the yellow light of the bathroom sconces seemed to waver, transforming into moonlight. Maybe this would happen for the rest of our lives. Like magic, we'd be transported back into that enchanted garden, back to our moonlit pond and its dark waters. What a gift that secret garden had been. I thought we'd left our sanctuary behind. I'd mourned it. But maybe we hadn't lost it entirely? Maybe Penn carried it with him. Maybe his body was a magic portal that would always take us back.

He stepped out of his clothes, and I pulled him into the water with me, hungry for him. Starved. The heat in his eyes told me he felt the same way. My back hit the cool tile wall behind me, and I gasped. With his body pressed against mine, our lips soft and wet, we breathed into each other as if air didn't exist outside our bodies.

My skin prickled. It had never been more sensitive in my life, and even though I'd scrubbed away the chemicals until every part of me felt painfully raw, I wanted to feel Penn's hands on my body.

I pulled him closer. "Touch me."

"Where? Here?"

His hand slid down my back.

"Or here?"

It circled around my hip and dipped lower.

I gasped, and he smiled against my lips.

"Your skin is so soft," he whispered, trailing his fingertips back up the center of my body. "I've never felt anything like it. This doesn't hurt, does it? After all the chemicals…?"

I shook my head. "Keep going."

He kissed me, desperate, and I whimpered against his lips. How could I tell him what it felt like? Pain and pleasure existing in the same touch, as if the two feelings had woven together, covering me from head to toe. Sharp and smooth. Hard and soft. Every feeling became both the front and back of the same coin, sending me spinning.

His mouth moved down my neck, across my collarbone, as his hands glided over my stomach, fingers feathering across the sensitive skin, before traveling back down, down, down.

My head tipped back, my eyes closing as the water spilled down across my chest. There was no place in the world I'd rather be than in Penn's arms. Why couldn't we freeze time and stay in this moment? There was no complication, only the two of us.

Here.

Together.

$\mathcal{P}$enn and I emerged from the shower pink skinned and smiling. Even though my body felt tired in a way it never had before, bone deep, like I could crawl between the white sheets and sleep for days, I felt hopeful again. There was still so much to fight for, and I still had Penn beside me.

I combed my fingers through my hair and stepped out into the dining room where everyone sat bent over the table.

"What's all this?" Penn asked as we walked up.

Both Markus's backpack and leather satchel lay open at the end of the table. Apparently he'd been down to the van while we were showering and had brought up all of the group's belongings, because everything we now had was spread across the glass tabletop.

"This is it," Markus said. "The sum total of our resources. Don't let it overwhelm you."

The sarcasm dripped from his lips. He stared at the items on the table like they'd personally disappointed him, as if these things had betrayed him instead of one of his friends.

There wasn't much. Next to Jane, all of the phones sat lined up, a row of useless black faces we couldn't even turn on for fear we might be tracked. Farther down the table, Dave was looking over the stun guns. And next to those sat the now useless-looking saws and metal cutters. There was a small pile of rope and climbing equipment, a few canisters that must have contained the same chemicals that had saved us the night before, and a pile of masks and gloves that Ian sat sullenly wiping.

At the head of the table, Markus was flipping through a stack of papers.

Penn and I each pulled up a chair.

"How can we help?" I asked.

"You can try to talk some sense into these idiots," Jane said.

"Maybe he's not so off the mark," Ian said, continuing what I assumed was the conversation we'd just interrupted. "We've been backed into a corner. What are we supposed to do?"

Penn and I looked around the group, confused. "Do you mind filling us in?"

Jane shoved the phones away from her. "These testosterone-filled warriors think the next course of action is to blow someone up."

Blow someone up? Again? My stomach lurched. They had to be kidding. How could any of them be thinking about resorting to violence after what we'd just been through?

"That's an oversimplification," Markus said.

"Is it? You said we need to bomb the NuPet headquarters."

"They need to realize we're a threat," Markus countered.

The sickness worked its way up my throat. "We just set off a bomb in that warehouse," I practically shouted. "We've already blown people up!"

Markus scowled. "That was self-defense, and you all know it! Besides, do you think any of their executives are going to feel that? No. They're sitting in their cushy offices ordering their peons to do their dirty work. Those assholes need to feel something for once!"

Jane threw up her hands. "Listen to yourself!"

Markus started pacing, waving his arms around as he spoke. "You make it sound like this is something I *want*. This isn't what I want. This isn't what I asked for. I don't want people to get hurt. It's what I'm fighting *against*. But it's pretty clear no one is doing anything to help our cause. If we want to make any sort of change, we're going to have to do it ourselves."

"Violence isn't the answer," I insisted.

Markus stopped pacing and folded his arms across his chest, his eyes narrowing as he looked me up and down. "What do you suggest we do?"

My mouth went dry. I could practically feel his disgust. What was he thinking? That he'd chosen a useless little waif to help him in this fight? That I was taking up more space and resources than I was worth?

"We can't just sit here licking our wounds and hoping something will start going our way," he said sharply. "We have to make people pay attention to us."

I studied him, trying to come up with the right words to defuse his anger. I'd seen his passion over the past week, but I'd never seen him like *this*. His hair stuck out from his head in clumps where he'd been running his hands through it. His eyes were bloodshot and twitching with the injustice of it all.

The only thing I could think to use was our history. We'd both been wronged in ways no one in the room other than Ian would ever understand. Maybe reminding him would help.

"I hate these guys as much as you do," I tried, keeping my voice calm, "but there has to be some other way."

"You know we don't have the luxury of time," Markus said. "We've already wasted a week on this last raid. Your friend isn't going to last much longer."

I nodded. Missy's face swam in front of me. The skin along her jaw, bruised and raw. The new wound cutting across her cheek. The pain in her eyes.

Dave, who'd been unusually quiet, piped up, "Come on, man, get creative. We start bombing people and we're going to end up in prison."

"I'm not afraid of prison," Markus said matter-of-factly.

Dave glared. "You might not be, but I am. Listen, we all signed up for this, but you never said anything about killing people."

"He's right," Penn said. His face had gone a little white.

I knew how much he hated his father, but it was not enough to kill him.

Penn didn't talk about his dad much, but he'd told me a few things. Sometimes I wondered if he was trying to prove to me that his father hadn't always been bad. That he'd come from someplace good. This was the man who'd tucked him into bed when he was a little boy. He had carried him on his shoulders, taken him to the fair, taught him how to fly a kite. There were beautiful memories mixed in there.

"What about those papers?" I asked, pointing to the white sheets spilling out of the files in front of him.

Markus had taken a few of the pages out. From what I could see, they were photographs of people. Not the best images, all pixelated and faint, photos that had been taken from a very great distance and blown up a thousand times. Underneath each photograph there was a paragraph thick with type.

Markus flicked through the pages. "This is just information. Facts. What am I supposed to do with any of this? Words. Numbers. A bad picture. It's just a summary of these people's lives. Who cares where they work, who they play cards with, what day they were born on?"

"It's important information," Jane said, defensively.

"Fine," Markus said. "Then tell me how to use it."

He dumped the file across the table. The pages fanned out across the glass, forming a sea of black-and-white faces.

Jane glared down at the pictures.

"That's not my job," she said. "I gather the information. I can't work magic."

"But you expect me to?"

"I expect you to try everything before you start killing people," she said. "You've said it before: lives are worth saving."

"I was talking about the pets."

"So you think these people should die?"

"Of course not. I didn't — "

"Wait a second," Penn interrupted.

We all turned to look at him. He leaned far across the table, staring at the pictures.

Mouth clamped in a tight line, he narrowed his eyes. "Who took these?"

"I did," Jane said.

"What's *she* doing here?" He snatched up a paper and waved it at them. "Someone tell me what the hell she's doing on this table."

No one answered. I squinted at the paper, trying to make out what he saw, and gasped.

The picture was clearer than most of the others. In it, Penn's mom walked down a sidewalk clasping Ruby's hand. Elise was wearing dark sunglasses and had her hair pulled back in a tight ponytail, but it was unmistakably her. The curls sticking out of Ruby's hat made her look younger and more vulnerable than ever.

Why was Ruby on this piece of paper? What had she and Elise done?

"My mother is not one of your enemies, and don't even *think* about pinning anything on my little sister!" Penn shouted. "I don't know where you're getting your information, but they're not involved. My dad is, yes. But my mother and my sister are *not* targets. My sister's just a kid!"

"Calm down," Ian said.

"Don't you dare tell me to calm down!" Anger radiated off him like heat. He spun on Jane. "Tell me why you're following them. Now!"

"They're not targets!" Jane yelled. She held her hands out in front of her, shrinking back in her chair.

Penn pinned her with an icy glare. "Why should I believe you?"

"Because I'm telling you the truth. She's not a target. I promise." Jane's face brightened, though she couldn't hide her desperation. "These people aren't all targets. They're people of interest, important people who might be able to help. They might be able to provide information or skills or leads."

Markus pointed to the paper in Penn's hand. "We've had our eyes on your mom for months. We've known she could be a beneficial resource for us, considering how close she's been to your father. Spouses can be treasure troves of information."

"Sometimes they have information they don't even realize they're holding," Jane added.

"And my sister?" Penn demanded.

"She just happened to be there," Jane said. "I promise. I'm not tracking her."

Markus waved her off. "We're not. I give you my word. It wasn't even until last week that we realized your mom might be an attainable source."

Penn set the paper down in front of him and regarded Markus with the same assessing look I'd seen on his father's face when he didn't trust someone. "What happened last week?"

Jane fidgeted uncomfortably, and the group of them cast a quick glance among one another. Were they trying to decide whether or not to tell us the truth, or were they gathering up the nerve to lie?

"What aren't you telling us?" I asked.

Jane nodded to Markus and he sighed, spreading his hands out flat on the table in front of him, laying it all bare before us. "Six days ago, your mom took your sister to the city."

Penn's jaw clenched tighter. "So? They go to the city all the time."

"She *moved* to the city," Jane clarified. "Your mom moved out of your father's house and took your sister with her. We don't know if it's permanent, but it looks like they're staying with a friend in SoHo."

Ian dug through the papers and pulled out another sheet, handing it to me.

"Do you recognize it?" I asked, tilting the paper so Penn could see. In the photograph, his mom was entering a narrow brick building.

"Yes," Penn said, the barest hint of relief drifting across his face. "That's my uncle Stephen's place."

"Is your mom close with him?" Markus asked.

Penn shook his head. "Not really. He's kind of the black sheep of my mom's family. He's an artist. Once, my mom took us to one of his art openings, but that was a few years ago. My dad hated it. He paints a lot of nudity, but not the pretty, classical kind. It's gritty and dark."

"So, you don't think he'd be in contact with your father?"

Penn snorted, his shoulders relaxing another inch.

"No. I think it's safe to say they haven't been in touch."

Markus smiled. "That's good."

"Is it?" Penn asked.

"If we want to use her as a source, it is," Markus said.

Penn looked at me with a swirling mixture of anger and fear in his eyes. "And what if we don't want to use her as a source?" he said. "What if we want to leave her out of this whole freaking mess all together?"

I knew he'd do anything to protect me, and to help the cause I cared so much about, but I had no doubt he'd draw the line at endangering his mother and his sister.

I reached for his hand. "Penn," I said, gently. "We need her."

He closed his eyes. "What good is she going to do?"

"Of all the people in the world, she knows your dad the best, doesn't she?" I asked. "She might know something that will help."

"Or we could always go with my other plan," Markus said.

I glared at him. "*Bombing* people? I'll never agree to that."

Penn sank into one of the chairs and stared out the window. Below us, cars whizzed along the street, cabs darting in and out of traffic like small, yellow beetles. A steady stream of people flowed down the sidewalk, unaware of us looking at them from above. In the distance, a siren wailed.

Jane scooted closer to him, resting her hand gently on his arm. "She'll talk to you," she said. "It would take us weeks to make a real connection with her, but if you go there, if you ask her to help us, she'll listen. It'll save so much time. It could really work."

"We have to try," I said, squeezing Penn's hand. "Please."

He stared into my eyes, his expression blank. Did he regret it, loving me? I wondered if he sometimes wished I'd never come to his house. Without me, he'd still be worried about getting girls to kiss him in his swimming pool, or finding a venue for his next gig. He wouldn't be thinking about bombing people or putting his mom and his sister in danger.

He took a deep breath, holding my gaze. "Okay," he finally said. "We'll try."

Five

*M*y feet ached. Penn and I had been standing on the corner across the street from his uncle's apartment for the past three hours. Cars honked and people rushed by, talking into phones or lost in their own worlds. The scent of hot dogs drifted past on the breeze, making my stomach growl.

Every once in a while, someone would glance in our direction, and my heartbeat would quicken. Markus was fairly certain we weren't being followed, but he wasn't taking any chances.

"We should just go up," Penn said for the thousandth time. "We're wasting time sitting out here."

"She'll come out," I assured him half-heartedly, staring at the hot dog in the hand of a businessman as he walked by. I knew I should be keeping my eye on the door to the building, just in case Elise or Ruby emerged, but for the past hour I'd been obsessed with the long brown sausages that passed by every few minutes.

"Or she won't," Penn said.

"She can't stay in there forever."

He kicked at a piece of gum stuck to the sidewalk. "We would have noticed if someone was watching us."

I stared down the street at the little café a few doors away. People sat sipping cups of coffee and reading newspapers.

"Markus and Jane must have their reasons," I said. "What if we go sit down there for a little while? It'll look less suspicious than standing here for so long."

Penn glanced over at the van parked midway down the block. The sun hit the windshield, making it impossible to see inside, but we both knew that Markus sat at the wheel, watching us. Next to him in the front seat, Jane would be snapping pictures with the camera she'd borrowed from Dave's sister. It wasn't until we were about to head out that she realized how much of her equipment had been left behind at headquarters. As we'd driven across town to SoHo, she'd grumbled the whole way about telephoto lenses and wireless microphones, annoyed she had so little to work with.

With a sigh, Penn grabbed my hand and led me down the sidewalk toward the café. "They can't get mad at us for moving twenty feet." He reached into his pocket and pulled out a small stack of bills. "We could probably share a croissant or something."

The wad of cash in Penn's pocket wouldn't last us too much longer, and he couldn't use the debit card he still kept in his wallet. It was tempting, especially now that all of us were basically homeless and broke. Markus and his group had plenty of cash at their headquarters, but it was as impossible to get as the equipment.

I wasn't much help, either. All the money Missy had stolen from her old master had been left behind when she and I fled the safe house. I'd give anything to have her old backpack again, if only to have a piece of her safe in my hands.

We sat down at a small metal table next to a couple drinking coffee while their baby slept tucked in a stroller next to them. A woman sat on the other side of us writing in a notebook. They all looked completely content with the day ahead of them. It would probably be filled with mundane things, like doing laundry and going to the grocery store. They didn't even know how lucky they were to move through their ordinary lives. People like Markus and Ian and I were fighting for just a piece of what they took for granted.

Penn picked up a menu. "Can you see the door from where you're sitting?"

I nodded. It was basically the same view we'd had for the past few hours: the empty doorway to Penn's uncle's building, and next to it, the newspaper stand where people stopped every few minutes to buy candy bars and magazines. The only difference was that from where we were sitting now, I could see the newspaper man's face instead of the back of his head.

"Does a chocolate croissant sound good?" Penn asked. "Or just a plain—"

I leaned forward. "Penn," I interrupted.

He glanced up, following my gaze to the front of

the building where the door had just closed behind a woman in dark glasses. His mother. She paused for a moment, looking both directions as if she was only now considering where she was headed. A moment later, she tightened her grip on her purse and turned south, heading away from us.

In a second, Penn and I were up, winding our way back through the tables and out onto the sidewalk, which seemed so much busier than it had all morning. We jostled our way past a woman pushing a stroller and a young man out walking his dogs.

"Where'd she go?" I asked.

The sidewalk in front of us was peppered with businessmen and young couples, but I didn't see Elise anywhere. It was like she'd just vanished, evaporated into the air along with the car exhaust and steam from the hot dog vendors.

Penn's brow wrinkled, and a moment later he was pulling me along, rounding the corner past the newspaper stand. There, halfway down the block, was his mom. As if she'd sensed us there, she glanced back over her shoulder. Her lips were pursed, her face tense.

Why hadn't she noticed us?

"Something doesn't feel right," I said, pulling on Penn's hand.

He didn't answer, only sped up.

My stomach flipped. It hadn't occurred to me until this very second that the congressman could be nearby. "What if she didn't leave him?" I asked. "What if he's here?"

What if he had convinced Elise to fool us into thinking

she'd left him? I wouldn't put it past him. Right now he could be waiting just past one of these doors, waiting for her to draw us closer to him, a spider drawing us into his web.

We closed in. In front of us, the *clack* of Penn's mom's heels smacked the sidewalk. The sound of them filled my head, pounding like a drum, noisier than the honk of the taxis and the squealing of brakes.

Penn dropped my hand and lurched forward. His hand tightened over his mom's shoulder, pulling her into a little alleyway. He pushed her into the dark alcove of a doorway, and she shrieked, bringing her hands up to fight, ready to slap and claw her way away if she needed to.

"It's okay. It's okay," Penn said. He stepped away from her, lifting his hands. "Mom! Calm down. It's me."

She froze, her body shaking and her hands hovering in front of her face. Slowly, she raised them to her eyes, lifting away the dark glasses.

Penn's face blanched. "Mom! What happened?"

No response. No recognition. Nothing.

He traced the arch of her brow. Beneath it, her eye was puffy and red. The dusty purple of a bruise ringed her lower lid. Her hand flitted up to the mark, delicately touching the skin as if she'd forgotten it was there.

"Mom?" Penn repeated. "Did Dad do this to you?"

I shrank away, my stomach churning at the thought. What had the congressman done?

As if a switch had been flipped, she blinked and gave her head a little shake, her face coming back to life. "Darling!" She swept him into her arms. "What are you doing here? My God! I was so worried."

He let her embrace him for a moment, resting his head on the top of hers, but then he pulled away. "You haven't answered me. Did Dad do this?"

She swallowed, looking away from him, her gaze landing on me. Her lips pursed, but she caught herself. It must be terrible to see me. I was the embodiment of everything that had torn her family apart. But I didn't feel she hated me. I used to, but not anymore. Not after everything she'd done to help Penn and me escape his father.

"You two shouldn't be here," she said.

"We need your help," Penn said. "We've been working with—"

"Honey, the city isn't safe," she interrupted. "Your dad has eyes everywhere." She turned back to the street, as if she'd actually just reminded herself.

"Does he know where you are?" Penn asked.

"Oh, I'm sure he does," she said. "You know your father. He makes it a point to know everything. And if he doesn't know, he'll pay someone to know it for him."

His mouth tightened. "We'll go, but first, we need information—"

"Penn!" she cut in. "You aren't listening. We cannot do this here." She looked toward the road again.

"It's okay," I said. "We have people with us, watching."

She shook her head. "It won't help. However many people you have, he has more. Always."

"But—"

"We can't talk about this here," she said firmly, leaving no room for argument. "I can't be seen with you. If he's already spotted us together…" Her face blanched.

"There's a woman he's posted to watch me. I don't think she suspects I'm aware of her, but I'm not blind. I see her everywhere, pretending to window-shop or write in her stupid little notebook. She's so ordinary looking. I know that's why he picked her. He thought I'd never notice her, but I do. I do."

I thought of the woman I'd seen sitting next to us at the café. She'd been writing in a notebook.

"Have you seen her today?" Penn asked.

"Not today, but that doesn't mean she's not there. This is what I need you to do," she said, bringing her hand almost reflexively to her bruised eye again. "I'm going to walk out of here first. Do not follow me. I need you to wait. Ten minutes at least. And when you *do* leave, turn left, not right, which is the direction I'll go."

Penn frowned. "But if there's someone, that woman… Won't she just follow you?"

His mom nodded. "Yes. That's why I'm going to have to try to evade her. I'll do my best, and hopefully she won't suspect. Usually, I just let her follow me. It's a nuisance, but what does it matter? I'm not going anywhere. My life is on hold here. I'm just trying not to go insane sharing a house with your uncle Stephen. He's as peculiar as he was when we were kids. But at least Ruby loves him, and he's wonderful with her." Her face softened at the mention of Ruby's name. "I haven't told any of my friends what's happening. It's too embarrassing." She caught herself. "I'm rambling, aren't I? I'm sorry."

"So you're going to try to lose that woman?" Penn asked.

"Oh, yes." Her expression soured. "I'll do my best. You

don't worry about me. Go to the Herald Square station. I'll meet you there. Wait for me just inside the turnstiles."

"And if you don't lose her?"

"It will be busy in the subway. If for some reason she follows me, get on the D train and take it all the way to Brooklyn. Meet me at Coney Island."

Penn's expression changed. For a moment, the worry melted away. "The Wonder Wheel?"

Elise smiled, nodding. "Where else?"

She took a deep breath and pulled Penn into a hug. "God, all I want to do is hold you."

I cast my eyes to the ground. Why did it feel like I was intruding?

After a minute, she let him go. "I'll see you there?"

We both nodded, although the looks on our faces must not have instilled much hope in her.

"Don't worry," she said. "I'll see you soon."

She turned and strode back out onto the street, carrying herself with the sort of confidence I was used to seeing. Elise Kimball was a powerhouse. If we were going to have one of Penn's parents on our side, I was actually glad it was her.

Penn and I pressed ourselves against the side of the alleyway and watched his mom move briskly down the sidewalk. It didn't take long for the sea of pedestrians to close in around her, but before she completely disappeared, I caught a glimpse of a woman following behind her, a woman with mousy brown hair pulled back in a loose bun. I strained to get a better look, to see if she was carrying a notebook in one of her hands, but before I could, she was gone, too.

• • •

*T*he inside of the subway station buzzed and churned and whirred. There was so much noise and energy in one place, it felt as if we'd descended the stairs into the belly of a roaring beast. Noise had never been more alive, echoing off the walls, bouncing and moving around us along with all the people. Where had they all come from? A continuous stream of them funneled down the stairs into the tunnel.

A group of kids surged past us, and I scooted closer to the white tiled walls, wishing there was a way to disappear. If the congressman's spies had spotted us, there was no place to run.

"What's taking her so long?" I asked.

I was already nervous, but this place only made things worse. Every few minutes a train would rumble down the dark tunnel, barreling toward us with such force the walls shook. The brakes would squeal, and the sound would squirm through my chest like a serpent.

"She'll be here," Penn said, but I could see the question in his eyes. *What if she doesn't come? Then what?*

"What's the wonder will?" I asked, trying to distract myself from the doubt creeping over me.

"The what?"

"The wonder will," I repeated.

Penn laughed. "Oh! The Wonder *Wheel*! It's a Ferris wheel. Coney Island is an amusement park."

I shook my head. This sort of thing was happening less and less, being utterly lost in a conversation, but it still bothered me when it did. I'd gotten good at piecing information together, but every once in a while, there were words that just didn't make sense, words I'd never heard before.

Penn studied me. "It still blows my mind," he said. "I'm sorry. Sometimes I forget you didn't grow up in front of a television like the rest of us."

"So, it's a wheel in a park?" I asked.

"An *amusement* park," Penn said. His face lit up. "It's not the same as a regular park. There are huge rides and roller coasters. You'll just have to wait and see. It's kind of hard to explain. My parents used to take me there when I was little. My mom and I both liked the Wonder Wheel the best. It's this giant wheel with little cars you ride in."

He gestured with his hands, showing how the ride would spin around and around, carrying him into the air with each rotation.

"My mom and I were the only ones in my family who liked it. We liked looking out over everything like we were birds. Sometimes, if you're lucky, the ride stops when your car is at the very top and you sort of rock there for a little while. It's awesome. I'll take you up on it. Sometime when life isn't crazy and scary anymore, we'll go up to the top of the Wonder Wheel and we'll just sit and look at the world together, okay?"

"Okay." I smiled at the sweet hopefulness on his face. Maybe someday we would go there for fun, up on that wonder wheel. It sounded both terrifying and amazing.

My gaze flitted over the people descending the stairs, and my heart quickened. Coming down the stairs was the woman with mousy brown hair. She was dressed in a plain brown sweater and jeans, so ordinary you might look right past her. She certainly wasn't the type of woman that usually made people nervous. That must have been why they picked her. Penn's mom was right.

A lock of her hair had fallen from its loose bun, and she swept it out of her eyes, scanning the crowd beyond the turnstiles. I tugged Penn's arm, pulling him behind a group of tourists.

"It's the woman, the one following your mom," I said, pointing her out to him as she pushed her way onto the platform.

A train rumbled into the station, and people shoved forward, but the woman stayed behind, glancing over the crowd. She was looking for someone, that was clear, and I knew exactly who.

The swarm of people jostled onto the train, and the platform cleared a bit. There weren't many of us left. A few people stood listening to a man playing a squeaky violin by the bench to our left, and we stepped up beside them, hoping that if the woman looked our way, she wouldn't guess who we were. But I didn't want to take my chances. If she'd been hired to follow Elise, she would know about Penn and me. She would have seen pictures of us.

There was a screech, and the train pulled away. The woman glanced up, and her eyes fixed on something across the tracks. Her body tensed, and her eyes narrowed ever so slightly. It was the stance of a hunter, a cat stalking its prey. Penn and I followed her gaze. On the opposite platform, his mother stood close to the edge, staring down the tunnel with a determined scowl.

"I thought she said to go to Brooklyn," Penn muttered. "What's she doing over there?"

He started pushing his way to the turnstiles, ready to make his way to the other side of the tracks, but I held him back. In front of us, the woman in the brown sweater was also hurrying back through the turnstiles.

"She said to stay on this side," I said.

"But she's over there!" Penn gestured, annoyed, to the other side of the terminal.

Just then, a train rumbled into the station on the opposite side of the tracks. Penn's mom disappeared behind the painted steel as it squealed to a stop. Through the scratched windows, a stuttering image of her flickered on the other platform. The train slowed to a stop, and the doors puffed open. From where we stood, we could see Elise frantically searching the people flowing toward the doors.

"She's looking for us," Penn said.

"Just wait."

"No. We must have misunderstood her."

I shook my head. "I'm not going over there." Maybe Penn was right. Maybe his mom wanted us on that side of the platform, but I wasn't going to follow her. Not when that other woman was over there.

Through the glass, I caught sight of the woman in the brown sweater. She was standing close to Penn's mom, close enough to reach out and grab her hand. The woman leaned forward and spoke into Elise's ear, and my stomach lurched. I backed up, bumping into Penn. Maybe I'd seen it wrong. The glass was foggy and scratched. My eyes could have been playing tricks on me. But then Elise turned ever so slightly and nodded.

Penn let go of his hold on my arm, and his hand fell to his side.

So, he'd seen it, too.

"What…" His voice trailed off.

But I understood. The same question was roaring in my ears. Was Elise one of them? Was she working with the congressman, too?

The woman didn't linger for long at Penn's mother's side. The doors to the train slid open, and she stepped on. Elise followed behind.

Did she think we were on that train, too?

Penn and I stood paralyzed. Even from outside, we could see the train car was packed. She stood next to the door. The woman in brown was only a few steps down from her, pressed between two young men. Through the window, we had a perfect view of Elise's profile: her elegant nose, her high cheekbones, her sleek hair. She didn't look like a traitor. But I guess I didn't know what a traitor looked like. On the outside, they were human like the rest of us. It was inside the ugliness lived.

"How could she do this," Penn said. "How?"

## Six

The doors to the train let out a puff of air and began to shut.

I grabbed Penn's arm. Was this it? Was Elise really betraying her own son? His whole body stiffened next to me like he was bracing himself for a blow.

And then suddenly Penn's mom was slipping through the crack and back onto the platform. She moved in one fluid motion, like a dancer, her tall, thin body, twisting to fit through the sliding doors.

Penn's muscles tightened beneath my hand, and he lurched forward.

It only took a moment for the woman in brown to catch on. Her body jerked toward Elise as if she could catch her. Elise landed on the platform. The woman elbowed the men who were standing next to her, trying to free herself from the crowd. She stumbled toward the door, fumbling to open it, too, but the doors held tight. The train was already moving, speeding away from the station.

The last train car clacked past, and Elise came into full view, standing alone on the platform across from us. She made eye contact with us, and a wicked little smile sneaked across her face.

She'd known exactly where we were the whole time.

"Are you crazy?" Penn yelled. His voice echoed through the tunnel, but there was no anger behind it, only relief.

"Stay there," Elise called.

Her face was flushed, her eyes bright. In all the months I'd known her, I'd never seen her like this before. She'd always been reserved and proper and intimidating. At times she'd even been kind, but I'd never seen her alive like this. She reminded me of Ruby. I'd never seen the resemblance before, but there it was, and it made my heart swell for her.

Penn and I collapsed onto one of the wooden benches lining the walls, and a few minutes later Elise was standing before us.

"Sorry if I scared you," she said. "I couldn't lose her."

"God, Mom! My heart feels like a freight train," Penn said, his voice winded like he'd just run a race. "Are you trying to kill me?"

"I'm sorry, darling." She smiled.

He huffed and stood, still looking shaken. "You're pretty pleased with yourself."

Elise grinned, but it didn't last long. "At least for the moment," she said. "It was probably a stupid move.

There's no way they're going to let that woman keep following me now that they know I'm on to her. They'll send someone new, and I won't have any idea who's keeping tabs on me."

Something about the way the woman with the notebook had stood so close to Penn's mom nagged at me. Yes, Elise had made a big show of losing her, but how did we know we could trust her? I studied her face for some clue she was lying.

"Are you alone?" Elise asked, looking around.

Penn nodded. "The rest of the—"

"What did she say?" I interrupted.

"Excuse me?" Elise said.

"The woman who was following you," I said. "She said something to you right before the train came."

Elise's brow crinkled, and the worried look returned to Penn's face.

He folded his arms across his chest. It was a protective move, as if he was trying to put a barrier in front of his heart. "Mom?" His voice was uncertain.

"But she didn't speak to me," Elise said, defensively. "You don't think..." Her gaze flicked between the two of us. "You can't possibly think I'm working with her. You have to believe me."

Penn stepped away from her. "I saw it, too. She whispered something in your ear."

Elise shook her head, confused. "No one talked to me. I was standing on the platform, and then the train came and then..." Her face lit up. "Wait! Someone did say something to me. But I didn't realize..." She closed her eyes as if she were trying to replay the moment. "There was a woman behind me. She asked if this was the train uptown, but I didn't actually speak to her. I only nodded. Was that her? Was that the woman who's been following me?"

She opened her eyes and stared at Penn imploringly.

He gave a small nod. "It was."

"And you think, what? That I planned something with her? What are you implying?"

"We just have to be safe…" I said. "It's not that we don't trust you."

Elise's eyes clouded, looking from me to her son. "Oh, honey, I would never betray you. Never. I'm your mother, for God's sake. I'd do anything for you. I'd die for you." Her voice cracked.

He studied her. I had no idea what he was seeing. Maybe he was remembering what it had been like to have her for a mother? That was an experience I'd never get to have.

Finally, he nodded. "I'm sorry. It's just been a really difficult couple of weeks."

She wrapped her arms around her son, and he bowed his head, placing a soft kiss on her brow.

It didn't take long for another train to rattle into the station. The doors whooshed open, and the three of us climbed on. Elise and I sank into two empty seats near the back of the car, and Penn grabbed onto the hand railing above us.

The train was full, packed with tourists in *I heart NYC* T-shirts and hats, people carrying shopping bags, and families pushing strollers.

"This is better." Elise sighed, eyeing the people around

us. "It's crowded, but it's the good kind of chaos. No one here will pay any mind to what we're talking about."

I studied the faces: so many colors, so many emotions, but they did all seem lost in their own worlds. Still, I couldn't shake the feeling we were being watched. What if the woman in brown wasn't the only person following Penn's mother? "Are you sure it's safe?"

"Yes. I believe so," Elise said. "We have an hour's ride until we arrive. That should be plenty of time to tell me where you've been." She reached out and touched Penn's arm as if she wanted to remind herself that he was really next to her. "I've never been more worried in my life. God, Penn. It's been a nightmare, truly. One day you were spending all your waking moments in your room, and then you were just gone! And your dad…" She shook her head, swallowing back her words.

"Did he hurt you?" Penn asked.

"Please, let's not talk about him yet. Let me just sit on this train and look at you. I can't think about your father right now."

Penn scowled, but he didn't press her for more. "It's hard to even know where to begin," he said. "I guess maybe the story needs to start with Ella."

Elise turned to me, and I took a deep breath, trying to figure out how to explain everything that had happened since the night we stood in her driveway and she pointed us toward Canada, where we thought I'd be safe, thinking she might never see either of us again.

The train rocked beneath us, lulling me, reassuring me, and the words poured out. It was amazing that we were zooming along underneath the city, but not impossible. If there was one thing I'd learned, it was that the world and every person in it had depth, layer upon layer that often didn't have anything to do with the way they appeared from the surface.

By the time I finished telling Elise about Missy coming for me, about what it had been like in the black market, and the girls I'd met in the kennel's breeding program, Elise's eyes were wide and we were nearing our stop. Somewhere along the way, she'd grabbed my hand in both of hers as if by holding on to me, she could protect me from the things I'd already been through.

"I'm sorry I never saw you for who you are, Ella," she said. "I'm sorry for the way I mistreated you...before."

I shook my head. "You don't need to apologize."

"No. I do," she said. "I've always considered myself a feminist. It's one of the reasons I abhorred the pet program so much to begin with. It made me so angry thinking girls could be bought and sold like objects. But deep down, I wonder if I was as guilty of thinking of you as an object as everyone else. I underestimated you. I let myself believe you were weak because you're small, that you were dumb because you're pretty. But I was so wrong. You're smart and brave, and I'm proud to know you."

I opened my mouth to thank her, but I couldn't speak. It was absurd that a compliment could make my throat constrict this way, could make my eyes sting. Luckily, the train squealed, slowing down, and Penn and his mom both turned to watch the subway station rush into view through the windows. Quickly, I brushed a tear out of the corner of my eye.

We got unsteadily to our feet, and the train lurched

to a stop. A group of tourists shuffled from their spot on the other side of the train car and a young couple I hadn't noticed before caught my eye. Next to them, their baby slept peacefully in its navy-blue stroller, just a lump underneath the blankets. The woman's eye met mine for just a moment before she quickly glanced away.

A cold dread snaked through my stomach. Maybe it was just a coincidence. Maybe they weren't the same people I'd seen earlier at the café.

The doors slid open, and I made my way toward the front of the crowd, watching the couple out of the corner of my eye as they stood, too, jostling their stroller as they made their way out of the train.

The crowd of passengers flowed up and out of the subway terminal, blinking in the bright afternoon light outside of Stillwell station. A big family strode past us with arms full of beach bags and strollers. A little boy with dark-brown hair skipped happily down the sidewalk. "I'm going to get a cotton candy!" he called out to his parents. "And if I get sticky, I can let the ocean wash me off."

Elise squeezed Penn's hand. "When did you stop being that exact little boy?" she asked. "I mean it? When?"

"You can get me a cotton candy," Penn teased. "I promise I won't even get sticky."

I peered back over my shoulder. The couple with the blue stroller had stopped a few yards back and was stooped over their baby, messing with the blankets.

"Hey, did you see that couple when we first got on the train?" I asked.

Penn and his mom gave them a quick glance. "No. I don't believe I've seen them before," Elise said.

"Maybe you just never noticed," I said. "You were distracted by that other lady. There could be more than one person following you."

We turned the corner, and Penn's Wonder Wheel came into view. It really was a sight to behold, a giant wheel turning on the horizon like magic. Beyond it, the ocean rested calm and blue. Cars rushed past us, but in the distance, the rattle of rides and the shrill screams of little kids drifted over to us. Mixed in, the shriek of white birds drifting overhead made the hair on my arms stand.

I wished I could enjoy the sight.

I reached for Penn's arm, pulling him to a stop beside me. "Look."

The people with the stroller had turned the corner as well, and the couple stopped, seemingly admiring the view. The woman smiled, pointing down the street, and said something I couldn't hear to her husband. But the more I watched them, the more it looked like they were a pair of actors up on stage, their movements played out for my viewing.

And then, abruptly, they turned and headed the other direction.

Penn frowned. "I don't think they're following us. And if they are, they're doing a pretty crappy job. C'mon."

We hurried to catch up to Elise before the crowd swallowed her up, but I couldn't help but look over my shoulder one last time. They were gone.

I wanted to believe Penn. To trust his judgment. But I

couldn't shake the alarm pricking my skin.

That couple felt…off.

"It looks so small," Penn was saying.

"You haven't been here since you were twelve," his mom said. "It isn't any smaller than it used to be."

"Maybe we shouldn't stop to look," I said. "It's probably better if we just keep going." I grabbed Penn's arm and dragged him—as best I could anyway—toward the Wonder Wheel in the distance. Elise followed close on our heels.

The gates to the amusement park loomed large ahead of us, huge pinwheels of lights flashing in reds and pinks. I stole a glance behind us. A steady stream of people was lining up to buy tickets, and sandwiched in the middle of them, I could just make out the front end of a baby stroller.

The congressman might not have found us yet, but I was pretty sure someone had.

"We need to find a safe place soon," I whispered in Penn's ear.

There were so many people, everywhere I looked. Why had we come to the one place that was even more crowded than Manhattan?

Penn nodded. "We will."

We wound our way through the gates and a few minutes later we stood staring up at the giant metal wheel. Tiny cars teetered in two rows, one on the outside and one on the inside of the brightly colored metal as it turned slowly in a giant circle. My head spun. How could I be dizzy just standing on the ground? The amusement park was an overdose of colors and sounds: screeching and clattering and flashing lights. Even the air smelled too sweet.

"You get into one of those little cages on *purpose*?" I asked, staring at a group of people who were climbing into a small purple car encased in a crisscross of wire bars.

Penn smiled. "You wanted somewhere safe. This is it."

This was his idea of *safe*? I swallowed. "There's no place else?"

"Come on," he said. "We'll take one of the ones on the outside. They don't swing as much. It'll be fine. I promise."

I squeezed my eyes shut and reached for his hand. It seemed impossibly crazy that people would go out of their way to scare themselves, when there was already so much terror in the world.

At least it would get us off the ground and out of sight.

We sat down on a white bench, and they closed the door behind us. A moment later, the car swung backward, lifting us from the ground. My stomach swung, too, every bit of the world dropping away: the Liberationists and Markus and the people following us, all of them stuck on the ground while I flew away. My hands tightened around the edge of the seat beneath me. It was there, solid and real, so why did it feel like my body had forgotten which way was up and which way was down?

Penn's hand closed over mine.

I opened my eyes a sliver. I couldn't remember closing them, but I had. And as the darkness parted, my breath slipped away, too, but not from fear. It was the kind of awe I felt when the sky turned gold at sunset. This was what a bird felt like. Below, people zigzagged past the colorful tents like beetles. And out past the park's fences, their little bodies spotted the beach as far as the eye could see. Tiny forms, coming and going. It seemed impossible that things so small and inconsequential could hurt one another the way they did.

"That view," Elise gasped. "I'll never grow tired of that view."

I pressed my face closer to the wire grid. I needed to know if the couple with the baby stroller was still down there, but the view made my head whirl.

"Mom," Penn said. "We can't avoid talking about him anymore."

She sighed, resting her head against the metal while she stared out over the horizon. "I know, I know. But it's difficult for me to talk about him. After you left the second time, he snapped. I've never seen him so upset. He went mad. It's like I was living with a psychopath. I'd wake up in the middle of the night and he would be sitting in the chair in his study staring into the blackness with the most wicked smile on his face."

"Why didn't you report him?"

She shook her head. "For smiling wickedly?"

Penn rolled his eyes.

"But really, who would I tell? Who would even listen?"

"Mom, he's an elected official. People would care. Couldn't they take his office away from him or something? If he's doing illegal stuff?"

"Oh, sweetheart, it's not that simple. What am I supposed to say? He's turned into a villain whose only purpose in life has become to exact revenge? There's no proof. *I* would sound like the crazy one."

"Then tell them something else. Call the police. If he did *that* to you!" He pointed a shaking hand at his mom's eye.

Our car rounded the top of the wheel, and it slowed to a stop, sending us rocking back and forth. I gripped the sides of the bench and took a deep breath. Below us, I thought I caught sight of the blue stroller.

"Penn must be right," I said. "There are laws protecting you, aren't there? Couldn't someone put him in jail?"

Elise leaned her head in her hands. "No one is going to arrest him. Leaving him was the only thing I could do. At least it removed us from the situation so he couldn't…" Her voice trailed off, then, seemingly pulling herself together, she took a deep breath. "Your father has spent the last twenty years of his life building an empire, and he hasn't been stupid about it. For a long time, I thought he was obsessed with his connections. He needed to know everyone. He needed to be invited to all the parties. I thought it was about financial support. You can't build a campaign without donors, but it wasn't that."

The wheel jerked forward again, sending my stomach lurching. The thought of the congressman usually did that to me all on its own.

"What do you mean?" Penn asked.

Elise leaned forward and looked him in the eye. "He's been blackmailing people. I've known for a while. I just never suspected how serious it was going to get. And now that he has his eyes set on bigger things, a run for the senate, maybe even the presidency, it's only going to get worse."

"And you didn't do anything about it?" Penn threw his hands up, sending the whole car rocking.

"What could I do?" she asked.

"I don't know. Report him. Confront him." He gestured wildly.

"Report him to whom? This is what I'm trying to tell you. He had information on *everyone*: affairs, drug deals, embezzlement. You name it, he's got something to use for collateral. Some way to extort whatever he needs. Sometimes it's pictures. Sometimes it's videos or recordings. Sometimes it's just a bit of information someone else can use to further their own political career, and after he's given them that, they're beholden to him. And maybe this is politics. Maybe this is how they *all* do it. It's everyone: police chiefs, senators, county clerks. He collects them like stamps. He has people's lives strung out for him like puppets, and he's the master."

She waved her hands like a puppeteer, and I could almost see the little people hanging from the strings, dancing for us. I knew what it felt like to be one of his marionettes. All of us did.

"So how do we stop him?" Penn asked.

Elise sighed. "I don't even know if you can."

The wheel brought us to the ground and began another loop around. As our car began to climb again, I caught sight of a stroller. The crowd parted, and the couple from the train—and I was beginning to think from the café outside Elise's building, too—came into view. They sat on a bench near the base of the ride. Both of them had turned away from the stroller and held phones pointed toward the Wonder Wheel. In their distraction to record us, they hadn't noticed that the wind had blown aside the blanket covering their baby.

The stiff plastic arm of a doll glinted in the sunlight.

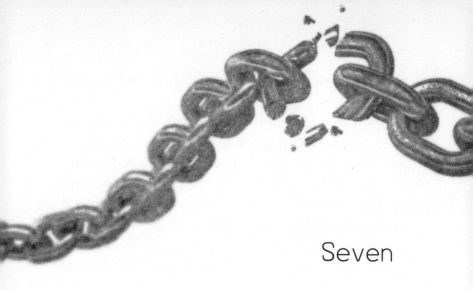

# Seven

"We *are* being followed," I said. "There! The couple I was telling you about. The one with the stroller."

I pointed, and Penn and Elise peered over the side of the cage, trying to get a better look.

"It has to be a coincidence," Elise started. "I've never—"

"It's a doll," Penn said. "In the stroller." He fell back in his seat, eyes wide. "What are we supposed to do now?"

"Calm down," Elise said. "It won't do any good to panic."

"What else are we supposed to do?" Penn said, peering back down at the couple. "Ella was right. They were following us, and now we're stuck on this stupid ride. Those people have probably been recording our conversation, and they've probably already told Dad we're with you. He's probably on his way here right now!"

My body jerked, the instinct to run so hardwired inside me that I had to beat it back to keep myself from jumping to my feet. "I don't think they know we've spotted them yet. That gives us the advantage, right?"

Elise's gaze darted between the couple and the ride's exit. "Yes. It's going to be okay," she assured us. "They can't hear what we're saying. That's why I picked this spot. Believe me, there's far too much distance between us, and this place has enough ambient noise to block out anything they could catch on tape. And even if they want to try to blow up their video and read our lips, they're not going to be able to see anything unless we press our faces against the bars and look down at them."

"What about Dad?" Penn asked.

"We've still got time," she said. "One more rotation and we'll get off. You two can go one way. I'll go another. The crowd here will only help you get away."

"But we haven't solved anything," Penn insisted. "Dad's blackmailing people, and you're telling me there's no way to take him down?"

"What if we get rid of the blackmail?" I asked.

Penn's face lit up. "If he's got videos and documents, couldn't we destroy them? Then he wouldn't have anything to hold over anyone. He'd lose his leverage."

"I doubt it," Elise said. "Your father is not the type to risk losing his power. You've seen the vault he keeps in his study."

Penn ran a hand over his face. "So we should just give up?"

"Maybe not," she said. "There's a man I used to go to school with at Cornell. We've reconnected over the last few months. Your father and I were both friends with him for a while, but we grew apart after we graduated. He never trusted your father, even before he made his way into politics. He used to accuse John of being a wolf dressed up in sheep's clothing, pretending to want to help the little man when really all he wanted was to grab more power for himself." She shook her head thoughtfully. "If only I could go back in time. I should have listened to him."

"But you think he might be able to do something for us now?" Penn asked.

"He's a brilliant man," she said. "He's bound to have connections that could help. I truly believe you could trust him. He's the only person I feel like I can confidently say that about."

I reached out to her, placing my hand gently on her arm. "Will you ask him to help us? Please?"

She nodded. "If you tell him I sent you, I know he'll do everything he can."

Penn studied his mom's face. It was clear there was another question he wanted to ask her, but something was stopping him.

"Who is he?" I finally asked.

She reached into her purse, scribbling some information down on a scrap of paper before she pressed it into Penn's palm. "His name is Erik Vasquez. He's a prosecutor for the district attorney's office. Don't let anyone follow you there."

"We won't," I promised.

She smiled, but there was worry written all over her face. The wheel was beginning its descent. Time was running out.

"When will I see you again?" Penn asked, unable to hide the way his voice wavered.

"Your uncle has friends at the Cornwell on Prince Street. If you need to get in touch with me, you can always go there. They'll find a way to get a message to me." She pulled him into a tight hug. "God, Penn, please be careful. *Please.*"

When the wheel slowed to a stop, their eyes were red, but their chins were lifted, their shoulders squared. The girl operating the ride opened the door, and we climbed back onto solid ground.

"I love you," Elise said. "Both of you."

Without hesitating, she took off toward the exit where the couple with the plastic baby now waited nonchalantly, the blanket once again covering the doll's painted face. Penn and I turned and pushed back through the line of people waiting to board the Wonder Wheel.

We rushed past whirling red-and-blue rides, and I had to grab Penn's hand for balance. Our feet might have been on pavement, but my head still spun. As he pulled me onward, I turned to look back into the crowd. The rainbow-colored dragons and spinning horses were blocking the one thing I needed to see: the couple with the blue stroller. Had they followed Elise, or were they behind us?

I scanned the swarms of people, but they all blended together. I needed to concentrate. For a moment, the noise died away, and then a sound brought me back. Three words. "Greenwich Training Center."

I dug my feet into the asphalt, scanning the crowd for the voice I'd just heard.

"Don't stop," Penn urged, tugging at my arm.

Next to the line for the small green roller coaster, a group of adults huddled around a tall man who was reading from his phone. "They're saying it was that Liberationist group," he said. "Friggin' terrorists if you ask me. You don't like this country, then leave."

"He said something about Greenwich," I said, turning to Penn. "Something happened."

"We don't have time to figure it out right now," he said.

I scanned the park. The rides still clattered, but something had changed. The mood had darkened, as if a cloud had just passed overhead, casting a shadow across the bright colors, dulling them.

He was right. We needed to get out of there. I turned toward the exit. In front of me, the back door to the snack shop was open, filling the air with the hot perfume of frying desserts. In the doorway, a boy in an apron stood with his hands on his hips, staring up at a small television mounted inside. On the screen, the camera zoomed in on the smoldering shell of a building. The front doors had been blown off their hinges, but there was no mistaking it was Greenwich. Or it had been.

"Penn!" I pointed to the screen just as the image changed.

In place of the now destroyed building, photos of a dozen faces filled the screen. The television was small and far away, but that didn't matter, I recognized all of us: Markus, Dave, Jane, Ian, Penn, and me, not to mention a half dozen others who might still be at headquarters.

Who knew where the news station had gotten the photos. They weren't great. Some were obviously candid shots, taken from a bit of a distance. They weren't too different from the photos Jane had taken of the people our group had been monitoring.

The photos of Penn and me were the exceptions. They hadn't been snapped as we ducked into a car or glanced behind us on a city sidewalk. Penn's was from his high school yearbook. I could imagine where the book still sat on the shelf in his room. In the picture, his hair was still messy and long, the way it was when we met, and he smiled a dashing white grin at the camera that seemed totally inappropriate now, like he found some pleasure in the idea that one of the training centers had been bombed.

I'd never seen the picture of me before, but I remembered sitting for it. A few months before the sale to our new owners, Miss Gellner had posed us, unsmiling, in front of the same white wall we'd been documented in front of every year since we arrived. In the picture, my hair was the light strawberry blond that was just starting to show again at my roots. It was pulled away from my face in a low braid they'd purposely positioned to accentuate the delicacy of my features.

I brought a hand to my bangs, combing them down onto my forehead. I'd never been more grateful to Missy's handiwork. With my short, dark hair I looked similar to the girl on television, but not the same.

Penn gaped at the screen. "What the hell?"

The boy in the apron turned, and my muscles tensed, ready to run. What if he recognized us? What if he started yelling?

But he hardly glanced at us. "I know! It's messed up,

right?" He turned to look back at the television just as the image of our photos disappeared.

"What happened?" Penn asked.

"Terrorist attack," the kid said. "Those pet protestor people bombed that place and killed the lady that worked there."

As if on cue, an image of Miss Gellner filled the screen. I hadn't seen her face in months, but the familiar yet strange combination of dread and awe spread through my body. I grabbed on to Penn's arm for support.

I'd never considered Miss Gellner a woman I cared about. She'd been cruel to me, ruthless, harsh, demanding. But she'd been important to me, a figure that had filled my days and given me a sense of purpose. There was no denying all the girls at Greenwich had meant something to her. We were her legacy. We made her proud. And as messed up as it might seem, a part of me loved her.

"Who would do this?" I asked.

The boy at the snack stand turned back around as if I'd been talking to him. "Sickos," he said. "They pretend they care about life, like it's all important, and then they just go and kill people? That doesn't even make sense."

Penn and I both gaped at him. Of course, he thought the news was telling him the truth. They showed him the images. They told him who the bad guys were. It didn't need to make sense to him. He only needed to trust it was true.

That didn't make his blind belief hurt any less.

The image changed on the screen once more. This time the view of the devastated training center zoomed in from above. The camera swept over the wreckage. It was a place I'd spent years of my life, but it was almost unrecognizable now. Most of the outside walls still stood, but the blackened roof had collapsed in the middle, revealing a pile of blackened beams, scattered like matchsticks.

I tried to imagine what lay beneath this burned-out shell, tried to walk its halls in my mind, but all I could imagine were the pianos in the music room. They'd been my first love, my first taste of passion. And even though I knew they weren't alive, my stomach clenched at the thought of them burned and broken. I could still feel the cold touch of their keys against my fingers. They'd saved me in that place.

"Dude, I've got to get back to work," the boy said. "Sorry. Stupid funnel cakes aren't going to fry themselves."

Penn helped me steady myself, but as we turned to leave, the boy cocked his head and narrowed his eyes, studying us as if he was actually seeing us for the first time.

I froze. *Please don't recognize us, please don't recognize us...*

Finally, he shook his head. "You can stay and watch it if you want. I'll leave the door open. Just don't let anyone steal anything, okay?"

Penn swallowed and pasted on that beautiful smile of his. "Thanks, man," he said, and for a second even I believed he was just another teenager at an amusement park.

The boy disappeared behind the counter, and the smile slipped from Penn's lips. "We've got to get back," he said. "Someone needs to tell me why our pictures are being flashed all over the news."

We took off toward the exit, Penn practically running.

"Slow down," I said, pulling on his arm. "People are going to notice us."

Penn slowed his pace. "You're right." His gaze darted among the faces of people passing by. I knew what he was thinking. In the last few minutes, the rules had changed. When we'd entered this park, the sea of faces had been a sanctuary, hundreds of bodies to hide behind. Now there were hundreds of eyes that might recognize us. Hundreds of fingers that might point us out. Hundreds of mouths that might shout our names.

A group of kids rushed past, giggling and pointing at the ride behind us. In the chaos of their excitement, I plucked a hat from a spinning rack standing outside of a souvenir stand, hiding it behind my back.

"Here," I said, stopping just outside the gates. "Try this on."

I slipped it on his head, tugging it down low on his forehead. It wasn't much of a disguise, but it was the best we could do.

Penn adjusted the hat, his eyes still a little too wide. "You don't think it was Markus, do you?"

Of course we were both thinking the same thing. How could either of us forget the anger on his face, the passion in his eyes? He wanted to bomb them. He said so himself. What if this was the violence he'd been craving? Was this the reason he'd sent us on a wild-goose chase after Penn's mother?

"But he told us to follow your mom?"

He shrugged. "I guess it was a pretty good distraction.

It got us out of the way, didn't it?"

The noise of the amusement park receded behind us, but my head was still full of that clattering din. I couldn't think straight.

Penn stopped outside the subway station. "What do we do now?"

"We need to go back to the others," I said.

He scowled. "How can we trust them after something like this? What if we're just walking into an inferno? If the police track us down, we'll go to jail. *Jail*, Ella. And not for something small. That bomb wasn't just destruction of property. It was murder."

I knew all that. "We have to go back anyway," I said. "We can't believe that stuff on the television without proof. What if it *wasn't* them?"

Penn nodded, but he didn't move.

"Here's what I know for sure," I said. "I know you and I had nothing to do with this. Nothing. And if our pictures were all over the news and we had nothing to do with this, maybe Markus didn't, either. We owe him enough to find out."

# Eight

*My* legs and arms were quaking by the time we reached the apartment. Every muscle in my body had been on high alert during the train ride. Even huddled against each other in the back of the subway car with Penn's hat pulled down as far as it would go over his face, we'd stiffened at every glance from every stranger, like the next time the doors opened, the police would rush in to grab us.

But none had.

Penn gripped my shoulders in his big hands. "Are you sure this is the right choice? Maybe we should just run. We could go south this time. To Mexico. We could live on the beach in a tent and fish for our food. We could forget any of this ever happened. These people aren't our responsibility."

I smiled sadly. "You know we can't."

Penn closed his eyes, leaning his forehead against mine. "I know." He sighed and then released me. "Let's do this then."

I knocked on the door and held my breath.

Jane's face, streaked with mascara, appeared in the doorway. "Thank *God*!" she said, pulling the two of us into a hug. "We didn't know what to think. There was no way to get ahold of you with the phones gone. We thought about heading out to look for you, but it'd be like trying to find a needle in a haystack, and with the news coverage..." She stopped talking, her eyes wide. "You guys, something really bad happened."

She led us into the living room where Markus and Ian sat slumped on the sofa, their gazes glued to the TV. Dave stared out the window with his back to us.

"We heard," I said.

Jane glanced uncomfortably at Markus, who muted the sound. The television continued to flicker, recycling the same images we'd seen earlier.

"Please tell us it isn't true," Penn said.

Markus threw his hands in the air. "See!" he said. "This is exactly what I'm talking about. If *they* believed it, we're screwed."

Jane sighed.

"It wasn't us," Ian said, leaning forward. "If that's what you mean."

Penn caught my eye and held my gaze. Could we trust they were telling us the truth? I gave him a little nod. It wasn't just that I wanted to believe them. I needed to.

"Honestly, we were afraid," I said, looking straight at Markus. "After what you said yesterday, we couldn't help it."

My gaze drifted to the television screen.

"That's exactly what they wanted," Markus said.

"Who?" I asked.

"The people who did this." He pointed to the burned shell of the training facility, his hand shaking. "They know we're weak. They know they've debilitated us with that attack at the warehouse. This is their last blow. They just severed the limb from the head, and now they're just waiting for us to bleed to death."

"So you think it's NuPet?" Penn asked.

"Of course it's NuPet," Markus said. "Who else would it be?"

"It doesn't seem too crazy to believe it could be another group like us. Or even our same group," Penn said. "Maybe everybody else at headquarters felt the way you did. Maybe this was their way of striking back. You can't know that for sure."

"Yes, I can!" Markus's voice exploded, echoing through the room.

Dave's sister appeared in the doorway. "Dave! Can I speak with you?"

He turned slowly from his spot at the window with a dazed look on his face, taking the group of us in as if he was only then noticing he wasn't alone in the room.

Markus glared at him. "Go ahead," he said. "It's not like you're being a big help here."

"Lay off him," Jane said. "You aren't making this any easier."

"I'll be right back," Dave muttered, ignoring Jane's words as much as he ignored Markus's. He followed his sister out the front door.

As soon as the latch shut, Jane turned on Markus. "Are you trying to tear us apart?" she asked. "Because it's working."

"He's useless," Markus muttered.

"He's just as stunned as you are," she said.

"Well, he can't tune out and give up," Markus said. "It's that sort of worried, weak attitude that's going to get us all killed."

Jane rolled her eyes. "Maybe you should be less worried about Dave's attitude and more worried about the fact the police might show up at this door any minute and arrest us for a bombing we had nothing to do with."

"Don't tell me what to worry about."

Jane folded her arms over her chest. The skin on her neck had turned red and blotchy. "It wouldn't matter if I did. It's not like you listen anyway," she said. "I'll be in the bedroom if you decide you want to have an actual conversation about this."

She stormed out of the room, and Markus glared after her. When the door closed, he sank back into the couch and blew out a breath. "I'm sorry," he said. "Maybe I overreacted."

Ian snorted. "It's been a shitty week."

"The pinnacle of shitty," Markus agreed. "I don't know how much more of this we can handle before we completely fall apart. It's bad enough we're fighting an uphill battle against people who are richer and more powerful than we are, but at least that's a real fight. I'll chase down those NuPet bastards and every single person they have wrapped around their fingers. At this point, I'm not sure I'd even feel bad bombing those assholes. But let *me* bomb them. Let *me* decide my own evil. I'll own it. I'll own every drop of blood I shed. But this…" He gestured at the television. "This isn't my fight. It's fake!"

The scene on the TV looked all too real to me, but I understood what he meant. Those weren't our sins being broadcast across the nation. Miss Gellner's death wasn't ours, even if they wanted to thrust it at us.

Penn backed away from the TV, his jaw clenching and unclenching as if worry had become something solid to chew on. He looked even more unsettled than he had during the subway ride back to the apartment.

I took his hand and led him toward the door. "I think we should get some air."

"I wouldn't go far," Markus called after us.

In the hallway, Penn dropped my hand and distractedly pressed the elevator button until the bell dinged and the door slid open. Inside, he leaned against the wall, and repeatedly tapped the button for the top floor.

Penn was normally a rock, steady and solid, but that newscast had clearly upset him. "Are you okay?" I asked.

He rubbed a hand over his face. "I just need some air," he said. "I don't like apartment buildings like this."

We came to a stop, and I followed Penn out into a small atrium. Above our heads, the glass ceiling was grimy with dirt and pigeon droppings, but a bit of sun filtered down. I caught sight of the city skyline and, past it, blue sky spotted with clouds.

Penn pushed his way through the atrium's doors onto the small rooftop patio. A gust of wind whipped past our faces, and he raised his head up, breathing deeply.

It was clear not many people used the space. There

were a few wooden benches, gray and weathered, pushed up near the wall, but it didn't look like they'd been used in years. A few neglected topiaries withered in pots by the building's edge where a brick pathway wound past the atrium to the other side of the roof.

Penn sank down onto one of the chairs and dragged his hands through his hair. "This isn't good."

"We can go downstairs if you'd rather."

"I don't mean *this*." He gestured to the roof. "I mean all of it: the bombing, the stuff on the news. It seems like it's all spiraling out of control."

"But at least it wasn't our fault."

He shook his head. "*We* know that, but nobody else does. Everyone I know will have seen it…my face all over the news. Like I'm a murderer. Do you think my mom knows yet?"

"We were *with* your mom," I said. "She's not going to think it was you."

"No, I know, you're right. I wasn't even thinking…" His voice trailed off and he stared into the distance with a blank look on his face. "Maybe we should call the cops. You said it yourself—we were with my mom. They can't pin it on us if we have an alibi."

I didn't know what to say. "Penn…"

"The police can't all be bad, right? This is the United States. This isn't Russia or something."

I could hear the hope in his voice, and it broke my heart. Sighing, I shook my head. "It doesn't matter. We can't take the chance," I said. "Someone is making it pretty clear we're a target. If they were willing to kill Miss Gellner to frame us, imagine what else they could do."

"I've *been* imagining it," Penn muttered. "That's the problem."

Another gust of wind swirled around our heads, and I wrapped my arms around my chest. From somewhere on the other side of the rooftop came raised voices, caught up in the breeze. A woman was yelling.

"...think what would happen to *me* if you get caught?"

I froze, and Penn sat up straighter.

"Is that Dave's sister?" I whispered.

"Maybe," he answered. "We should leave."

He stood, and the voices drew closer, moving as if they were about to round the corner.

"Over here," Penn said, pulling me behind the large metal tube of an air vent.

"We'll be fine. Stop worrying." There was no mistaking Dave's voice. "These are my friends. They've got my back."

"You're talking about them like you're all in high school or something," his sister said. "Half of them are pets, remember? They aren't like you." She shuddered. "You promised me it wouldn't be dangerous."

"I didn't know this would happen."

She laughed, but it was a mean sound. "You always underestimate things. It's your biggest problem."

"Can we not start this now? We hardly ever get time together. Do we need to spend it fighting?" he asked, trying to put his arm around her shoulders.

She shoved him away. "People are getting killed! I'm not really interested in a happy little reunion right now. You stuck me in the middle of a huge mess. I could get sent to jail for aiding and abetting criminals."

"That's not going to happen."

"How do you know?"

He threw up his hands. "It's only going to be a little longer. We're so close to winning this thing, and then all of this terrible stuff is going to pay off. I promise."

The confidence in his voice surprised me. Normally it was Markus with the passion and the certainty that the cause we were fighting for was just. Dave could get excited about his gear, but I'd never seen him speak about the movement this way.

Vanessa sighed. "We should get you back. They might be planning things without you there, and it's important for you to know what's going to happen."

The door to the atrium opened, and their voices died away.

"We should get back, too," I said.

Penn stood and looked out over the city. "I need a couple more minutes," he said. "Come here."

The cool wind climbed over the edge of the building, twisting around us so my hair whipped like a halo around my head. Penn slid behind me, smoothed down my hair, and rested his chin on top of my head. I sank back into his warm arms and shivered.

Down below us, the sounds of the city rose like a song, haunting and distant. If I ever got to make music again, I would remember these sounds. I would remember the sirens and the horns. I would remember the sound of jackhammers, of a city being built up and torn down at the same time.

• • •

*B*ack inside the apartment, everyone sat around the television again. Even Jane had reemerged from the bedroom and was sitting between Markus and Dave. If there had been a disagreement between all of them, there was no way to know it anymore. Maybe grudges couldn't last very long when the rest of the world was out to get you.

Penn and I lowered ourselves onto one of the sofas.

"Is there anything new?" I asked.

"Oh sure," Markus said. "They've got some guy on who's claiming he saw us all driving away from the scene of the bombing."

"It's pretty convenient," Jane said. "Our car drives past him at thirty miles an hour and he gets a good look at all of our faces. I don't understand how that reporter isn't calling him out on it."

She jabbed her finger at the man with the microphone, and the screen flickered as if sensing her outrage. A moment later the picture disappeared, leaving only blackness.

"That's weird." Ian picked up the remote and switched the channel, but the screen stayed dark. "There must be something wrong with—"

The screen flickered and a new picture filled the monitor.

A face we all recognized stared back at us. My mouth opened in a gasp, but there was no air in my lungs for breath. It felt like a huge pair of hands had just clamped down on my throat.

## Nine

The congressman sat in the dark leather wingback chair in his study with his legs crossed loosely at the knee.

The camera didn't show his desk or the chaise lounge on the other side of the room, where I'd once sat shackled and chained, but I could picture it all. I could feel the thick carpet under my feet, could smell old wood and leather. Paper. Cologne.

Penn glared at the TV. "What the hell?"

The congressman seemed to smile in response. "Hi," he said, leaning forward as if to take us all in. "I'm Congressman John Kimball."

"What is this?" Markus yelled, looking at Penn and me like we had any idea what was going on.

"As many of you know, I've been instrumental in fighting for the ethical treatment of genetically modified pets," the congressman went on.

"Turn this bullshit off," Markus said.

I held up my hand. "No, don't."

The congressman made my skin crawl. He filled my stomach with the lead weight of dread, but I couldn't ignore him. I refused to close my eyes and hide under the bed. I'd stare him in the face until the day I beat him.

His plastic smile gleamed. "Today I'm proud to be premiering a new video showing you the wonderful improvements happening in the lives of our genetically modified friends. Over the next few minutes, you'll get to experience firsthand the rehabilitation already helping to make it possible for these girls to become a respected part of our society."

The congressman's smiling face faded out accompanied by the uplifting strains of "America the Beautiful," and a new scene faded in: a half dozen girls sitting around a dining room table, laughing and talking as if they didn't have a care in the world. The music continued, a chorus of pure female voices rising together, and the montage continued. The girls now sat at computers, listening intently as instructors walked among them nodding and smiling. Next, the girls knelt in a garden, their hands buried in dark, freshly dug soil as they learned to plant bright-green seedlings.

The congressman's voice came in, describing the scene. "Their future is bright. With extensive training provided by top-notch instructors and educators, NuPet is ensuring its girls are being given the best chance at making a full transition into society. Not only are they being taught valuable life skills including computer technology, gardening, finance, and first aid, but they're being provided the encouragement to follow their dreams."

"One day I'll be a world-class chef," a girl said, smiling stiffly while she stood in front of a large industrial stove with bright chopped vegetables spread out in front of her.

They expected us to fall for this?

I clenched my hands. "None of this is real," I said. "What about the pictures of the girls we've seen? What about the warehouses? The chains? Where are *those* girls?"

"It's propaganda," Ian said. "It doesn't matter if it's real or not. The people who made this video obviously knew what they were doing."

"I'm on the road to becoming a school teacher," another girl said, a forced smile on her face. She sat posed at a desk in a library with a textbook open in front of her.

"Look at them!" I said, waving at the screen. "They're like dolls being posed in different positions. Can't people see that? Ask her to read that book," I yelled. "She can't do it! They're not teaching her anything."

"Am I the only one who noticed they're just showing the same five or six girls over and over again?" Penn asked. "This isn't real. This is a commercial. They're selling lies."

Jane shook her head. "It doesn't matter. People won't notice."

The scene changed one last time, zooming out to show the congressman and the president of NuPet standing among the same half dozen girls. The men shook the girls' hands, smiling charitably as if to congratulate each of them on finally becoming a real person.

Ian switched the television off, and we all sat in silence.

Maybe lies were the most powerful weapon. They didn't even need to win. They could just rewrite reality. What did truth matter when someone could just go on television and lie about it? They could turn us into murderers. They could dress up a handful of girls and kill the rest. It wouldn't matter because the world would believe whatever they told them.

"They're baiting us," Markus said. "They want to distract us from the real fight. They want us to match each swing they take, but it'll only waste our time." He steepled his fingers and tapped his lips. "We need to attack them. We need to fight back…but not where they're looking. It's the only way we're going to win. They think they've got the upper hand, and we need to let them believe that for now."

"So what are we going to do?" Dave asked.

Penn reached into his pocket and pulled out the piece of paper his mom had given him earlier. Since we'd heard the news of the bombing, I'd completely forgotten she'd given it to us.

"I don't know if it will lead to anything," he said, handing the paper over to Markus, "but it's a place to start, and I'm pretty sure my dad and his buddies at NuPet won't expect it."

Markus unfolded the paper and stared at the name penned across it.

*Erik Vasquez*

He was just one man, but maybe he held the secret to beating the congressman at his own game.

...

*I* smoothed down the thin wire running from the small mic attached to the front of my shirt to the battery pack taped to my lower back.

It didn't feel right to record Mr. Vasquez, not when he was going out of his way to help us like this, but Jane had assured me, over and over, that there was nothing unethical about it. There was simply no way for the entire group of us to meet with him all at once. It wasn't safe, and it would certainly draw way too much attention.

As it was, Markus thought we were already pushing our luck by having both Penn and me show up to meet with him instead of having Penn go alone, but Penn had been adamant that he wouldn't go without me. I wasn't arguing. Too much could happen. What if someone recognized him and called the police? If Penn was going to be arrested, I was going with him.

Penn grabbed my hand as we approached the little pizza place on First Street. Next door, a group of people poured out of a bar. They bumped into us, laughing and joking, hardly noticing us as they continued on into the night. Jazz music spilled out into the street with them, mixing with the squealing of car brakes and the rumble of motors. This city felt so alive. What would it be like to sit down at one of these restaurants and soak in all the bustle and commotion without worrying about who was watching? What would it be like to let go, to become one of them, just another face on the street, another voice in the crowd?

"This is it?" Penn asked, coming to a stop outside Vic's Pizza.

Through the window, we could see the tiny dining room with its wooden tables and ripped red vinyl chairs. The dark brick walls were covered in writing where visitors had jotted their names down in layer after layer of ink.

"It doesn't seem very private," I said.

The look of worry on Penn's face told me he didn't think so, either, but there was nothing we could do about it now. This was the place where Mr. Vasquez had asked us to meet him.

The bell above the door jingled as we stepped inside.

"Just sit wherever," the boy at the register said, gesturing to some empty seats near the back of the room.

We scanned the restaurant. There were men and women lifting greasy slices of pizza to their lips and sipping tall, sweating glasses of beer. And even though no one looked up as we made our way to the back, I still wondered if any of them had been sent here to watch us.

A man sitting alone at one of the booths along the back wall looked up at us as we approached. He was handsome, with thick dark hair just beginning to gray on the sides. He wasn't dressed in anything fancy, but you could tell right away he was important.

He lifted his hand in a small wave and nodded for us to sit.

"Mr. Vasquez?" Penn asked.

He reached out a hand. "Please, call me Erik. You probably don't remember, but I met you when you were just a little boy. You and your mom came to dinner with me in Chicago."

Penn frowned. "Wait, were you the guy that did the magic tricks?"

Erik laughed. "Ahhh, yes! You have a very good memory. Although, I find objection with the word 'tricks.' Not just anyone can make a steak knife disappear."

He winked and turned to me, his bright eyes crinkled at the edges as he took me in. I'd had plenty of men look at me over the past few months, but his gaze was different. There was no hunger in his eyes, only kindness and curiosity and delight. "And you must be Ella," he said, extending his hand. "It's a pleasure to meet you."

Penn relaxed back into the booth a bit, and I reached out to shake Erik's warm hand.

"Thank you for meeting us," I said. "And on such short notice."

"Anything for Elise," he said, turning back to Penn. "I'm not sure if you know this about your mom, but she saved my ass more times than I can count when we were in school. If it wasn't for her, I'd probably still be trying to pass my philosophical methods course."

"I didn't," Penn said. "Know, I mean."

"Well, she was brilliant. You didn't hear it from me, but a few of my papers might have ended up with more words written by her than by me by the time they got turned in." He chuckled and leaned back in his seat. "Your mother is a special person. I'm sorry your family has been going through this."

In the middle of the table, a candle inside a red glass jar flickered, and Penn's gaze traveled to it. Was he thinking about his family?

"Are you sure this is an okay place for us to talk?" I

asked. "There might be people trying to listen in on our conversation."

"I know it seems like a strange choice," he said. "But this is the place I trust the most. More than my office. More than my house. Whenever I've got confidential business to attend to, this is where I come. I've been friends with the owner for years, and he keeps an eye out for me while I'm in here. Almost twenty years working for the district attorney and he's never let me down. So don't worry. Whatever we say stays right here." He patted the worn wooden tabletop.

Guilt flashed over me. It would stay at the table…and with Markus and Jane, who were hearing everything.

"They're blaming us for the bombing at Greenwich Training Center," Penn said. "But we didn't have anything to do with it."

Erik raised an eyebrow. "I guessed as much."

"And now we need to find a way to fight back, not just against all the terrible things NuPet has done to girls like me, but for trying to frame us," I said. "NuPet and the congressman have all the power, even if they're making it seem like we're the ones to be scared of. They still have hundreds of girls like me held captive, and we're pretty sure they're going to kill them soon if we don't do something to stop them."

"You have proof?" he asked. "That's not the story I've been hearing."

"If you're talking about that commercial, it's a lie," Penn said.

One of his eyebrows rose.

"They're dressing them up and using them like props,"

I said. "But if you look at that video, there are only a half dozen girls. It's just for show. They want the public to stop asking questions and forget about us so they can go ahead and kill the rest without anyone noticing."

"That's a pretty big accusation," Erik said.

"But it's the truth," Penn said.

"Truth is subjective."

"What's that supposed to mean?" Penn asked.

Erik sighed. "I'm not accusing you of lying. I'd love to believe in one real truth, but it's never that easy. What might be true to you is false to someone else. All I'm saying is you can't rely on generalities and presumptions. You need to show proof if you want to convince people of truth. And right now, NuPet is doing a pretty good job of offering up evidence to back its claim."

My face grew hot. "Even if that evidence is a lie?"

Erik shrugged sadly.

"So, what if we made a commercial of our own?" I asked. "We could offer our own evidence. Real evidence."

"There's a moment in the video that was filmed in a room I recognized from the Yale campus," Penn said. "My dad has a lot of buddies on the alumni board, so he must have convinced them to let NuPet film there. What if we go there and catch them on camera? What if we switch the narrative? We could expose their lies. We could tell the public the truth."

"It's not a terrible idea," Erik said, "though, I don't know much about making videos. But I'll tell you this. Even if you did succeed in recording their lies, if you made a great film and found someone who would actually agree to air it, I doubt it would do much good."

"But we'd prove NuPet is trying to manipulate people," I said, incredulous. "They could see the truth with their own eyes."

"It doesn't matter if it's truth or not," Erik said. "I'm sorry to disappoint you, but this is bigger than a few videos. You might convince a few people, but only until the next batch of propaganda gets released. They're a huge company. And they'll always be one step ahead of you. They have more funds. More power. More connections."

"So it's pointless to try?" I asked.

"That's not what I'm saying." He took a sip of water and swallowed. "This is the thing that's nearly impossible for me to explain. I've been trying to fight corruption since I was just a little bit older than you two, but it's not cut-and-dried. It's not like you can arrest one person and fix everything. I've seen the kind of damage it can do to our country, to cities, to businesses, to families. But this kind of thing isn't easy to fight. It's complicated. It's a web. A sticky, tangled, mess of a web."

My hand climbed to my neck. I knew what he meant. I was just as trapped in it as anyone.

Why had Elise sent us here with such confidence if there was nothing this man could do for us? I dropped my hand and picked at the chipped edge of the table. There must have been something we were missing, some way this man could help us…

I turned to Penn. "What about those files your mom was talking about?"

Erik leaned forward. "Files?"

"The congressman has files he's using to blackmail

people," I explained. "Elise said it's the reason he's convinced so many people to help him. They're afraid if they don't, he'll expose them."

"It's probably how he got the police to blame us for that bombing," Penn said.

Erik considered him. "Maybe."

"Ask my mom," Penn said. "She's the one who told us. Apparently my dad has a ton of information he keeps in his study at our house. Can't you get someone to search it? I bet you'll find more than enough stuff to prove what he's been doing."

Erik shook his head. "I can't search a person's home without probable cause. Believe me, my people want this as badly as you do, but our hands are tied."

"But there is probable cause. I'm *telling* you."

"In a case like this, your word just isn't enough. I can't search private property."

"Isn't this sort of thing your job?" Penn said. "Don't you have people that can get warrants or whatever? Or are you afraid? Does he have dirt on you, too?"

"No," he said. "Not me. Not directly."

"What's that supposed to mean?"

For just a moment, I thought I caught a glimmer of fear in his eye. "Listen, I have no real way of knowing how deep any of this goes, but I do know this: your father is a dangerous man. I've known it for years. He doesn't think the way a normal person does. He's brilliant. His brain could do a lot of good or a lot of bad. He knows how to read people, how to use them. He always has." He shook his head sadly. "You can bet he has ties to the police in precincts all over New York and Connecticut, so it's not going to do us any good to get the police involved. And that means my hands are tied. I can't break the law."

"But he can?"

"That's his prerogative. Not mine. I can give you advice, but that's as much as I can offer."

"What advice?"

"Well," he said, leaning forward onto his elbows, "your mom might not be totally off base about those files, but I can guarantee your father isn't keeping them solely at his house. He's not stupid. Files like that are worth millions, and he wouldn't risk keeping them somewhere unsecured. I've heard rumors that he keeps all his information on a server in the Catskills."

Penn looked at him eagerly. "Where?"

"I wish I knew, but it's just a lead," Erik said. "I don't have anything solid."

Penn's hands balled beneath the table. "So your advice is a hint. What are we supposed to do with that?"

"I'm sorry," Erik said. "But this is reality. Nothing is ever going to just fall into your lap. You have to search for it."

Penn scoffed. "So I'm supposed to just *search* the whole Catskill mountain range hoping I stumble upon my dad's secret files?"

"Maybe the reality is that, for you to have any real impact, you're going to have to take down the whole corrupt system allowing these guys to exist," Erik said.

"Isn't that your job?" I demanded.

He frowned. It wasn't an angry look. There was real sadness on his face. Real regret. "I wish there was more I could do," he said. "Can you at least let me buy you dinner?"

My stomach turned. How could a slice of pizza fix anything?

"No thanks," Penn said, standing. "We should probably get back."

Erik stood, too, reaching out to shake our hands. "I'm sorry this didn't work out the way you planned. But please, don't hesitate to contact me if something new comes up."

"All right," Penn said.

"And send my love to your mom."

Penn stiffened. "I will."

Was that what this was all about? Elise? Did Erik want to seem like he was being helpful because he had feelings for her? Maybe he'd never had any intention of helping us. It was impossible to know, but it didn't matter anyway. We were on our own.

No one glanced up at us as we left. We were inconsequential, just two kids leaving a pizza place. And that's exactly what we felt like—kids. Powerless. Weak. Alone.

The bell on the door jingled lightly once more, and we stepped back out into the night. Once again, the sound of jazz music drifted out of the bar next door. I paused, listening to the soulful cry of the saxophone. For a moment, I closed my eyes, focusing on the full, round tone.

And then, just as the last note of the song died away, the bomb went off.

# Ten

*O*ne single note rang in my ears.

High pitched.

Whining.

The saxophone… It had just been playing, wasn't it? I could remember the low, sweet crooning, but that wasn't what this sound was.

I shook my head and tried to bring a hand up to my eyes, but something held it clamped down at my side. I tried to wiggle free, but there was something pressing my back, too, making it hard to breathe.

I coughed. My mouth was dry, thick with dust and the taste of metal.

"Penn," I croaked. "Penn?"

I blinked, trying to turn my head.

In front of me the ground spread out like a battlefield. Red-and-blue lights blinked behind a cloud of dust. Dark forms moved left and right, up and down. Long limbs waved to one another.

My cheek pressed against something rough.

"Penn!"

"Here's one," someone said. They sounded far away, a voice inside a bubble floating somewhere high above my head.

The weight on my back lifted, and a hand slipped beneath me, lifting me from the ground. I choked in a deep gulp of air and balanced on my wobbly legs. Even with the world tipped vertically once more, I couldn't make sense of it.

"Ella!"

I turned.

The dark outline of Penn stumbled toward me. Behind him, the building crumbled in on itself. Brick and cement. Wire and steel. Here and there a tipped table, a smashed chair. Broken glass littered the ground, glittering with the orange light of flames that glowed inside the hole where a door had just been. A door. A door. The door that had just jingled shut behind me.

"Miss, we need to get you checked out," the man with the faraway voice said.

My hand flapped up weakly, pushing him away from me. "Not now."

"Miss?"

Penn, face smeared with dirt, stood before me, and I slumped into him.

"Are you okay?" His hands darted up to a large gash on my forehead. "You're bleeding."

"I'm fine." I tried to shrug away the pulsing in my head.

Penn held me, his hands traveling up my arms, across my shoulders. They brushed my cheeks, touched my ears, my eyes, his fingers double-checking that every other part of me was still intact, still whole. Alive.

"What happened?" My voice stuck on the grit inside my mouth, and my gaze wavered to the sidewalk in front of me where a candle sat seemingly unharmed, the flame still flickering inside the red glass jar.

"It was an explosion," Penn said. "Inside the restaurant."

"Is Mr. Vasquez…?"

"We need to get both of you checked out," the man said, still standing beside me.

I turned to look at him, a youngish man with red hair, dressed in a dark-blue shirt and pants. "Not now," I said, my voice rising in irritation. He was trying to help, but we didn't have time for him. "Please, go help someone else."

"Ella, are you sure we shouldn't get you checked out?" Penn asked.

"I'm fine. Really," I said, ignoring the pain as I turned back. The hole in the side of the building beckoned, and I tugged the neck of my shirt up over my mouth.

"Miss, you can't go in there," the man said, sensing what I was about to do. "You need to come with me."

"Our friend's in there," Penn said.

The man grabbed his arm. "I'm sorry, but you two need to come with me. You need to let the professionals do their jobs."

Penn shrugged off the man's grasp and followed me, stumbling over the rubble. Both the front door and the large glass window were gone. We stepped over the place where the threshold had been, our feet crunching on gravel-size bits of glass and plaster.

To our left, behind a tipped-over table, another man in blue rushed to uncover a woman's face. He struggled to lift a piece of plaster from off her body. Her arm stuck out from a pile of bricks, unmoving. I tried to imagine her face. I must have just seen her, whoever she'd been. I'd walked right past her, minutes ago. She must have been sipping her soda or taking a bite from her pizza and now... I clutched my chest, trying to catch my breath. I was one of the last people on earth to see her alive, and I didn't even remember what she looked like.

Penn and I made our way over shards of wood and plaster that had fallen from the ceiling, trying not to look too closely into the wreckage.

Only a portion of the back wall of the restaurant still stood. Most of the brick had broken loose, collapsing across the booths. Which table had we been sitting at? I couldn't remember. Nothing looked the same anymore.

At my feet, the red-checkered corner of a menu stuck out of the mess.

"Ella," Penn called. He knelt in front of a body.

The man lay facedown, his head tipped ever so slightly to the side. The dark hair, only slightly messed up, was coated in white dust, like he'd aged years in just a few minutes' time. His skin was coated in dust, too, except for the line of dark red trickling down the back of his head and soaking into the fabric of his shirt collar.

I dropped to my knees. "Help me uncover him," I said, clawing at the debris. The bricks fell to pieces in my hands. The fine, powdery dust covering Mr. Vasquez puffed up in clouds of white while I dug, clinging to my skin, my hair, my lashes.

"It's too late," Penn said.

"Get one of those men to help us!"

"*Ella*." Penn grabbed my face and forced me to look at him. "It's too late."

I stopped digging, letting his words settle over me. My vision flickered, darkness closing in at the edges. I tried to blink it away.

"We need to get out of here," he said, looking over his shoulder at the gaping hole in the side of the building.

"We can't just leave him."

Penn pulled me closer so all I could see were his eyes. Those eyes. Would I ever be able to look into them again without seeing all this agony staring back at me?

"We can't stay here," he said, shaking my shoulders a little and sending icy spirals of pain through my brain. "This wasn't an accident. Someone planned this."

"You think this is our fault?" My gaze fell to the stain of red slowly congealing on Mr. Vasquez's neck.

"We don't have time to think about that right now," Penn said. "Whoever did this is going to find out you and I are still alive soon enough."

The front of the building was bustling with rescue workers. On the sidewalk, the boy from the front desk lay across a white stretcher. A bandage wound around his forehead, blood blossoming across the white fabric. His eyes stared right past us as we walked by.

"There you are!" It was the same man who'd been so adamant earlier that we see one of the medics. Why couldn't he just leave us alone? "You really need to come with me."

He took me by the arm, steering me toward a large white ambulance parked in the center of the street. Its dancing red lights cut through the air above our heads.

"We're fine," Penn said, following behind. "Really, there are other people that need you more than we do."

We stopped beside the back doors, and the man grabbed a stiff, black blanket from a small shelf inside, draping it across my shoulders. "Hey, Carter," he called out to a woman crouched in the back of the van. "Will you wait with these two for just a sec?" He turned back to us, his face serious. "Stay here. You've been in a very serious accident. You can't just leave the scene. Understand?"

We nodded. But as soon as he rounded the corner of the ambulance, Penn pulled me behind the van's open doors. "We need to get out of here," he whispered. "As soon as that woman looks away we need to make a run for it. Got it?"

I nodded.

"Excuse me, do you have any water?" Penn asked the woman. "I need to rinse this dust out of my mouth."

"Yes, of course," she said, "Hold on just a second."

She turned away to open a small cabinet and Penn squeezed my hand. Just one squeeze, but it meant *go*. Together, we rushed away from the ambulance into the dark.

We rounded the front of a cab and stopped short, me gripping the hood to find my balance.

The red-haired rescue worker leaned against the back door of a dark sedan, flipping through a stack of papers on a clipboard. He looked up when he saw us. "Where are you going?" he asked. "You need to be cleared before you leave."

"I know. We were just trying to find a phone," Penn said. "We need to get in touch with...my mom."

"Mmm-hmm," he said, setting down the clipboard and nodding to a man who stood on the other side of the car. He opened the back door and grabbed another blanket from the back seat, this time draping it around Penn. "I'm worried you two might be in shock," he said, keeping his hands on Penn's shoulders. "Why don't you have a seat? Then we can see about getting you a phone, okay?"

He lowered Penn down onto the edge of the back seat, careful not to hit his head against the roof.

I glanced between the two men. Something didn't feel right. "My head really does hurt," I said. "Maybe we should wait in the back of the ambulance."

The other man wasn't dressed in dark blue like the ambulance worker. He wore a white shirt, rolled up at the sleeves. The skin on his wide face was pocked and rough. It was the kind of face that looked like it had seen terrible things, too many to count, and now it had grown bored of tragedy.

"I'm sorry. We just have a few questions we need to ask you first," this man said.

Penn struggled to stand, but the ambulance worker pushed him back into the car, slamming the door.

Eyes wide, Penn tugged at the handle, but it was locked. "Go, Ella!" he yelled, smacking the window. "Run!"

I twisted away from the car, but the man's hand clenched my arm. "Nope, darling. You're not going anywhere, either," he said simply, clasping a pair of handcuffs around my wrist. He pulled me toward the front door to the car and shoved me inside. "We've got some questions to ask you, too."

"We didn't have anything to do with it," I said for what felt like the hundredth time.

The man with the weathered face didn't even look up from his paperwork. He'd only said a few words to me since we arrived at the police station. He wanted a confession. That was all. If I wasn't willing to confess my guilt, or Penn's for that matter, he wasn't interested in talking. They'd separated us the moment we'd arrived, smacking a pair of handcuffs on Penn as soon as the door to the car had opened.

I stared at the cement wall. Was Penn on the other side, staring back at me? My head ached from where it had smacked the ground after the explosion. The pain seemed as solid as that cinder block, something living that had taken up residence behind my eyes.

I sat up a little straighter in my chair. The metal was cold and hard, but I hardly noticed it anymore. I concentrated on that pain, focusing on it instead of the way I could hear the air whistle through the man's nose each time he took a breath.

I could sit here forever. That was the thing they didn't realize about me. Sure, I wanted to lay my head on the cool table or, better yet, sleep, but I'd never give them the pleasure of seeing that weakness. I'd been trained to sit still, to ignore discomfort and boredom. This room, with its cement walls and its solitary table, couldn't break me. I didn't need food or water. I didn't need sun or fresh air. Miss Gellner had given me a gift, even if she hadn't realized it at the time. She thought she was teaching us how to be showpieces, ornaments, perfect in their stillness, but that was just what we looked like from the outside. What she hadn't realized was that she'd been teaching us to meditate, how to turn inside ourselves to a serene and self-sufficient place where we could exist for as long as we needed, even when that place was filled with pain.

"You're wasting your time with me," I said. "It isn't going to do you any good to keep me here."

The man grunted. "We'll see."

Retreating back into my bruised mind, I rubbed my finger and thumb together. The black ink had dried, but I could still feel the way the intake officer had held each finger, pressing it against the paper, the swirls of my prints appearing like magic on that white page. I tried to picture the pain in my head leaving my body and seeping into those black swirls.

But then, for the first time in hours, the door to the room opened and a new man walked in. "Hey, Metcalf," he said, "the body count is in. They're reporting five fatalities and six more in critical condition."

Metcalf nodded, staring directly at me instead of the man at the door.

Five people were dead. Is that what he wanted me to hear? Did he want to watch that information sink in, see how my face would give away my guilt? Well, it wouldn't.

"Also, the bomb unit called. They've got the prints."

He sat up, interested. "And?"

"It's a match," he said, giving him a thumbs-up before he closed the door again.

Metcalf stared down at the table, smiling. It was an ugly smirk, self-satisfied and gloating. It was the kind of smile a mean child would get after they'd won a game, realizing that bragging was even better than victory itself. I'd seen that smile on Ruby's friends.

And even though he wasn't looking in my direction, I knew his smile was for me. My fists clenched under the table. I wanted to reach out and smack him. I wanted to feel my fingernails tear the thick skin on his cheeks. I let myself imagine it. Maybe I was a terrible person, reveling in the joy I would get from his pain, but I didn't care.

He cleared his throat. "Don't you want to know what that was all about?"

Honestly, I wasn't sure how much more information my brain could handle, but I relaxed my gaze, barely tensing the muscles in my cheeks so my lips would lift ever so slightly at the edges. My sweet, rosebud mouth would never show him the pain and disgust I felt inside.

"Would you like to tell me?" I asked.

His eyes narrowed. I wasn't playing his game the way he wanted me to, and he couldn't hide his anger from me. "You're a nasty little thing, aren't you?"

I blinked, inviting him to go on.

"I'm sure you fool a lot of people with that pretty little face of yours, but it doesn't work for me," he said. "I know what sort of person you are. You're greedy and conceited. You think you're so special. You think you deserve to be treated differently than other people, but you're just a doll somebody created to play with. And now you're angry because you can't figure out why you can't get your way. But I'll give you a hint. It's because you're stupid. They gave you a pretty little head, but they didn't put anything inside of it."

I didn't move, didn't look away. He could insult me all he wanted to, but I didn't need to listen.

He snorted. "Oh, you can sit there pretending it doesn't bother you, but you'll feel different when they're playing with you in prison. You'll make quite the toy in there, you know. But that's probably what you're good at, isn't it?"

He stood up and prowled around the table until he was standing directly over me, so close I could feel the front of his legs pressed against my arm. I wanted to pull away, but I didn't.

"That's where you're going. Prison," he said, resting one of his huge paws on my shoulder. "The fingerprints came back. From the bomb. Your boyfriend's prints are all over it. Did he think he was clever, making a bomb out of a guitar amp? Is that the sort of hipster shit he thought would be cool?"

My heart pounded in my ears, pulsing in time with the throbbing in my head, as the reality of what he was saying crashed into me with the same force as that bomb.

"Got your attention, did I? You didn't know they could fingerprint a bomb, did you?" He laughed. "You were too stupid to realize that."

His voice faded away, drowned out by the roaring in my ears. Guitar amp… Guitar amp… Those two words played over and over in my head, and my eyes glazed, imagining the inside of Penn's room. I could picture his bed, his desk, his wall of instruments, and below them, the amplifier boxes with their waffled fronts and dozens of small knobs.

And then I remembered the last time I'd been in Penn's room, the night I sneaked in through his window. The room had looked so different, all of its uniqueness stripped away so it looked more like this concrete cell than the messy explosion of personality it had been before. I remembered how empty the wall had been with his instruments gone. I hadn't thought to ask where they'd been taken, but I bet if I did now, he would tell me his father had been the one who'd gotten rid of them.

Of course those amps would have had his fingerprints all over them. Had his dad been planning this all along? Or had he believed at first that he was hurting him enough just by taking his things away? At what point did he realize he could use Penn's most beloved possessions to frame him for murder?

There was a knock at the door, and Metcalf snatched his hand away from my shoulder, taking a step away from me as the door opened.

A woman poked her head in. "Sorry to interrupt," she said. "But they need you up front. The news is hounding us for a press conference and everyone's saying you should do it since you have the most information about the case."

"Edwards isn't going to do it?" he asked, surprised.

"No, he thinks you should."

"Oh, sure. I can pull something together," he said, picking up his papers and tapping them against the tabletop to straighten them. The pleasure on his face was unmistakable. Any gratification he had been getting from tormenting me was nothing compared to his obvious desire to feel important.

"I'll stay with the suspect," the woman said, sliding into the room, where she stood next to the door with her hands clasped in front of her.

"Yeah, sure." Metcalf didn't even glance at me as he left the room. "Thank you, Agent Marks."

The clack of his shoes faded down the hall, and the woman, Agent Marks, tilted her head, listening as if to make sure he was really gone before she reached out and pulled the door closed.

"You're the pet?" she asked. "The one they brought in for the bombing?"

I swallowed. Her eyes were intense, unblinking. A kind of nervous energy radiated off her.

My gaze traveled to her waist where the black butt of a gun stuck out of the holster strapped to her hip.

"Answer the question," she ordered.

"Yes. I am."

Standing with her back pressed against the door, she slowly reached behind her. Her fingers closed around the lock and she twisted it, locking the two of us inside together.

# Eleven

*A*gent Marks wiggled the doorknob, making sure it was locked, and then she was in front of me. It only took her three long strides to reach the table. She leaned forward against it, her palms spread on the cold metal top, and stared me directly in the eyes. This close, I could see the specks of yellow in her irises.

"You're bleeding," she said, studying the gash on my head. "No one cleaned you up?" Her eyes twitched with a look of annoyance or revulsion. I couldn't tell.

I sat up straighter. "I'm fine."

"Somehow I doubt that." Her breath puffed in my face, but I didn't back away. "They've got your friend's fingerprints all over the bomb."

"I know," I said, my voice sticking in my throat so it came out more of a squeak than an answer. "He told me."

"It's all they need to charge him," she said. "Do you

understand that?"

Was that anger in her voice? Satisfaction? I couldn't read her, only that she wasn't kidding around.

Underneath the table, my legs trembled with the need to run. Not that I believed I *could* run at the moment. I turned my head away from her, not wanting to look her in the eye anymore. She wasn't telling me anything different from what Metcalf had said, but her words frightened me in a way his hadn't. He'd wielded his words like a weapon to my throat, a threat he'd wanted to cut me with, but hers felt different. These words weren't meant to threaten me. They were simply facts when she spoke them. Cold, emotionless facts.

My throat tightened. "He didn't do it."

She glanced back at the locked door before she reached for the belt at her waist.

I sucked in a deep breath, closing my eyes, waiting for the bullet. Was this it? If the congressman had sent her to finish me off, I only hoped he'd finally be satisfied.

But the bullet didn't strike. Instead, a cold hand wrapped around my wrist. I opened my eyes to find Agent Marks inches away from me. Her frizzy brown hair had fallen like a curtain in front of her face. A second later, my right hand slipped free from its cuff.

"We've got to hurry," she said, standing up so her flushed cheeks came back into view as she buckled the empty cuffs to her belt.

"Where?" I asked.

"We'll take you out the back door."

"I don't understand," I stuttered.

"The case is a sham," she said. "The fingerprints...the

witness list... Someone set this thing up to make it look like you two were responsible for that bombing, and for some reason most of the people in this department are going along with it. It's insane. And the ones who realize something is up are too freaked out to say anything. But there's no way I'm going to be one of those sheep. I'm not just going to sit here doing nothing while they pin this on the two of you. I'm sorry there's not anything I can do for your friend, but I can get you out if we hurry."

"Wait." I held up my hand, forcing my throbbing brain to digest what she was saying to me. "I can't just leave Penn." That's what she was asking—for me to just abandon him. "You said it yourself. He didn't bomb that place."

"I'm afraid his innocence is inconsequential right now."

"It isn't to me," I said.

She shook her head sadly. "I'm sorry. But if we're going to get you out, we have to move quickly."

"No. I can't. I can't go," I said. "He'd never leave me. He wouldn't. Besides, I'm the reason he's in this mess in the first place. There's got to be something we can do."

Her face grew serious. "Listen. I know it feels like you should let your emotions lead you right now, but I promise, it's not the time. You have to be smart. Strategic. And the best thing for you to do right now is leave."

I swallowed. "You're sure there's no way to get him, too?"

She shook her head and strode to the door. Her hand hovered over the lock, waiting for me to give her the go-ahead, but I sat in my chair. Frozen. In some other room in this building Penn was getting framed for killing five people. It was clear from what Agent Marks had said that not everyone believed it, but that didn't mean anyone would protect him. If I left, he'd be alone here with no one to support him. No one to protect him. And even though there was nothing I could do, I wanted to believe he could feel my presence. That the air I breathed would leave my lips and find his, and he wouldn't feel so alone.

"You're not going to do him any good in here," Agent Marks said, sensing my hesitation. "The best thing you can do is to get out, get that gash on your head looked at, and then get to the bottom of this. Something stinks, and I'm afraid to find out how much of it is coming from right inside this department."

I got shakily to my feet.

"Won't you get in trouble for this?" I asked.

"Don't worry. I've got it covered. Someone in processing owes me one. And they don't have enough to keep you here for much longer anyway." She paused, finally twisting the lock on the door. "I've been watching your story for a long time…yours and the other pets', too. I'm sure a lot of people have. I've never known how I could help. It feels good to finally find a way."

"Thank you."

She pushed the door open and grabbed my upper arm, throwing her head back in confidence. This woman knew how to put on a show. Her confidence reminded me a bit of Penn's mother.

We strode past a few open doors, me leaning on Agent Marks more than I probably should have. A few people looked up from their desks, and Agent Marks gave them each a curt nod, moving on without consequence. At the end of the hall, she led me down a short flight of stairs, pushing her way out a pair of glass doors that led onto a busy side street.

She released my arm. "You're going to need to hurry. You don't have long," she said. "This isn't a normal case. The DA is saying they want to prosecute. Someone has already assigned him counsel from the public defender's office, and I'd bet you anything the guy they picked is in their pocket, too."

My mind raced, trying to concentrate on what she was saying, but the pain purred inside my head, growing stronger, distracting me. The DA, those were the people Mr. Vasquez had worked with. It seemed like ages ago we'd sat with him in that booth in the pizza place, but it hadn't even been a day. I tried to remember what he'd said about the people he worked with. Had he mentioned them? Did he say the congressman might be blackmailing them, too? I tried to replay our conversation, but all I could picture was the way he'd looked lying facedown on the floor, blood pooled on the back of his shirt.

I shook my head. It was a jumbled puzzle, made even worse by that explosion, and I was struggling to piece it all together. "The counsel. What's that?"

"His lawyer," she said. "And if he doesn't have someone real to defend him, anything could happen. My guess is they're going to move him through here so fast he'll be rotting in a prison cell with a life sentence in a week."

"What am I supposed to do?"

She looked at me resolutely. "Don't you have anyone who can help?"

"I thought I did," I said, "but that bomb killed him."

• • •

*T*he sun had already set by the time I found my way back to Penn's uncle's apartment building. My clothes were stiff from my own sweat mixing with the fine, white dust the bomb had created. My fingers kept climbing to the spot on my forehead where my skull had met the ground. My bangs covered the small cut, but they were stiff with blood and dirt.

My whole body ached, but the throbbing in my head drowned out most of it. The pounding had started on the stone-size bump on my forehead, but it had soon spread, reaching its fingers around my whole skull so it felt like a giant pair of hands squeezing with such pressure my eyes threatened to burst from their sockets with each step.

By the time I shuffled up to the newsstand where Penn and I had waited for Elise to emerge from her building the other day, the pain had taken on a life of its own. It had a smell, like the moist breath of a horse in one of the fields by Penn's house. The arms it had wrapped around my whole body were covered in dark-gray fur, matted and dense, so thick it drowned out all the sounds of the city. Now, the only sound I could hear was the pain's low voice, singing softly in my ears.

I collapsed against the wall in the alleyway beside the apartment, staring up at the fire escape climbing the side of the building.

"Stop holding me," I muttered, swatting at the air around my head, trying to get the beast to let go of his grip on me long enough so I could think clearly.

I couldn't remember how long I'd been talking directly to the pain, but I wondered now if it was the reason so many people had steered wide paths around me while I'd walked down the middle of the sidewalk.

I stumbled to the front door of the building and tried the door, but it was locked tight.

On the brick beside the door, a brass panel with a few dozen labels listed the names of the people who lived inside. Beside each of the labels there was a round button. If I pressed them one by one, maybe Elise would answer. None of the names looked familiar. If Penn had told me his uncle's name, the pain had pushed it out of my mind. I stared at the letters printed on the little tabs, but they only blurred, the alphabet twisting and swimming in shapes I couldn't even remember the names of.

"Can I help you?" a man asked, stopping beside the door. "Wait. Your head…it's bleeding."

I glanced from the buzzers to his face. "Oh, yes, that." My hand hovered above the cut. "I'm all right. I'm trying to find someone."

"Do they live in this building?" he asked.

I stepped away from him, scrutinizing his face, and his eyes narrowed ever so slightly. He wasn't old, even though there was a bit of gray sprinkled in his beard. Had I seen him before? I turned to look across the street to the small café. Maybe it had been a mistake to come here. There would still be people following Elise, wouldn't there? I'd forgotten that. And this man…was he the one who'd followed us at Coney Island? Was he the man with the baby stroller? I couldn't remember what he looked like. His face swam in front of me, blurred and fuzzy at the edges.

I stepped away from him.

"I… Never mind," I said. "This is the wrong place."

"Wait." He reached out for my arm. "Who are you looking for? You look like you need help. Please, let me help you."

I twisted away from his grasp. "I'll yell," I said, looking around at the people who strolled down the street. "I will. If you touch me again."

I could feel the scream pressing against the back of my throat, ready to burst out like the howl of a wounded animal. Would any of these strangers even help, or would they just keep walking, pretending I didn't exist?

"Whoa!" The man held up his hands, stepping back from me. "Take it easy. I was just trying to be helpful."

"You can tell him he won't get away with this forever," I said. "People are going to find out. People…people are going to…" I shook my head, unable to finish.

What would people do? Nothing. They would keep ignoring me the way they always had. That was the truth of the matter.

"Sweetheart, you need to get some help," the man said, unlocking the door and pushing his way inside. He pulled the door closed, making sure it locked securely behind him.

Maybe I'd been wrong.

Maybe I hadn't seen him before.

*A*gain, I leaned against the wall in the alleyway and looked back up at the building. The brick mocked me, reminding me of one of the stories Ruby had read to me when she was trying to teach me all the letters. I blew a puff of air from my lips, wishing I could huff and puff and magically make the walls fall down. If I could only blow away this throbbing wolf inside me, it could tear down this whole building.

My gaze followed the black vertebrae of fire escape up to the top of the building, trying to remember what Penn had said when we were here last. He'd pointed out his uncle's apartment, the one with the metal sculpture winding around the railing like a snake.

I walked over to the place where the fire escape started, about ten feet up the side of the building. I tilted my head back, gazing up between the black, slatted steel to the night sky above me. It might as well have been a witch's tower, and me, I was waiting for a princess to send down her golden hair. Ruby's stories pulsed inside my mind, churning as if they were trying to escape. Who could have guessed there was so much truth inside of all those fairy tales she'd read to me?

All I wanted was to curl into a ball and go to sleep.

Up above me, Elise sat inside one of those rooms. I wondered if she even knew about Penn. Had someone told her that her boy was locked inside a cement room being blamed for killing all those people? Maybe she couldn't help us take down the congressman, but surely she could help get Penn out.

The bottom rung of the fire escape ladder started high above my head. Even a six-foot-tall man wouldn't be able to jump up and grab it. I pushed on the side of a Dumpster sitting a couple of yards down the alley, but it didn't budge. I peered inside at the black bags of trash, the old rolled-up carpet and broken bottles. It was packed full, but even if I spent an hour trying to empty it out, I doubted it would be light enough for me to move.

The stench of trash was strong, sickly sweet with soured food and water-logged cardboard. I lowered the grimy plastic lid, covering my mouth with my hand, and reached up, hitching myself up the side. My foot slid against the metal, trying to find traction. It was only six feet high, at the most, but my body was exhausted. Maybe if I'd been rested, I could have pulled myself up with my arms alone, but not now. Finally, my foot found a small notch, and I wedged the tip of my shoe in, my arms and legs shaking as I pulled myself onto the sticky top.

I lay on my stomach panting. The alleyway was dark, but if people passing by turned to look, they'd be able to see me, which meant…which meant…

I took a deep breath, trying to push away the blackness that lurked at the edges of my vision. I needed to concentrate.

Which meant… I didn't have much time. It would be obvious, even at a glance, what I was trying to do, and if someone called the cops, I didn't think I'd have the energy to run from them.

I got shakily to my feet, the plastic lid on the Dumpster bowing slightly under my weight. It slanted at a pretty steep angle, and I stuck my arms out to get my balance before I inched my way up to the very highest point. The Dumpster wasn't long enough, or sturdy enough, for me to get a running start, so I worked my way as close as I could to the edge.

Reaching my arm out toward the ladder, I stretched my fingers as far as they could go, but they only brushed air. I was almost as tall as the ladder now, but it had to be at least six feet away.

I choked back a small sob. I couldn't do this. I couldn't. I was too tired, too small, too beaten down from so much running. Maybe if I could shake this pain. But it clung to the back of my head with nails so sharp they cut. When was it okay to just give up? There had to be a point at which anyone would break, even the strongest person. Even Markus. Even Penn. Even Missy.

A tear slid down the side of my cheek.

None of them would give up, would they?

I focused, shutting out the rest of the world. Shutting out the claws that bit into my skin. Maybe if I just imagined I was one of them, just for a minute, they could climb inside this body of mine and make this leap for me.

My knees bent, the muscles in my thighs tensing like a spring, and my arms swung back. I opened my eyes, zeroing in on the rung of the ladder. All I had to do was reach it. That was all.

The fears clouding my vision fell away one by one. It wasn't my job to worry right now. It was useless, squandering my energy on the things I had no control over. I could spend the last of that energy holding on to that image of Penn being pulled away from me by the police officers, or blood dripping down the side of Missy's face. I could focus on that memory of Mr. Vasquez's lifeless body...or I could let it go.

I breathed out and concentrated on that black metal

rung. I could feel it clasped between my palms, cold and smooth and real.

My feet pressed against the top of the Dumpster and I let go of it all. Right now I wasn't Ella. I wasn't a pet or a friend or a lover. I wasn't bound by pain or obligation. I was only muscle and skin and bone. I was lift and thrust and concentration. I was the tightening muscles inside my eye, focusing on the thin metal goal in front of me.

For a moment, I could fly.

My body soared. Free. Pain hung behind me like a dark cloak in the air.

And then my hands struck steel, and my fingers clamped. The full force of that ache smacked into me, cloaking me once again. It wrapped around my body. Tight. Encompassing. My left hand slipped. The fingers slid from the rung as the momentum of my body swung me, twisting so my legs flew out in the direction of the street beyond.

I winced. My body continued to swing, but I hung on with my right hand, squeezing so tight my fingernails bit into the palm of my hand. I wouldn't let go.

My body twisted again, and I grunted, throwing my left hand up, but my fingers slid past metal. I cried out, as if that last desperate howl from my lips would be enough to hold me there. The wail from my lips mixed with another sound, pain's mournful baying, desperate and feral, billowing out from inside me. We were one.

I lurched upward again, pulling both of us, and finally, *finally*, my fingers closed around the rung. The pressure of my full weight tugged on the ladder, releasing it so it rattled to the ground. I held on tight. The pads of my hands were sticky with sweat, but I held on.

I looked down. My feet almost touched the ground, but I was afraid if I let go, the ladder would retract back up to the first platform. I swung my legs in front of me and then behind me. They pumped higher, and I tightened my stomach, giving one final kick so my right leg wrapped around the side of the ladder.

I pulled myself up, grunting. Slowly, I walked my hands higher up the rungs until finally both feet were solidly beneath me on the bottom rung. I clutched the ladder, leaning into it, and closed my eyes, breathing heavily.

But I didn't have time to rest. We didn't have time to rest.

I raised my face.

Pain raised its face.

We looked up, up, up. Above was the platform where Penn's uncle's sculpture loomed, beckoning.

"Hold on tight," I grunted to the pain.

Then I took a deep breath and started to climb.

# Twelve

My legs trembled. They'd never been this tired. Even if I hadn't been pulling this monster with me, with its matted fur and stinking meat, they would have been exhausted from climbing the steep fire escape stairs up eight stories. Now, looking down between the slats under my feet, I could see the dark ground far, far below me. Pain's claws sank deeper into me.

"What are you afraid of?" I growled at it.

With each level I'd climbed, it had clung on tighter, my heart and its heart throbbing in a peculiar synchronized beat as I'd scrambled past people's tall windows, praying they wouldn't turn to see me sneaking past.

Now I crouched outside the dark window to Elise's apartment. Inside the room was empty. I could just make out the dark mass of a bed.

*Take us there*, the pain purred, pointing to the bed.

But light spilled out of another room down the hallway. Maybe Ruby was in that room, sitting on a couch next to Elise with a book open in her lap. The image gave me courage, and I tapped on the window.

*Go in. Go in. Go in*, the pain whispered impatiently, its voice echoing off the walls of my head.

I held my breath, waiting, and then tapped again, a little louder this time.

If anyone could make me feel better right now, it was Ruby. For a moment, the thought of her dimmed the pain.

It seemed so strange that her family had purchased me to be her pet, but she'd ended up being my first taste of unconditional love. That love felt like a soft blanket. A salve. A cool cloth draped over my eyes. Sure, she was just a child. She couldn't set Penn free or rescue Missy, but she could wrap her arms around me and snuggle her sweet head against my shoulder, and for a moment, I would know the world could be a good place.

I knocked again, louder, and pushed up on the window, expecting to find it locked, but the pane slid up easily. Now that it was open, I could hear music drifting in from the other room. It was the soulful crooning of a jazz singer. I couldn't place the voice, but I was certain it was the kind Penn had loved to listen to in his room on those hot days we'd shared last summer.

The sound filled me with an ache I'd never felt before, blooming up through my stomach and across my chest. It smothered the monster, pushing it further inside me, and I moved closer to this new ache. It was beautiful and sorrowful, the same feeling that music like this had always stirred in me, but now it was matched with the longing to go back in time, to feel Penn's arms around me, to spend just a few minutes in the past, when we had no idea what sort of pain the future was about to bring. What was the word for that? Nostalgia? I'd never really understood before how a person could long for the past, but now it made perfect sense.

I pushed the window up a bit farther and crawled inside, dragging the weight of my pain with me.

Down the hallway, another light flipped on, and the dark edge of someone's shoulder poked through the doorway, pausing as if they were unsure what direction the tapping had come from.

"Penn?" I called, crouching next to the edge of a small bookshelf.

*Be quiet*, my pain crooned. *Pay attention to* me.

Was it crazy to believe he could be here? I couldn't separate crazy from reality anymore. There were too many voices filling my head. Maybe his mom *had* found out he was being held at the police station. Maybe she'd known exactly who to call to get him out. It wasn't impossible, not for Elise. That was why I was here, after all, wasn't it?

And then the silhouette of Penn's whole body filled the hallway.

"Penn!" I called again, my voice cracking.

His footsteps sounded against the wooden floor, bringing him closer to me until he stood in the doorway to the bedroom. He reached out, flipping the light switch so the dark room was finally bathed in light.

"Hey." I frowned, blinking in the blinding light. My

monster hissed, reeling, and I grabbed my head to stop it from spinning. "How did you—"

Wait. The man standing in the doorway wasn't Penn. No, this was the man from the door downstairs.

Recognition washed across his face. "Hold it right there," he said, backing away. "I don't know what you're looking for, but you need to get out. Right now, got it?"

I squinted, trying to keep his face from spiraling. Maybe it had been the beard that had thrown me before. Of course he'd looked familiar. His face was made of pieces of Elise and Penn and Ruby, a mosaic. He hadn't been a spy. He was Penn's uncle.

"Please," I said, holding up both my hands. "I just need to see Elise."

He narrowed his eyes. There wasn't just fear in them now, there was anger. "I don't know who told you she was here, but your information is wrong."

"But…I just saw her…yesterday." My head throbbed and the monster thrashed inside me. If he would just let me sit down so the room would hold still, so I could get my bearings, maybe I'd be able to explain myself.

"I don't know who you think you saw yesterday, but it wasn't her. You can't just break into someone's home like this. I don't care who sent you! This is trespassing. I'll call the police."

He reached in his back pocket and pulled out his phone.

"I just need to talk to her," I said. "*Please*. They've got Penn!" My voice climbed. Maybe it was fear, or frustration, or the need to drown out this pain. Maybe I just needed him to hear me. Really hear me.

"You can't threaten us," he said. "You don't think she already knows…"

And then Elise emerged in the doorway.

"Stephen?" She stopped short. "What's going on?"

"Get in the other room. Now!" he ordered, trying to push her back through the doorway.

"Oh my God! Ella!" She shoved his arm aside and ran across the room, scooping me into her arms. All the strength I'd mustered to get from the police station to this building and up that fire escape dissolved, and I wilted against her.

She rested her head on mine, sobbing, and the two of us crumpled to the ground.

"They've got him," she cried. "They've got my little boy."

"Elise?" The man stood over us, confused, his hand reaching out for his sister. "Are you sure you should be doing this? You can't trust people right now. Not anyone. This girl could be—"

"Shut up, Stephen." She sniffled. "This is Ella, you idiot. Penn's Ella!"

His hands dropped to his sides. "Oh, *oh*. I didn't realize. I'm so sorry." He stared down at us for a few minutes, shifting uncomfortably on his feet. "Maybe you two should come sit somewhere more comfortable?" he asked, gesturing at the hard, wooden floor where we'd dropped. "And we'll need to do something about that cut." He pointed to my head.

"Oh my goodness!" Elise reeled back. "Oh, Ella, darling, what happened? Come in the other room. Let us take care of you. I wasn't thinking. I should have offered you a place to sit." She shook her head and got slowly to her feet. "I guess I haven't really been thinking straight at all tonight," she went on. "I took one of Stephen's Xanax earlier. Maybe that was a bad idea, but I felt like I was going to lose it."

As she talked, she led me down the hallway and into a small living room where they must have been sitting together before I climbed through the window. The music I'd heard earlier was still drifting out of a record player near the sofa.

I wobbled on my feet, scanning the room for a place to sit. The two oversize chairs in front of me were empty, and I collapsed into the nearest one. My pain slunk back, licking its wounds.

"Where's Ruby?" I asked, surprised she wasn't curled up in one of these chairs.

Even through my mind's fog I could see this was the kind of room she would love—cozy and a bit unkempt. It didn't feel anything like the perfectly manicured house they lived in. This apartment was stuffed with old books and carved wooden sculptures. Colorful rugs overlapped one another on the floor, and the walls were covered in oil paintings and watercolors and sleek black-and-white photographs.

"Is she in bed?"

It was dark out, but I had no idea how late it was. Hopefully we hadn't been so noisy we'd woken her. There was no way she'd go back to sleep once she knew I was here.

Elise's face blanched, and she lowered herself onto the chair next to me, staring off into the distance. Her hand climbed to her right ear where she started picking absently at a small red patch of skin.

"John took her," Stephen said. "He filed some petition and sent his attorney over with a woman from Child Protective Services this afternoon while Elise was off at the police station trying to help Penn."

"But he can't just take her away like that, can he?"

I looked frantically to Elise. It couldn't be true. But the pain on her face was all the proof I needed.

He shrugged. "John does anything he wants. He said Elise is unstable and an unfit mother and probably came up with a whole bunch of other lies. He wants to hurt her, and he's doing a really good job at it. She's not taking it well. First the thing with Penn and now this. That's the reason I gave her the Xanax. I was hoping she could finally get a little bit of rest."

My own pain receded a bit more, and Elise's personal agony seemed to step forward. I wanted to fight it off. I wanted to protect her from it, but my head felt like it was going round and round the Wonder Wheel, and I didn't think I'd be able to stand even if I tried. "I'm sorry," I managed. "I didn't know."

Stephen sighed, looking me in the eye. "It's a good thing you're here. Really. Please, forgive the way I acted earlier. If I'd known who you were I never would have…" He shook his head, embarrassed. "I've just been so angry about what these assholes are doing to Elise and her kids. It's no secret John and I have never clicked, but this is a new low, even for him. I just don't get how someone can do this to their own flesh and blood."

Elise stopped picking at her skin. She blinked, pulling

herself back into the moment. "Ella, you were with Penn when it happened, weren't you? You saw it all. Please tell me. Please say he didn't hurt those people."

I saw it all. She was right. The dust, the smoke, the thick, dark blood on her friend's shirt. The beast stirred inside me, my head throbbing anew and my ears filled with a high-pitch ringing. "Of course he didn't."

"I knew it," Elise said, smiling sadly. "I really did. My boy wouldn't blow up innocent people."

I nodded. It felt like there was so much I needed to ask her, but I couldn't think straight. The room darkened at the edges, and the pain in my head purred, flicking its tail as it curled around me. Was this what I was supposed to talk to Elise about, I wondered, or did she already know?

I blinked. The room was too silent. Elise and Stephen stared at me, concerned.

"Ella?" Elise asked. "Did you hear me?"

"I'm sorry," I mumbled.

"I think that's enough talk for tonight," Stephen said. "Let's get Ella to bed. We can figure this out in the morning."

Elise nodded. "Come on, dear," she said. "You can sleep in Ruby's room."

*I* didn't remember closing my eyes, but when I opened them, a bit of daylight crept past the curtains and across the floor. My head still ached, but the monster that had gripped it so tightly the night before had retreated. I rolled over, rubbing my eyes.

"Ah, she stirs," Elise said, scooting forward in the chair next to the bed.

"I'm sorry, I—"

"Stop right there," she said. "Rule number one: no apologizing. That goes for both of us. It's a waste of energy, and we don't have time for that. I'm just happy you're finally awake. That bump on your head isn't pretty."

I sat up, reaching for my forehead, and my fingers grazed a bandage.

"I got the blood off and put some ointment on, but you'll want to wash it in the shower. We can bandage you up properly when you're all clean." She pointed to the bottom of the bed where a T-shirt and jeans lay folded and stacked. "They're Ruby's, but I'm guessing they'll fit. The bathroom is down the hall, and there's a clean towel on the rack. Oh, and there's some medicine on the nightstand. The orange pills… They should help with pain."

She stood up, smiling. Her eyes crinkled at the edges. "I'm glad you're here, Ella. It probably seems weird, after what we've been through, but just having you here makes me feel better. Both my kids love you, and they're the best people I know. So I guess that makes you one of the best people by association, doesn't it?"

My throat tightened. "I love them, too."

She paused by the door. "All right. I have some phone calls to make. Stephen's got breakfast waiting for you in the kitchen when you're ready."

"Elise, wait. I know you said no apologies, but…" I

swallowed. "I'm really sorry about your friend. He seemed like a good man."

She closed her eyes, nodding. "So you *did* get to meet him?"

"Yes."

"I hoped so. But that's not what they want anyone to believe," she said, leaning her head against the doorframe. "They're saying Penn targeted Erik because he was going to be prosecuting the Greenwich bombing case."

"It's a lie."

She sighed. There was such sorrow in her small exhale.

"It was very clear he cared a lot about you," I said, watching her face. I hoped I wasn't crossing some sort of boundary, but I wanted to give her something, even if it was the tiniest morsel of happiness to hold on to.

She breathed deeply, as if she were inhaling those words, letting them sit inside her chest where they would make a new home. A moment later, she straightened her shoulders and slipped out of the room and into the hallway.

*H*alf an hour later, I sat down across from Elise at the kitchen table. My hair was still damp from the shower, and my skin was rubbed clean. Ruby's clothes fit almost perfectly. They felt good, these clothes, as if somehow when I'd pulled them on I'd cloaked myself in a little bit of Ruby herself.

"You look better," Elise said, sliding a plate of toast across the table to me. "That's good. We have a lot we need to do today."

"Elise?"

She carried on as if I hadn't spoken. "I've been on the phone with one of Erik's close friends. He doesn't work for the DA, but he's worked with criminal law for years."

"Elise?" I tried again.

"I want you to talk to him as soon as possible. We need a written statement of your account. I don't trust a word in those police reports. We all know they're fabricating these things."

"Elise!"

She looked up at me, surprised. "What?"

I clutched my head, keeping the echo of my voice from reawakening the monster. "I can't stay. You know that, right? It's not safe. For either of us."

She shook her head as if she could jiggle away my words. "Not if you stay inside," she said. "You came late last night. I doubt anyone saw you."

"Maybe," I said. "But if the congressman finds out I'm here, he'll punish us both. You don't think it's bad enough what he's done to Penn? What if he does something to Ruby?"

"He wouldn't." She gasped, but I could see the terror in her eyes. Something had changed inside her husband, and she knew it. He wasn't the same man he used to be. If he could use Ruby as a pawn in his game, he wouldn't hesitate to do it.

"He might not hurt her physically, but there's no telling what he's capable of," I said. "That's why I have to go. If there's anything I can do to stop him, I have to try."

"He can't be stopped," Elise said. "That's the problem. Besides, what are you going to be able to do by yourself? At least if you stay, we'll have each other."

The hope in her voice almost changed my mind. It was what I wanted, to be accepted by her, to be needed. It seemed crazy that the people who felt like family could change and grow this way. But maybe that was what it truly meant to be human. That no matter the horror or pain we experienced, we could always find love. It was how I knew for certain the thing I was fighting for was good and real and true.

"There's still a core group of Liberationists left," I said.

"The ones whose faces are still plastered all over the news?" she snapped. "The ones who let you and Penn walk right into a staged bombing?"

I bristled, wanting to protect them, to defend them. They were as much to blame for that bombing as me or Penn. "They aren't perfect. I know it. But they're the best hope we've got."

She buried her face in her hands. "I'm sorry."

"No apologies, remember?"

She smiled, even though it looked like it pained her. "So that's it? You've made up your mind?"

I nodded.

"And there's no hope of me changing it?"

"No."

"You and Penn sure have your stubbornness in common," she said. "You'll at least finish some breakfast before you leave, won't you? You're going to need to keep your energy up."

"I will."

But I hadn't just come here to rest and refuel. Making sure she knew about Penn and Erik wasn't the only reason I'd come, either. There was still something I needed from her.

# Thirteen

"Elise…" My stomach flipped. I knew I could trust her. That wasn't why my heart had begun to hammer. I knew she would tell me everything if it might set Penn free, but I was afraid the answer she was going to give me wouldn't be the one I needed. "It's about those files," I said, "the ones the congressman—"

"Can you stop calling him the congressman?" Elise interrupted. "He loved being called that. It makes him sound so important, and I just… It bothers me."

"Oh. Of course." I paused. "The files your husband has been blackmailing people with."

She cringed. "How about we just call him John."

"Fine. John."

Elise nodded, but she didn't look pleased. "I already told you," she said. "I don't know where he keeps them. I've looked. Believe me. I've searched his office a dozen times. I even made a copy of the key to his office in Washington and searched it, too, but there's nothing there. You've got to understand that if John has made a point to hide something, he's hidden it well."

"On the night we met with Erik, he mentioned something." I hesitated. This was the information I needed, and yet I was still scared of her answer. "Have you ever heard John mention the Catskills?"

Elise snorted. "Ella, you can't live in the Northeast and not mention the Catskills."

My stomach sank. "But that doesn't mean it's a bad tip."

"No, you're right," Elise said. "I didn't mean to dismiss you. What exactly did Erik say?"

"Just that he heard rumors that the congressman—" I stopped myself. "I mean, John—kept files on a server in the Catskills."

She sat silent with the information, and I picked nervously at my sleeve. Finally, she spoke. "There's the old hunting cabin John bought after Penn was born. His dad used to take him duck hunting when he was a kid, and he said he wanted to have that with Penn. It never made sense to me, the guns, shooting things, you know."

I cringed at the thought of Penn killing animals. He'd never even mentioned it to me.

"They only went a few times," Elise said. "They'd stay a couple of days, rough it without running water and heat. I only had to go up there once to know it wasn't for me. I don't know why anyone would choose to freeze all night in an unheated shack and pee in a dirt hole, but the boys seemed to like it. The last time they went, Penn was ten.

Up until then they only shot at old cans and targets, but John finally decided he was old enough for a real hunt. They came home a day early. Penn's eyes were red and puffy from crying. He wouldn't tell me what happened. Just went up to his room and stayed there for a day and a half. Apparently he shot a squirrel. It fell out of the tree, but it wasn't dead yet, and John wanted him to finish the job. He couldn't. Poor kid. I don't think he really understood, you know, that when he shot that gun, he'd actually be killing something. And when it sank in... He always had a tender heart. That's how I know he'd never hurt anyone," she said. "We've got to fix this, Ella. We can't just let him sit in that cell with people telling him he's a horrible person."

Her eyes burned with worry, and her hand gripped mine so tightly that my fingers ached. "We *have* to help him." Her hand drifted up to the spot near her collarbone again, worrying the sore she'd already rubbed raw.

"I'll help him. Don't worry."

"How?"

"That hunting cabin," I said. "I need to know where it is."

She buried her face in her hands. "It's pointless. You think that little hunting cabin is really it? It's a shack! It's a pile of rotten wood sitting in the middle of a couple acres of trees."

"We have to try," I said.

"You think they wouldn't have already found it if something was there? That Erik wouldn't have stopped him if he could?"

"Maybe he was about to," I said. "If Erik thought it

was a legitimate clue, it's worth looking into, isn't it? If someone found out Erik knew about the cabin…"

I couldn't finish the sentence, but it made sense, didn't it? If the congressman was blackmailing people inside the DA's office, he would have known if Mr. Vasquez had a new lead. If it was a false clue, the congressman wouldn't have cared, would he? But if it was true, if his private server really was at that cabin, it would make sense that he'd do anything in his power to stop Erik from finding out.

He might even kill him and frame his own son for the murder.

"Elise!" I exclaimed. "You need to tell me where that cabin is, and you need to tell me now!"

The directions to the cabin, which Elise had finally written on a stiff white index card, were tucked inside my pocket when I knocked on the door to Dave's sister's apartment. I hated going back without Penn, but at least I wasn't coming back empty-handed. Right now I had to keep believing our meeting with Erik had at least pushed us in the right direction. Markus would find a way to get us to the Catskills, and if the congressman was keeping his secret files there, he'd find a way to destroy them.

"Ella?" Dave stood frozen in the open doorway, staring at me as if he were seeing a ghost.

I sighed with relief. "I'm so glad you're still here," I said. "I didn't have any way to get in touch, and I was worried you guys would have moved on."

Still he stared, unmoving.

"Um." I frowned. "Can I come in?"

He blinked, seemingly bringing himself back from someplace far away. "Oh, yeah, of course," he said, stepping out of the way so I could pass.

Across the room, Jane looked up from the table. "Oh my God! Ella!" she screamed, jumping to her feet. In a flash, she was at my side, scooping me into a tight hug. "Markus!" she yelled. "Markus! She's back." She cupped my face in her hands. "How did you get here? We heard you and Penn had been arrested. The messages I intercepted from the police department made it sound like they had a strong case against you." She glanced behind me at the door as if she was expecting to see Penn there.

"He's not with me," I said.

The smile dropped from her face. "Oh… I'm so sorry." She shook her head. "I thought…"

"Where's Markus?" I asked, my fingers tightening around the paper inside my pocket. Elise was right, there wasn't time to feel sorry.

"We couldn't get rid of you if we tried, could we?"

I turned around to see Markus smirking in the doorway. He rubbed a towel through his damp hair. A clean, white T-shirt hugged his shoulders and chest. He looked new, fresh, ready for anything.

I smiled. "No, you couldn't."

It had never occurred to me before that Markus was like a brother to me, but now it struck me. He and Ian and Missy, along with every other pet NuPet had bred, were more than just genetic variants of me—they were my family. We weren't lonely, solitary souls NuPet had created. We were bound together.

"Do you have a death wish or something?" he asked, standing before me.

"Not really."

The weight of worry I'd been carrying across my shoulders lifted as he neared me. Markus wasn't perfect. He was hotheaded and idealistic and stubborn, but if there was anyone I wanted on my side to fight against the congressman, it was him.

"Good." He laughed, pulling me into a hug. "Because it seems like you're one of those cats with nine lives. How many do you have left anyway?"

I shrugged, pulling the paper from my pocket and handing it to Markus. "Hopefully enough to get some use out of this."

Markus scanned the carefully drawn map before he looked up at me, confused. "What is it?"

"It's a map to the congressman's hunting cabin in the Catskills," I said. "There's a good possibility this is the place he's keeping all the blackmail files he has on people."

"And how are you planning on getting rid of all these files?" Ian asked, plucking the map from Markus's hand.

I cocked an eyebrow. "Do you still feel like blowing something up?"

Markus grinned. "I thought you'd never ask."

. . .

*A*n hour later, the five of us sped along the interstate on our way to the Catskills. Out the window the towering buildings had been replaced with an endless sea of trees. They might have been the very same trees Penn and I had passed all those weeks ago when we drove from his house toward what we thought then would be the freedom of Canada, but they looked so different now. The summertime green of their leaves had changed, and now they flickered gold and orange and red, as if the leaves themselves had caught fire, burning away all the dreams we'd started out with.

Dave looked down at his lap, picking at a hangnail on his thumb. "Maybe I should have stayed behind," he mumbled.

"You're the one who knows how to operate this thing," Markus said, nodding to the backpack sitting at Dave's feet.

He inched away from the bag as if he was just remembering what was inside of it. "It seems stupid for us all to go."

"Are you serious?" Jane asked, pulling her hair back from her face into a high ponytail.

"I'm just saying maybe we should have kept it a smaller mission. We don't know if this is even good intel."

"Do you have anything better to go on?" Ian asked.

"No, but sometimes sitting still is better than acting. We could be walking into another trap."

"Grow a pair," Jane snapped. "Is this because of Vanessa? All of a sudden you think your sister knows more than the rest of us? News flash—she doesn't know shit."

"Leave her out of it."

It was pretty obvious where Dave's sister stood on the mission. She'd made it abundantly clear to him before we left, and the walls inside her apartment weren't as thick as she might have hoped. We'd all heard her shriek about suicide missions and collateral damage, but at least Dave was here.

"Come on, guys," Markus said. "Now's not the time for this. We need to be solidifying a plan, not tearing into one another."

"What more of a plan do we need than blow the place up and get the hell out of there without getting ourselves killed?" Dave asked.

Jane snorted. "Well, there's an oversimplification if I've ever heard one."

She was right. We didn't have a clue what we were getting ourselves into. The aerial footage she'd pulled from old satellite maps wasn't at all helpful. Even zoomed in at the highest resolution it was impossible to make anything out. The whole property was a blur of trees blending into the surrounding forest, acres and acres of endless green. The hunting shack Elise had told me about wasn't the only thing we couldn't see in the picture—even the road leading in and out of the property was obscured by the dense blanket of leaves.

"How can we be sure the place will be empty?" I asked.

"It's in the middle of nowhere," Markus said.

Dave glared at him. "That doesn't mean anything, and you know it. There could be guards. You think that prick's going to leave his most valuable information unattended?

He's not stupid."

"Dave's right," Jane said, unsmiling. It was clear she didn't want to be agreeing with him right now. "We need to think about the very real possibility that someone will be positioned there."

"You promised no one would get hurt," I reminded Markus. It was my one and only condition. We could use as many bombs as he wanted. We could blow that hunting cabin and the congressman's files sky high. We could make a crater in the earth the size of a football field, but I couldn't be responsible for killing anyone. I couldn't watch anyone else die.

"I told you. No one's going to get hurt," Markus assured me. "Here…"

He reached into the bag in front of him and pulled out the remote detonator. It wasn't big, maybe the size of a small cell phone. On the front of it, a red button about the size of a dime was enclosed in a clear plastic cover. Carefully, he passed it back to me. "Nothing blows until you give the go-ahead."

I stared down at the small box resting in my palm. It was lighter than I'd expected. How could such a little thing control so much power, so much devastation?

"Are you crazy?" Dave said. "She doesn't know what she's doing!"

"Calm down! She's not going to mess it up." Markus met my eye. "We'll need to be at least a hundred yards away from the epicenter before you push that button, but we can't get too much farther away or the sensor won't register. As soon as we're in a safe range, just lift the plastic case and hold the button until the red light starts flashing. You'll hear it beep. Once it does we've got about thirty seconds to get as far away as we can before it blows."

I ran my thumb over the plastic.

"And don't think about changing your mind," Dave said. "There's no undo button on that thing. You've got one chance. That's it."

*I*an slowed the van, pulling onto a smaller road that forked off of the side of the interstate.

"We'll park a mile or two away from the site," Markus said. "That way we can scope it out before we detonate the bomb, okay?" He looked straight at me as he spoke.

"And what if there's a guard?" Ian asked.

"The place doesn't sound big," Markus said. "If he's got a guy posted there, we'll find a way to divert him. Did we bring any smaller explosives?"

"It's not like you gave me a lot to work with," Dave complained. "You said we needed power, so that's what I brought. I thought you wanted the biggest bang for your buck. This thing isn't some wimpy little firecracker. You press that detonator, and there's not going to be anything left."

"And we can't break it into anything smaller?" Ian asked.

Dave rolled his eyes. "That's not how this works."

"Fine. We've got some flares though, right? We can't do any damage with them, but I bet they'll work for a distraction."

Dave threw up his hands and flopped back against the seat. "Dude, if we have to resort to using flares, we're screwed."

The paved road gave way to dirt, narrowing the farther we drove. We wound our way into denser trees, and the hills continued to climb higher and higher. Every once in a while, another small lane would jut off to the left or the right with the tip of a rooftop showing in the distance, but the farther we drove, the fewer houses we saw.

We rounded a corner, and to the left, the trees parted. Beyond, a glimpse of the valley came into view. I gasped, my stomach dropping in almost the exact same way it had on the Wonder Wheel. How had we climbed so high? The golden ridges of the mountains disappeared into the distance, row after row of hills, as if the wilderness stretched out forever.

"The directions say to take the next right." Jane compared the card Elise had written the directions on with the map she'd printed off before we left, paying no attention to the view.

"It can't be far now," Markus said. "We need to find a place to park the van."

Ian slowed to a crawl. "We're going to have to find somewhere over there," he said, pointing to the right side of the road. "It's too steep on the other side."

An embankment rose up next to the road, and he steered onto it. The van bumped over it and into the trees.

"Careful," Dave yelled, grabbing the backpack.

Ian slammed on the brakes, and the van lurched to a stop. "You can't just yell at the person driving!"

"This thing is sensitive," Dave said. "You want to kill us all before we even get there?" He swung the door open, holding the bag carefully pressed to his chest, and crawled out.

Ian rolled his eyes. "Anyone else want to get out?"

The rest of us shook our heads.

He took his foot off the brake, and we rolled forward slowly, bumping down the small hill and into the brush. The van was tall, but hopefully the embankment would help to hide it.

We scrambled out of the car, looking at Markus for direction.

He zipped up his dark-gray hoodie and motioned for us to do the same. "I doubt any cars are going to pass, but we should stick to the woods just in case." He hiked a pack up onto his shoulders and tromped off into the underbrush.

Jane and I hitched our bags up, too, and followed after him.

"So I guess I'm in charge of carrying this?" Dave grumbled behind us.

"I'd trade you, but you're doing such a great job complaining," Jane said. "I'd hate to take that away from you."

Dave picked up his pace, shoving past us and snapping sticks and twigs beneath his feet as if he was trying to make as much noise as was humanly possible.

"What's going on between you two?" I asked.

Jane didn't look at me. "What do you mean?" She ducked under a low-hanging branch, swatting at some bare twigs that caught in the back of her ponytail.

"Something's changed. Ever since the warehouse."

"I don't know," she said. "Maybe there wasn't ever anything *to* change."

"I just thought…" I clambered over a large fallen log. A few months ago, it would have been impossible for my body to move this way. And even though it ached, I was so grateful for its new strength. "It seemed like you two cared about each other."

"Yeah." She grunted, pulling herself up behind me. "I used to think that, too, but I guess I misread the data. I've been pretty good at that lately."

We pressed on in silence, the snap and crunch of our steps saying as much as our words could have.

I tried to think back to the last time Dave and Jane had been close. It used to be they had found any excuse to be next to each other, to reach out and touch the other's arm, to hold each other's gaze. But ever since we'd been betrayed at the warehouse, things had been different. It seemed crazy that Dave would blame Jane, but maybe he did. Why else would he avoid her the way he'd been doing?

We marched on. In my bag, the small rectangle of the detonator dug into my back with each step, reminding me just how easy it was to kill. Just pull a trigger. Press a button. Maybe that was what was wrong with the world. You could push a small red circle, and somewhere else people would die. Your hand wouldn't touch flesh or bone or blood, only plastic, cool and detached.

I stopped and wriggled off my backpack, dropping it on the leafy ground at my feet. The group, with the loud crunch of twigs and leaves under their feet, didn't notice my absence and kept going.

I unzipped the bag and reached in, past the flares and the binoculars. If I was going to be carrying a box that could rip a hole in the side of a building, I wanted to be holding it.

In the branches above me, a squirrel chattered noisily. Maybe it was screaming at me. Maybe it was telling me something important, but I couldn't understand. I just hoped it wasn't anywhere near the congressman's cabin when we blew the place up.

I tucked the small plastic box into my pocket and zipped my bag up again.

Ahead, the group had stopped and were crouched next to a large gray boulder.

"We must be getting—" I started to say as I approached them, but Markus raised his hand, signaling for me to be quiet.

I stooped next to them and peered around the huge rock. The road we'd been looking for wound through the trees only a couple dozen yards away. At the end sat the congressman's cabin. But instead of the small shack Elise had described, a huge cinder block wall rose up at the end of the driveway.

My stomach dropped.

This wasn't a little hunting cabin.

This was a fortress.

## Fourteen

"Well, this is a pretty good sign we're in the right place," Markus said, shrugging out of his backpack. He rested it at his feet, crouched down, and pulled out a pair of binoculars.

"Or it's a sign we should get our asses out of here and figure out a different plan," Dave said.

"No way we're leaving now," Markus spat. He zipped his bag up and readjusted the straps. "We just need to get a better handle on things. Dave and Jane, you two follow this little ravine around the back and scope out the rear. I'll take Ella and Ian up to that gate to see how well this place is fortified."

"Great, send me with the guy who's already figuring out how we should run away," Jane said. "Just don't be surprised if he hides in the car instead of coming with me."

Dave glared at her. "Go to hell."

Markus scowled, his eyes traveling between the two of them. "Fine… Dave, you have the bomb anyway. You come with Ella and me. Ian, you and Jane get eyes on the back."

Jane smiled sourly.

"This whole plan is screwed up," Dave said. "We should have taken some time to plan this, not just rush in like idiots. We're all going to end up dead."

Markus rolled his eyes. "Thanks for the optimism. Do you want to back out now? Because if that's what you want, fine. You can walk back to your sister's and hide there, but you're not ruining this for the rest of us."

Dave's jaw clenched, and his lips pulled into a tight line. "I'll come."

Markus studied our group, his gaze traveling head to toe over each of us as if he was double-checking that everything was in its proper place. Dressed in our dark hoodies and military boots, we looked like a group that actually might be able to pull off this sort of mission. Finally, he nodded, seemingly satisfied, and motioned for Jane and Ian to break off down the small wash running between the trees.

"I doubt there's surveillance, but we should try to stay covered as much as possible," Markus said to me and Dave. "We can move between these boulders."

He pointed to a row of large gray rocks like the one we stood behind. They jutted out between the trees in a jagged line stretching between us and the wall. Most were only a few feet off the ground, but we could still crouch behind them.

"See that large pine tree over there?" he asked. "That's our endpoint."

Near the corner of the wall, a massive pine towered above the compound. Its branches were wide and sweeping, but it looked like they'd been trimmed back so they no longer hung over the top of the wall. If Markus was thinking about using it to climb over, it would be tricky. Even from here I could see the coils of barbed wire that lined the top of the cinder block.

I tried not to imagine the way those barbs would cut into my skin if I got caught in that wire. There were only so many more injuries my body could take before it refused to give any more. But if Markus had his mind set on scaling that fortress, there would be no persuading him.

We covered the distance in a flash, ducking beneath the pine tree's dense branches. The three of us pressed our backs against the tree's massive trunk.

"Ella, do you have binoculars?" Markus whispered.

I nodded, slipping off my backpack and reaching inside for the heavy black lenses like the ones he already wore draped around his neck.

He pointed at the huge pine tree. "I'm going up."

"I'm coming, too." I swallowed, remembering the distance between the tree and the wall. I could climb it, but if he needed me to clear the wall and its barbed wire, we were in trouble.

"Dave, you feel okay about being our eyes on the ground?"

Dave nodded. His face was unreadable, set in a deep scowl that could have been anger or resolution.

"Good," Markus said, unsmiling. "We'll have a better idea what we're up against soon."

He grinned at me, gesturing up at the tree with the wide sweep of his arm as if it were a grand carriage I was about to climb into and he was the king and I the queen.

The branches fanned out from the trunk like a perfect ladder spiraling upward. I jumped, grabbing hold of the lowest branch, and my feet scrambled against the rough bark. Markus caught hold of my leg, boosting me up and over the first branch. I hung on tight, straddling it as I found my balance.

Sweet-smelling sap stuck to my fingers and my palms, and with it, the gritty crumbs of bark and dried needles. I reached above me, grabbing on to the next branch for leverage. A few sharp needles dug into my skin, and I winced, pulling myself to my feet. Below me, the ground receded. Head spinning, I tightened my fingers around the branch.

If I'd learned anything from the Wonder Wheel and the fire escape outside of Penn's uncle's building, it was "don't look down." Did Miss Gellner not think to train us not to fear heights? I guess she figured we'd never have to climb a tree or drag ourselves up a fire escape.

I could do this, though. I'd just concentrate on the next branch and then the one after that. It wasn't far. I fit my foot into the elbow between the limb and the tree and propelled myself higher.

Markus pulled himself up onto the branch below me. "You're halfway there," he encouraged.

My knees shook, and I fumbled for the next handhold. The tree's limbs sagged around me, heavy with needles that hid me from view, but in here at the center of the tree, it felt open, like a grand green tower.

The binoculars thumped against my chest, but on I climbed. One branch. Then another. I needed to see what was on the other side of the wall. This place was more important than Elise or Mr. Vasquez had realized. This was the key. I could feel it.

My feet scuffed against the rough bark, finding a pattern, a dance, between the levels. Glancing down at a particularly difficult foothold, I caught sight of the ground beneath me, a faraway blanket of brown. Mixed with the dizziness, a surge of pride washed over me. I'd done it.

Markus made good time, crossing to a branch a few feet to the left of me a second later. From our perch in the tree, I could see clearly over the wall and into the large compound that everyone had assumed would still be nothing more than a dilapidated hunting cabin.

The gray slab walls looked cold and stark and sterile, a series of thick cement blocks in the middle of the forest. A few narrow windows ran along the top of the building, but nothing big enough to allow a good view inside. Even the tall black door at the front was one solid panel, without so much as a peephole.

In the driveway, a pair of black SUVs sat parked side by side.

"If there are cars, there must be people," I whispered.

Markus frowned down at the vehicles. "Not necessarily."

As if it heard us, the large black overhead door on the side of the building slowly rolled open, and a minute later, two men in dark suits emerged. I scrambled backward on the branch and dropped the binoculars. Thank goodness for the strap around my neck. They fell with a thud against my chest.

"Don't move," Markus hissed.

The men didn't look up. They stopped beside one of the vehicles, talking quietly to each other.

My legs felt too unsteady, too unreliable to be up so high. I wanted solid ground beneath them. "We should get out of here," I whispered.

Below us, Dave must have detected the low hum of human voices because he waved frantically up at us, signaling toward the wall.

Markus shook his head, raising his finger to his lips. He lifted the binoculars to his eyes once more, undistracted from the target of his attention.

I took a deep breath, trying to settle the flock of birds taking flight inside my chest, but it felt like my madly beating heart was trying to lift me away from here.

Steadying my hands, I brought the binoculars to my eyes once more. It was worse not knowing. If the men were going to spot us balanced here, I wanted to know.

Just then, a third figure emerged from the darkened carport. He wasn't wearing a dark suit like the others. The khaki pants and woolen sweater matched the surroundings, but they filled me with cold fear. This was his casual weekend wear. I recognized it immediately—recognized the slow way he sauntered into the sunlight, the confident way he held his shoulders back, his head high, as if he owned the world, with all its trees and hills and creatures.

The congressman.

My body jerked away, trying to put as much distance between us as possible, regardless of what I wanted. My foot slipped off the narrow branch, sending a cascade of dead needles to the ground as I landed on my bottom with a painful thump. Frantically, I grabbed at the trunk.

A hand clamped tight to my upper arm, steadying me. Below me, a few pinecones bounced onto the ground near Dave's feet.

"Just stay right there," Markus said.

I wasn't going anywhere. Maybe ever again. Pulling in a shaky breath, I wrapped my arms and legs around the tree's broad middle.

In the driveway, an engine roared to life.

I pressed my cheek against the tree, concentrating on the sound of a motor whirring near the wall. The metal gate rumbled open, and a moment later the vehicle's tires hummed down the long driveway.

I could see the road from my place in the tree, and I watched the SUV disappear around the bend, only a bit of shiny black flashing between the trees as it drove away.

"Come on," Markus said, scrambling down from the branch next to me. He held out his hand to help me. "Now's our chance."

"Did they all leave?" I croaked. I couldn't say his name.

"Just the two in suits," he said, steadying me as we made our way down. "This is perfect. It isn't just a chance to get rid of the files. This is a chance to rid the world of a pestilence."

My feet hit the soft needles padding the ground, and I sank to my knees. This wasn't what I wanted. My hate for the congressman grew inside me like a disease. It wormed its way through the middle of me, seeping into everything good. It was a sickness, this hatred—it fed itself, that sour taste inside me, suckling the bitter need to make him suffer. But just because he was a monster didn't mean that I'd allow myself to be turned into one.

"I can't do it," I said.

"What do you mean? This is everything! Everything we've been trying to do!" Markus said. "We've been handed a *gift*."

"It's still killing someone," I said.

Markus's eyes narrowed, his lips pulling back into a snarl. "Have you forgotten what he's done to you? What he's done to all of us? What he's *still* doing?"

Of course I hadn't forgotten. I could live a hundred years and I'd never forget how small that man had made me feel, how used. But that didn't change things. That didn't excuse murder. "That's Penn's *dad*."

"The dad that framed him for murder? God, Ella! Think of the bigger picture. I realize life is precious, I *do*. I understand what a gift it is. He's the one who doesn't understand." He waved at the house, his eyes shining. "He plays with people's lives like this is a game to him. This man is a parasite. He needs to be stopped."

I glanced over at Dave, who stood silently, holding the heavy bag in front of him. His eyes were wide. Was it fear I saw in them? Compassion?

"Even if I agreed to kill...*him*...what if there are more of them?" I asked. "More guards? More visitors?"

Markus grabbed his head like he couldn't believe what I was saying. "So what if there are? This is *war*. There are going to be casualties."

Snatching the bag from Dave's hands, he strode out from under the cover of the pine boughs. He stopped by the edge of the wall, and in one fluid motion, he swung the bag high into the air. His strong arms propelled it farther than I could ever dream of throwing it. It flew up, suspended above us all for a long moment before it fell with a *thunk* onto the flat roof.

Dave shoved him. "What the hell, man? Are you insane? What part of 'explosives' don't you understand?"

Markus ignored him. "Press the button, Ella."

I backed away. "No."

"Press it!"

"Are you out of your mind?" Dave said. "We don't know who else is in there. We don't even know where Jane and Ian are."

Markus's face fell. The freight train of his fury, which had been barreling down on us, ready to flatten us beneath its steel and wrath, slowed.

"We'll wait for Jane and Ian," he said. "But I haven't changed my mind."

"This isn't a dictatorship," Dave said. "We're a group."

"Then we'll ask the others to vote," Markus said. He leaned against the wall, folding his arms over his chest. "We can wait right here. They'll be back soon enough."

"What if those men come back?" Dave asked. "Maybe you better go look for them."

Markus narrowed his eyes and rubbed his palms on his pants. Fidgeting, he stared out into the woods. "You two stay here," he finally ordered. "I'll loop around the back."

He took off, moving swiftly through the yellow leaves

littering the ground near the base of the wall.

I pressed my back against the tree trunk, staring at the cinder block wall in front of me. The congressman was on the other side. After the men had left, he'd retreated inside, but he couldn't be more than a dozen yards away from me.

I scanned the top of the wall where the metal posts stuck up out of the gray blocks, holding the coils of barbed wire in place. There didn't appear to be any cameras, but my skin crawled anyway, imagining the congressman could see me now, that he knew how close I was to him.

"You can't do it," Dave said, leaning up next to me. "Don't let him talk you into it."

"I can't believe he's doing this," I said. "Jane and Ian will agree with us. He'll see."

He frowned, glancing up at the wall like maybe he was just as afraid as I was that we were being watched. "It was a mistake coming here like this," he said. "If they find out…" He kicked the dirt, digging at the ground like a caged animal.

Markus emerged around the corner of the wall, followed by Ian and Jane.

They jogged up to us, their eyes bright.

"Tell him this is a bad idea," Dave said.

"What?" Jane looked to Markus, confused.

"We need to get the hell out of here," Dave said. "If you think we're in the middle of a witch hunt now, what do you think's going to happen if we kill their precious leader?"

Jane shook her head. "Kill who? The back's clear. No

guards. We're good."

"He's here," I said. "John Kimball."

Jane and Ian looked at each other, their mouths dropping open.

"You said the plan was a go," Jane whispered, turning to Markus.

"It is," he said, stony-faced.

"That's not what you agreed to. You told Ella—"

Markus groaned. "Would you guys listen to yourselves? You're bickering over trivialities. The answer to our problem has fallen in our lap. We'd be stupid not to do this."

Jane's face clouded, and she turned away from us as if the answer to this terrible dilemma was hidden somewhere in the woods. Ian reached out to her, resting his hand on her arm.

"Jane?" he whispered.

She took in a shuddering breath. "What if I do it for you, Ella?" she asked, still staring off into the trees. "Let me push it."

My hand flew to my pocket.

"You could go back to the car," Ian said. "You won't even be a part of it, not if you don't want to be."

How could they be agreeing to this? Were they all crazy?

"But I'd know," I blurted. "It's the same thing."

"It's not," Markus said, shaking his head. "Let us do it."

They'd do it. They would kill the congressman. They'd push that button knowing he would die. And maybe they'd be doing it for me, for themselves, for the other pets, but did that make it right?

I looked between their faces. They were good people, trying to take this weight off my shoulders. Maybe this wasn't about murder for them, or even revenge.

My head throbbed. How could they expect me to make this choice? Because that's what they were asking. Even if I didn't push the button, if I didn't take the congressman's life, handing over that remote detonator would be doing the same thing, wouldn't it? Turning a blind eye wasn't any different than committing the act myself.

But if I didn't, if I refused, was it the same thing as allowing the congressman to keep killing girls like me? Both answers were wrong. Both outcomes would cut me like barbed wire being tightened around my heart.

And then, from the other side of the wall came a voice, one that chilled the very center of me.

"Dad! Where's the sidewalk chalk?"

It was Ruby's voice, lacking some of its normal vibrancy, but unmistakable nonetheless. I could almost see her standing there, her hands folded in front of her chest the way they were when she was unhappy with something.

Markus's face blanched. "No," he muttered under his breath, his beautiful plan disintegrating before our eyes.

My fingers clamped around the detonator. What had I almost done?

## Fifteen

*I*t was dark by the time we got back to the apartment. We dragged ourselves through the door, and Markus slammed it behind us, heading straight for the guest room. None of us had been able to look one another in the eye since we climbed back into the van. Not only had we failed to destroy the files, but we'd almost murdered a little girl.

Although, I wondered if Markus was really that upset by the thought of killing Ruby. If I hadn't been there, would he still have done it? Even after hearing her voice? He'd muttered to himself on the drive home, his hands clenching and unclenching around the steering wheel like it was a neck he'd like to squeeze.

Who knew if he'd told the others what was driving him for vengeance. It must have been horrible, whatever had happened to him while he was still under NuPet's control, to make him this angry. But it didn't feel like the time to ask.

Vanessa emerged from her bedroom, stopping to stand in front of Dave. Her hair was a mess, her shirt untucked and crumpled.

"Don't start with me," he said, holding up his hand before she even had a chance to speak.

Vanessa raised an eyebrow. "Can I talk to you? In private?"

He sighed, but he didn't argue, following her back into her room.

"We need to get out of this place," Jane said, slumping onto the couch. "Am I the only one who doesn't like that woman?"

I shrugged and sank down next to her. How could I care about Dave's sister when I couldn't get Ruby's voice out of my mind? What if she hadn't spoken? What if I'd handed over that detonator to Markus? I'd spent the past two hours imagining the bomb tearing that concrete house apart. Imagining Ruby's body lying in the rubble, lifeless and bleeding, like Erik at the restaurant. Like I imagined Miss Gellner's body after the Greenwich bomb went off. Like the men with the guns at the warehouse.

My finger traced the outline of the rectangle in my pocket. Every few minutes my hand fluttered to the box pressed against my leg, the way it might travel to an injury. I didn't want to hold it any longer, but I was afraid to let it go. It was my responsibility to make sure that button was never pressed.

"I'm sorry about the little girl," Jane said after a few minutes. "That was Penn's sister, right?"

I picked at a thread that had come loose on the cushion. "She shouldn't be there," I said. "She should be with her mom."

Elise needed to know where the congressman had taken their daughter. She'd probably found some solace in thinking Ruby was at home at their house in Connecticut, in her bedroom with all her books. But no. Both her kids were locked in cement buildings, and none of us could do anything to set them free.

Yet.

"We'll plan a new mission," Jane said confidently. "Don't worry. Give Markus a day or two and he'll come up with a way to get the girl out and destroy those files. It's not like this thing is over."

"Thanks." I smiled weakly. Her words should have been encouraging, but it seemed like every move we made only made things worse. It was hard to remember what we were fighting for anymore. Was this even about the pets, or had it gotten mixed up and tangled into something else?

A few minutes later, Dave emerged from his sister's room, shoulders slumped, head hanging low like a reprimanded dog. At least she hadn't yelled this time.

He slipped into the guest room, a bold move considering Markus was in there, probably crouched and waiting, ready to rip the head off anyone who entered.

I leaned closer to Jane. "Why are you doing this?"

Her hands stilled in her lap, but she didn't respond.

"I mean, why put yourself through this if you don't have to?" I went on. "You could do anything. You're smart and brave and thoughtful. You could probably be an important person, with your own life—one that didn't put you in danger, one that could actually make a difference."

"I *can* make a difference," she said, facing me with a look of pure resolve. "I knew coming into this it wouldn't be easy. Causes like this never are, but I have to believe the right side will win out in the end. We're inching forward. I promise. It might not seem like it to you because we're in the thick of it right now. We're in the muddy trenches and it's dark and cold and it seems like morning is never going to come, but it always does."

Tears pricked at the corners of my eyes. I wanted so badly to believe her. "But they must be thinking the same thing, right?" I asked. "Nobody fights for something because they think it's wrong. Maybe we're the crazy ones. Maybe we're the ones on the wrong side of history."

Jane shook her head. "Human rights and social justice are never the wrong side of history."

"Yeah, but you have to think I'm human to believe that."

She cupped my face softly in her hand. "Oh, you're human, Ella. There's no denying that."

From the other room, there was a loud bang and then a shout. Jane and I flinched.

"Damn it! Dave and Markus have got to stop acting like children," she said, jumping to her feet. "I don't have the energy to deal with those two."

The door to the guest bedroom swung open, and Markus rushed out. "Get up. Come on," he shouted. "We've got to get a move on it. Shit! Do we even have our gear together?" He looked around the room wild-eyed, then rushed to the table and started cramming things into a bag.

"Whoa, slow down, man. What's going on?" Ian asked, scrambling up from his spot by the window.

Dave emerged from the bedroom, too. He stared down at a piece of paper.

Markus gestured at him. "Tell them," he said.

Dave swallowed and looked up from the paper. "I think I found something."

"You think?" Markus shouted. "Tell them! Tell them what you just told me."

He shrugged. "I was just looking through the transcripts from yesterday's intel."

"Which transcripts?" Jane asked, trying to get a better look.

"There's this call, one of our bugs intercepted it from one of John Kimball's guys. It says where they are—all the pets. But they're going to exterminate them tonight. We don't have a lot of time."

Jane's face burned red as she tried to pull the papers from his hands. "Which bug was it?" she demanded. "I didn't see this. I looked over everything we got yesterday. There wasn't—"

"Goddamm it, Jane, stop!" Dave bellowed. "Haven't you done enough damage already? You keep missing stuff. It's like you've totally forgotten how to do your job since we got here. You're more worried about my sister than you are with your own crap."

Jane shrank back. "That's not true at all."

"You've been screwing things up long before we got here," he went on. "You got so caught up worrying about our relationship that your brain stopped working."

Jane's whole body stiffened. "Are you kidding me?"

"She's right, man," Ian interjected. "That's unfair."

"Is it?" Dave asked. "If she hadn't been so distracted, maybe she wouldn't have screwed up the warehouse job."

"You can't blame Jane for that," Ian spat, covering the ground between them in a heartbeat. "You act like she was the one swooning over you. I saw the way you led her on. You were clearly together."

"This isn't high school." Dave sneered. "But I guess you wouldn't know, would you?"

Ian shoved him in the chest. "Why are you being such a bastard about this?"

"You and Jane are worthless," Dave said, shoving him back. "Haven't you realized it yet? What good do either of you ever do? Huh? You think you've done anything useful for this cause besides complain and suck up resources?"

Ian glared at him. "I've been with Markus from the beginning, asshole! You have *no* idea what the two of us have been through. No idea about the sort of shit those monsters put us through. You think you know this cause? Bullshit! You're just here because it's an excuse to play with your stupid toys."

He charged at Dave, hitting him square in the chest. The two of them stumbled back into the wall, and a painting clattered to the ground.

"Stop!" Markus said.

"Maybe if you hadn't been with him, he would have gotten some shit done." Dave panted, wriggling free of Ian's grasp.

"Go to hell!"

"Stop!" Markus shouted, his voice loud enough to

make all of us jump. "We don't have time for this. Ella, Dave, get your things."

"What about Jane and Ian?" I asked.

"Maybe it's better if you two sit this one out," Markus said. "I need to concentrate, and I'm afraid the two of you might be more of a distraction than a benefit right now."

"What? No!" Ian rubbed his shoulder and winced. "You can't go there without us. You need a team."

Markus zipped his bag closed and threw it onto his shoulder. "I really need you two to stay here," he said. "I want to keep this small. We need something tight. The intel says there's only one guard holding the place."

"That doesn't seem right," Jane said, reaching for the papers again. "Let me look it over."

"We don't have time for this," Dave said, pulling away from her. He folded the papers in half, and then in half again, and shoved them deep in his pocket. "He already told you."

Markus sighed. "I'm sorry, okay? But we've got to go. You two hold down the fort here. I'll give you a call as soon as we've got the girls. Jane, you look into finding a safe place we can take them all once we've got them. They might need medical attention. We've got to have these things arranged."

Jane blinked back tears, but she raised her chin and nodded.

"I'm sorry," I whispered.

She shook her head, not looking me in the eye. "It's not your fault," she said. "Just get them out."

"I will."

• • •

*D*ave pulled the van onto a narrow road. The pavement was pitted and cracked, the place obviously unused for long enough the congressman's men felt confident they'd chosen a well-secluded spot to hold the girls.

We'd been driving north for more than an hour. Markus followed close behind us in the large white box truck he'd stolen from headquarters without being spotted.

In front of us, a crumbling white steeple emerged from between the trees. It glowed in the moonlight, a decrepit finger pointing to the heavens.

The hairs rose on the back of my neck. "What is this place?"

"Abandoned church, it looks like," Dave said.

"Shouldn't you park here?" I asked. "We don't want to give ourselves away."

"Oh yeah… Yeah." Dave swerved off the road, and the car skidded to a stop in the gravel and long grasses.

Markus pulled up beside us, switching off his lights and killing the engine so we were engulfed in darkness.

"You ready?" I asked.

Dave nodded.

"Listen, I just wanted to say thank you, Dave," I said. "I know you're not really doing this for me. I mean, you are, but I know you're probably one of those people that believes in causes. In things that are bigger than yourself."

Dave shook his head. "You don't need to thank me."

"I know it's not done yet," I said. "But I want to. I

think it's a noble thing to do. Markus and Ian, all of us who've been told we aren't like you, that our lives aren't worth as much as yours, we owe you. You didn't have to fight for us, but you chose to anyway."

He shook his head again.

"Anyway, I just want you to know how much it means to me," I said.

"Can we just get a move on?" he asked, not meeting my eyes. He swung open his door. "I want to get this thing over with."

He hopped out the door, quickly grabbing his bag from the back.

Markus was outside my door when I climbed out. He raised a finger to his lips, and we made our way in silence toward the steeple. It only took a minute to come to the clearing where the building stood, surrounded by a field of overgrown grass and bushes. The weeds had encroached all the way up the front steps, ivy winding its way past the arched front door and through one of the broken windows framing the entrance.

"The place looks empty," I whispered.

"I think that's the point," Markus said. "No wonder they chose it."

From this close, it was clear the building had survived a fire. Part of the roof was blackened, revealing a gaping hole. The night air was cold against my skin, and I doubted these collapsing walls were offering much more protection to the poor girls inside.

"Where's the guard?" I asked.

"He's probably right inside the door," Markus whispered, waving for us to move forward.

We crept slowly toward the building. Markus and I glided more quietly through the weeds, picking each step carefully, like a dance with silence, but Dave's steps weren't so light. The gravel and broken glass crunched under his boots like he was purposefully making as much noise as possible. I kept my eyes glued to the arched double doors at the top of the steps, but no one emerged.

Markus took a deep breath. "Okay. I'll go—"

Buzzing sounded from inside his bag.

He scrambled to unzip it. In the silence of the abandoned lot, the noise sounded like an alarm.

"What are you doing with a phone?" Dave hissed.

I was just as surprised as he was. Hadn't we agreed it would be foolish to use our phones? We didn't know if the person who had betrayed us at the warehouse was still connected to the movement. They could record our conversations. Track our movements.

Markus reached for the small flip phone tucked at the bottom of the bag, quickly dismissing the call.

"Are you crazy?" Dave whispered.

"Calm down," Markus said. "It's not one of the old ones. I had Jane run out and grab a couple of disposables from the drug store."

The phone buzzed again in his hand, and Dave and I both glanced nervously at the building.

"Dammit, Jane, are you an idiot?" Markus muttered. He flipped open the phone. "This better be an emergency!"

Through the phone, we heard the high-pitched rush of Jane's faraway voice. I struggled to make out words. She was clearly upset.

Dave took a step back, looking from Markus to me. "We don't have time for Jane's bullshit!" he barked, lunging forward to snatch the phone from Markus's hand.

Markus's face contorted in rage, and he advanced on Dave, his jaw clenched. "Give me the phone back." He lunged, knocking the phone from Dave's hand. It flew through the air, skidding across the dirt a few yards away, and they both tumbled to the ground. Dave was clumsy, but his limbs were long, one of the only advantages he had against Markus, who was a better fighter, even if he was smaller. Dave struck him across the face, grunting and clawing. With his legs, he pinned him to the ground.

"Stop!" I shouted. "We don't have time for this."

Their uncontrollable anger was going to ruin this whole mission. If we were going to rescue these girls, I was going to have to do it myself.

I turned away from them and rushed toward the building. On the ground in front of me, the phone lay open. I grabbed it and bounded up the crumbling front steps, digging inside my bag for the stun gun. These weren't my mission instructions. I was supposed to find the girls, not subdue the guard, but obviously things had changed. I'd just have to improvise and find Missy.

Behind me, Dave bellowed into the night air. "Now! Now!"

*Idiot.* Couldn't he see I was already going? He didn't have to yell at me.

The heavy front doors groaned as I pushed them open, raising the stun gun in front of me, ready to shoot. Even though a bit of moonlight streamed through the gaping hole in the roof, my eyes struggled to adjust to the dark. Near the front of the building, dark forms huddled by the wall, crouched and unmoving.

My hand clamped tighter around the stun gun, and I stepped farther inside. It was too quiet in here. Where were the sounds of the girls moving around, or the gasp of their collective breath? If there was a song of blackness, this was it.

Outside, Dave continued to yell. Or was that Markus? I couldn't concentrate. The sounds all but disappeared at the door.

Missy! I needed to find her. Now, before I lost her forever. The odd feeling we were being pulled farther and farther apart circled through my mind. It felt like I was standing on a high cliff, watching in slow motion as everyone I loved fell away from me, tumbling closer and closer to the ground with no way for me to save them. With each slow second that ticked by, the feeling swelled.

"Missy!" I called out. I didn't care if the guard heard me.

And then, from the front of the chapel, clattering filled the air. A small beam of moonlight shone through a high window, illuminating the bodies rising up. Wings flapped, catching the light like small bursts of white flames.

My throat tightened, and I wished all the stolen girls had really turned into these birds, rising into the night sky, free, uncaged. They flapped toward the hole in the roof, disappearing like smoke into the night.

Behind me, the door thumped.

I turned to see the hulking body of a guard blocking the doorway, and down the steps behind him, the unmistakable forms of a half dozen more just like him, descending on Markus and Dave.

## Sixteen

*B*etrayed. We'd been betrayed. Again.

I spun around, frantically searching for a way out. A bit of light shone behind the form that blocked the doorway, turning him into a faceless silhouette, a monster whose thick arms reached forward, ready to squeeze the life from me.

"Run, Ella!" Markus shouted. His voice sounded far away, small, trapped, like there wasn't enough air inside his lungs.

My eyes bounced between the giant in front of me and the scene that lay beyond. Markus knelt doubled over on the ground. Above him, two more guards pummeled his head and shoulders. A deep gash had opened on his cheek, spilling blood down his face. On the ground next to him, Dave struggled to his feet.

How could we have fallen into another trap? It didn't

make sense. Not twice. The last time, we'd been betrayed by a snitch inside the group, but not now. We couldn't have when it was just the five of us—

Dave stood, brushing the dirt and weeds from his shirt, and backed away from Markus. The guards glanced at him, but they didn't make a move to stop him. They didn't grab him, and he didn't run. He simply stood panting next to them as if that was where he belonged.

Rage blurred my vision, filling my whole head with thunder.

Through the racket inside of me, the story fell into place. The veil that had been pulled down over my eyes lifted, and I could see clearly. Dave. This whole time it had been *him*.

How could he do this to us?

As if pushed by some invisible force, I charged forward, my finger tightening around the button on the black gun in my hand. The electric current surged like a lightning strike, hitting the man in the doorway directly in his chest. The giant fell, hammering into the ground with so much force the rotted wood splintered beneath him.

I climbed over his body, my hand tightening once more around my weapon. Markus lay crumpled over, gasping at the guards' feet. Dave looked from him to me, wiping a dribble of blood from the corner of his mouth.

"Don't let her get away!" he yelled. "She's the one we need."

Above me, the rotting steeple reached impossibly for heaven. It was useless to hope some sort of god could save me now. I glanced back over my shoulder into the dark chapel. Maybe long ago, people had sought asylum inside the walls of this church, but now it was just an empty cage. If I moved back inside, I'd be trapped.

I didn't have time to go to Markus. I couldn't. Maybe it was cowardice. I knew it must look that way from the outside. To Dave, I must have looked like a girl fleeing, but it didn't feel that way. This wasn't about saving myself.

It was about finishing a job.

Now that I knew what cancer had been infecting our group, I might actually stand a chance. These past few days had felt like the group of us had been spiraling into a black hole, pulled under by our own disappointment, our own failures, each one dragging us down.

I leaped off the blackened church steps, and the congressman's men looked up from Markus. That was their first mistake, assuming that just because he was on the ground, he was beaten. Their second was turning their backs on him. They locked their eyes on me, hungry and lethal, like a pack of wolves.

I took off at a sprint. The woods were my only hope. If I could take cover in the trees, maybe I could move faster in the underbrush than they could. Maybe I could make it to that box truck. Maybe I could get away.

Out of the side of my eye, I saw Markus reach for his bag. He rose from the ground, his shaking arm pointing his sleek black gun at the guards.

There was a blast, and the world slowed. I turned, straining to see. Across the field, one of the congressman's men went down, his black-clad body falling into the tall grass like a man diving into the sea. The weeds swallowed him whole.

Another shot rang out.

The guard chasing me didn't fall. No, his feet still beat the ground, gaining on me. Behind him, Dave stood with both hands clamped around a smoking gun.

Markus's body lay sprawled out in front of him.

I cried out, waiting for the next bullet to be mine. He might not shoot to kill. He needed me, after all. But I didn't doubt that he'd shoot.

The blast echoed behind me as I struck the tree line, bounding into the undergrowth. A dense row of bushes ran the length of the woods here, thick with thorns and berries. The barbed branches tore at my arms, my face, my hair, but I plowed forward, looping through the trees, hoping I was heading in the direction of the vehicles.

My ears strained to hear the guards. Surely at least the one would be close behind me, but I could only make out the sound of my own breathing and the crack and crunch of my footsteps through the brush. If I wanted to hear anything else, I'd have to stop.

Off to my left, a branch snapped, and I spun to face it, bracing myself for the pain of the gunshot, but the woods were empty. I panted, crouching next to a thick trunk. In my left hand, I still clutched Markus's phone; in my right, the stun gun. I tucked the phone into my back pocket. I didn't have time to think about what Jane had called to tell him. Had she figured out it was Dave all along?

The stun gun's plastic was slick with sweat in my hand. It wouldn't do me much good against a real gun. Maybe if I found a place to hide they wouldn't find me. If I disguised myself well enough, I could see them sneaking up on me, and then maybe the stun gun would do me some good—if I had a chance to fire. But if I missed, if they saw me first, if they'd already called for more men to come search for me...

I couldn't stay. I needed to get to that truck.

Trembling, I got back to my feet. I took a deep breath, gazing up through the canopy of the trees. The leaves and branches hid the stars, but the moon was round and bright.

I took off again.

It didn't take long to break back through the edge of the woods into the clearing where we'd parked. The box truck and the van sat exactly where we'd left them. They couldn't be more than fifty feet away. Relief washed over me. I was almost there. If I squinted, I could see the keys Markus had left dangling in the ignition.

And then I saw movement. Through the windows of the box truck, I made out a dark shape poking up near the mirror on the far side of the vehicle. It moved into view for just a moment, not long enough to get a good read on it, then it disappeared behind the other side of the truck.

My stomach dropped. What was I supposed to do now? I needed that truck. I could feel more of the congressman's men bearing down on me as I waited. They'd be close by now. Too close.

I had two choices. I could make a run for it and hope to slip inside the truck without the person behind it seeing me. Or, I could sneak around to the other side myself. I still had the stun gun, after all, and I knew how to use it. If I was quick, maybe I'd have a chance.

I snaked around the clearing, keeping to the edges. The grasses were high, and I crept through them slowly, moving with the wind. Once again, I found myself grateful for how much NuPet had actually given me. There was a beautiful irony in the fact that they didn't even realize what they'd created, even though it became clearer to me with each new situation. From the outside, all they saw were beautiful girls, trained to be quiet, petite, elegant, refined. They overlooked the fact that they'd created girls who were nimble and smart and independent and quick, girls who could learn to adapt to any situation. Maybe this was the most beautifully human thing about me, this ability to adapt, the ability to thrive and learn and grow.

My feet slipped silently over the dirt and rocks, my body bending and arching like a ballerina on stage. When the wind quieted, so did I, balancing as still as a flower on its stem.

A gust billowed through the grasses, shaking the dry leaves in a tree nearby, and I rushed the rest of the way forward. There was a large stone near the front of the van, and I ducked behind it.

In the quiet air, I could hear the choppy breath of someone else. I peered up over the side of the rock. There, standing with his back pressed to the side of the box truck, was Dave, his hands clutched around the handle of his gun. He glanced nervously in both directions.

He knew I needed the truck. When the other guard had followed me into the woods, he must have come straight here, knowing it wouldn't be long before I'd show up. And he would be waiting. Waiting to capture me and turn me back over to the congressman.

Hate swelled inside me. It branched out from my

chest, a hot web spreading across my arms, my legs, twining through my fingers and pushing at the backs of my eyes until they clouded with rage.

Without thinking, I bounded forward, my feet propelling me off the rock. I flew through the air, aimed straight at Dave. He reeled back, shocked, raising his shaking hands in front of him.

The jolt of electricity from my stun gun met its mark, hitting him in the center of his chest. The pistol dropped from his hand, landing with a crunch in the gravel, and he fell forward, his body stiff, each muscle tense and rigid. His neck arched back, the tendons pulled taut, bulging as if they might burst out of the skin that held them.

He cried out, and I let go of the trigger, the crack and sizzle replaced by the smallest moan escaping from his lips.

I crammed my weapon into my waistband, snatched up his gun, and pointed it at his head. My hands shook, still buzzing with anger.

Could I do it?

Could I pull the trigger?

There'd be no changing my mind if I did.

*Pull it*, rage whispered. *Kill him.* Hate's breath was hot in my ear. So hot. I blinked, trying to separate myself from the body of all that fury, but it was inside me now, devouring everything else.

*Pull it.*

If I did, the bullet wouldn't be forgiving. This I knew. There was no mercy inside its metal casing. It would burst forth from the muzzle of the gun and split the skin on Dave's head like butter, splintering his skull, tearing through his soft brain until it found its way out the other side.

Dave quivered on the ground. A bit of saliva bubbled in the corner of his mouth, and he groaned.

My hand went weak, and a cold rush of sorrow flooded my body. Maybe this was part of humanity, this hate, this rage, but I didn't want to be a part of it. If I killed him now, wasn't I just as much to blame as the rest of them? This was the problem with war, wasn't it? And this *was* war, just like Markus had said. Two sides battling against each other, each one convinced the other was wrong. But didn't they know no one would ever win? Not with killing, at least.

Dave groaned again, lifting his eyes to meet mine.

I bit my tongue. There was so much I wanted to say to him, but there wasn't time.

I flung open the door to the box truck, tossed the gun onto the passenger seat, and climbed in, scooting over behind the wheel. In the truck's side mirror, the moon lit the gravel road behind me, and past that, emerging from the dark woods, was the last guard.

I scooted forward on the seat, trying to reach the pedals. My legs weren't long, and the truck wasn't built for people like me. My toes touched the controls. I'd never driven before, but there was no time to think about that now. I'd watched other people, and I knew enough. The gas pedal on the right made the car move. The brake pedal on the left made it stop. That would have to be enough information.

The keys glinted in the ignition. At least one thing had gone right tonight. I twisted them, and the engine rumbled to life, so much strength beneath me. I'd never really thought about it before. Cars had always taken me places, but I'd never been in charge of all that power, tons of metal and rubber.

I pressed down on the gas, and the engine revved, bellowing into the night air like a monster's roar, but the car didn't budge.

I glanced in the rearview mirror. The guard had heard it. There was no mistaking that sound. Gun raised, he took off at a run toward me.

"Come on! Come on!" I hit the wheel. What was I forgetting? It had all seemed so simple when someone else was driving.

I took a deep breath, trying to imagine what they'd done every time we'd gone somewhere. I had the keys. The car had started. My eyes darted over the dash, and then I remembered the stick with the letters on it: P R N D. In most of the cars, it was near the seat, but in this truck, it was up by the steering wheel. It wasn't a word I recognized.

I pulled it down one notch to the R and pushed hard on the gas pedal again. This time the truck lurched backward. The tires spun madly, spitting gravel and dirt in front of me as I bumped over the main road and into the ditch on the other side. My head slammed into the steering wheel, and I took my foot off the gas. The gun slid off the front seat onto the floor.

A bullet struck the back of the truck and exploded against the metal.

Frantically, I looked in the mirror again, but the guard had disappeared from my line of sight. He could be anywhere.

My whole body shook. Out the front window of the truck, Dave moved in the beams of the headlights, slowly rolling over.

I slammed down on the lever again. If R moved the car back, maybe N would move it forward. Once again I stomped on the gas pedal, but the engine only roared, screaming louder the harder I pressed.

P R N D… I tried to make sense of it, but the letters only spun in my mind, whirring and circling, as useless as the engine beneath me.

Another bullet struck the back of the truck. Another. And Another.

"Please work! Please," I yelled. I pulled the lever one last time, pounding my foot against the gas so hard it hit the floor. This time the truck screeched forward. I clung to the wheel, cranking it first to the left before I jerked back onto the dirt road, making a wide, skidding turn.

At the side of the road, the guard finally closed the distance between us. His face loomed in the truck's side mirror, so close I could see the snarl of his teeth, his lips parting in an angry grimace. There was another shot, and the passenger window shattered beside me. Tiny bits of glass spread across the seat next to me, cascading onto the floor and crashing into the side of my leg.

I kept the pedal pressed to the floor. The truck flew wildly over the rutted road, the empty box in the back thudding like a huge drum with each bump. The tires skidded around the curves, but I didn't dare lift my foot from the gas. Behind me, the guard disappeared.

The small dirt lane opened up onto a bigger road, and I turned left, steering in the direction we'd come from. My memory wasn't perfect, but I could probably find my way back, if that was even the right thing to do. Who knew what direction the congressman's men would be coming from. Would they recognize this truck? And what would happen if they spotted me?

I couldn't think about it now. My hands ached from gripping the wheel so tightly, and my head pounded. Every time a pair of headlights appeared in front of me, my body clenched, waiting for the car to run me off the road, but each time, they sped past without a second glance.

After a while, a smattering of city lights appeared. On the right side of the road, the lit sign from a small convenience store beckoned. I tapped the brake, careening awkwardly up the driveway and lurching to a stop at the edge of the parking lot.

I shut off the car and laid my head against the steering wheel.

From outside, the store looked empty. Only one other car sat in the parking lot.

I'd never felt more alone in my life. Growing up, there had been nights when I'd lie awake inside the walls of the training center, staring up at the blank ceiling, feeling like I was all alone, but that sort of loneliness seemed so naive compared to this. At the kennel and the training center, I'd never been alone, not really. There were always other girls just like me only a few yards away, and even though we suffered in our own quiet ways, it was a world of sorrow we all shared.

My pocket buzzed, and I jumped. I'd forgotten all about Markus's phone. Quickly, I dug it out of my pocket and flipped it open. The screen lit up with missed messages. It must have been buzzing in my pocket the whole time I'd been driving, but I hadn't felt it.

I scanned the messages, but each one only showed a couple of words. *Call me right... The information is... Tell me where... Please respond, we're...* I tapped the screen, but it wasn't the same as the phones Ruby and Penn had, and nothing happened.

I pushed the green button on the front, and a line of numbers came up on the screen. A second later it started ringing.

Quickly, I pushed the red button and dropped the phone into my lap. I hadn't felt this stupid, this inept, in so long, but my body remembered. The feelings slid back over me again, like one of the white cotton gowns I'd worn for so many years. It draped against my skin, lay across my shoulders, rested in my lap, reminding me I could never do this on my own. I was just a useless pet. I couldn't change the world. I couldn't even use a phone.

The phone buzzed again in my hand, ringing.

I stared at it. What if it *was* Jane? Markus had said it had been her on the phone back at the church. Likely, this would be her again, but my stomach rose in my throat anyway. How would I know if I could trust her?

I pressed the green button again and slowly raised the phone to my ear.

## Seventeen

"Hello?"

"Oh my God! Ella!" Jane's voice filled the speaker. "I've been trying to get a hold of you guys for an hour. I thought… I was afraid…" She swallowed loudly. "Where's Markus? Can you put him on the phone?"

I tried to find the words, but I could only remember the sound of the bullets and the way his body had fallen onto the ground. It was impossible to shape those things into sentences inside my mouth.

She must have sensed my hesitation. On the other end of the line, she sucked in a sharp breath. "No. Please tell me he isn't…?"

"I'm sorry," I said. "There wasn't anything I could do."

Something muffled the phone, but I held on, waiting. The sound of grief was clear, even hundreds of miles away. I hung my head and let go of the tears I'd been holding on to myself. Somewhere, Jane was doubled over in pain, too. It connected us, the same way the phone connected us. I didn't know how, but it was there.

After a minute, Jane's choked voice came back on the line. "I'm sorry," she muttered. "I was hoping I'd warned him in time."

"It was Dave?" I asked. "This whole time? It was him?"

"I feel like an idiot," Jane said. "I should have seen it. And maybe I would have if I'd been looking at him with more objective eyes. If I hadn't let myself…" She choked up again. "I'm sorry, Ella. I'm sorry I let you down. All of you."

"This isn't your fault," I said. "He was a part of our group. We trusted him."

That was the thing that hurt the most. We'd opened ourselves to Dave, and he'd betrayed us. Not just the group, not just the Liberationist movement in this fight against NuPet, but each of us individually.

"I know," she said, and then her voice perked up. "Wait, where are you?"

"I'm in the box truck," I said. "I got away from Dave and just started driving. I'm at a store by the side of the road. I wasn't thinking about where I was going. I must be a half an hour away from the city, but I'm not sure."

"I can't believe I almost forgot…" Jane said. "I got distracted by what happened and I… We've got to hurry!"

"What?"

"We've got to hurry," she repeated.

My stomach jumped. Something about the urgency in her voice made my nerves zing. "Why? What's going on?"

"It's the intel about the girls. The papers Dave showed

to you guys—"

"But he lied."

"Yes and no," she said. "After you left, I got curious. I wanted to look at the information myself, and something felt…off. So I logged back in to the program. The page Dave had showed you guys was still open, but it wasn't linked to the original information the way it should have been. He was sloppy. It might not have looked suspicious to anyone else, but I could tell a bunch of data had been exchanged. I had to rewrite some code, but I finally reverted the file back to its original state."

There was that feeling again. A spark, a zip, like electricity. "And?"

"And it showed that Dave changed the location."

"Wait." I stared off into the dark where a pair of headlights had emerged. They grew brighter, closer, and it seemed as if the words Jane was trying to tell me were getting closer, too. Clearer. Just a little nearer, and I'd see clearly what she was saying.

If Dave had only changed the location, that meant… "The intel is still good," I blurted. "Does that mean we know where the girls are actually being held?"

"We do," Jane said. "And you and I are going to go get them."

*I*t took Jane and Ian less than an hour to get to me, but that didn't leave us much time. If we were going to get to the girls, it had to be soon.

They parked their van beside my truck and climbed up into the cab next to me. In the dim light of the dashboard, I could see both Jane's and Ian's eyes were red and swollen, but underneath the sorrow they were alight with something just as obvious: determination.

I scooted over, grateful to give the driver's seat to someone else.

"It's a good thing you took this," Ian said. His voice sounded peculiar, quiet and raspy. "There's no way we could fit fifty girls into two vans."

I still hated the idea of cramming all of them in the back of a truck like they were packages, but if it saved them, it hardly mattered.

"I'm so sorry—" I started.

His body slouched against the steering wheel. He looked like a man who'd been crushed. I didn't know how long he and Markus had been together. But they were as good as brothers. I knew that.

"Ian," I said, "what happened to you and Markus? At your kennel?"

He stared off into the dark night. "It was bad."

I clasped his hand in mine. "Will you tell me?"

His face was stony. Unreadable. "Does it matter?" he said. "It's over now."

"I need to know."

He swallowed. "I'm sure it's not any worse than what they did to you girls. They bred us each with a particular client in mind, didn't they? As males, they knew we'd be valued for our strength. But they also knew that with that strength, we'd pose more of a"—he paused, carefully picking his words—"a threat, to our trainers and to our potential masters."

Jane shifted uncomfortably, and I wondered if she'd heard this story before.

"And so, if they were going to sell us, they'd have to break us first."

"Break you?" I asked.

His jaw clenched. "Have you ever heard of the way people used to break the elephants in the circus?"

I shook my head.

"I've heard about it," Jane said quietly. She swallowed. "The things I heard are barbaric. They start at a really young age. They keep them in small cages where they can hardly move. They tie their feet with ropes and stretch their limbs. They poke them with sharp metal rods. They yell at them. They starve them."

"Yes, that and more," Ian said.

My eyes stung. I knew what he was telling us. These weren't just the things they did to animals. Someone had done these things to Markus. To Ian.

"But why? Why would they do that?" I asked.

Ian squeezed the steering wheel until his knuckles went white. "It breaks the spirit. Break the spirit, and you control the body, the mind. Male pets weren't bred to serve in the same way female pets were. They needed us strong. They needed us to be able to do the work of five men without having to obey any of those pesky human rights labor laws," he said, bitterly. "And there were plenty of clients that wanted that sort of pet. But there was no way they'd buy us if they couldn't be assured that we'd be kept under control."

"You were too big of a threat?" I asked.

"Yes. Ultimately, that's what ended the program," he said. "But not before they did everything in their power to break us."

A syrupy blackness of silence filled the cab.

He straightened, shaking his head. "But I'm not broken anymore," he said, cranking the ignition. The truck rumbled to life beneath us, our huge white steed, our roaring dragon that would deliver us into battle.

Jane dug into her bag and pulled out a folded piece of paper. She handed it over to me.

I opened it up and scanned it. "This is it?" I asked. "The transcript Dave changed?"

She nodded as we pulled out of the parking lot and onto the black road. "This, right here," she said, pointing to the paper. It was dark in the cab, and I could hardly make out the writing. "He didn't have to change a whole lot. I'm pretty confident the date hasn't been messed with, which means we've got at least a few hours left before—"

"Before those bastards murder each and every one of those girls," Ian finished.

"You're sure about that part?" I asked. "You don't think Dave changed that, too, just so he'd be sure we'd go with him quickly?"

"I'm afraid not," Jane said.

"Tell her the worst part," Ian said, shaking his head.

I turned to Jane.

"These people are sick," Ian spat.

Jane didn't argue. She took a deep breath. "The address Dave changed... I Googled it. The building is owned by a trust that bought it from the state of New Jersey, part of a big buyback. Do you want to guess who helped facilitate its purchase?"

I shook my head. I didn't want to say his name.

"Tell her the worst part," Ian pushed.

I braced myself. Wasn't it bad enough all the pets were going to be taken to a building owned by the congressman to be killed? How could it get worse than that?

"It's BP Packing—an old meatpacking plant." Jane's voice cracked.

I just stared at her. Was this supposed to mean something to me? I'd never heard the word before.

Jane looked at Ian. "Don't make me explain it."

He shook his head. "We can't let her go in there without knowing what it is."

I knew the terrible things humans could do. I wouldn't try to hide from it. And being blinded from the truth was even worse. I would face the ugliness, the grotesque, distorted face of cruelty. I would look that monster in the eye if it meant I had a chance to slay it. But I was sick of being blind. "Tell me," I said.

Jane took a deep breath. "The place we're going was built for killing animals. Cows and pigs mostly," she said. "It wasn't pretty, and it wasn't humane. They didn't care how much pain or fear these animals felt, and you can sense that when you're there. It's a slaughterhouse."

I covered my mouth with my hands. I was going to be sick. It wasn't just the idea of death that disgusted me—I understood there had to be a place where meat was packaged. But the fact the congressman had chosen *this* as the place to murder all the pets made bile rise in my throat.

"He chose it on purpose," I whispered.

Jane's expression soured. "Of course he did."

He didn't pick the slaughterhouse because it was a convenient place to dispose of his problems. This was revenge. Just another way to dehumanize us, to spit on us, to show us just how inconsequential we all were.

"But you needed to know before we got there," she said. "I need you to be focused. We can't take any chances."

"I can handle it."

She squeezed my hand. "I know you can."

We drove up over some old railroad tracks and pulled to a stop behind a dilapidated wooden shack. A decade or so ago, this must have been a bustling district, but now it was deserted, strewn with abandoned cars and bits of rusting machinery.

The slaughterhouse sat, dark and looming, in front of us, a huge brick edifice with a line of cracked and broken windows running along the top of the building. Next to it, a vacant lot was littered with empty railroad cars and piles of old scrap metal. An old boat dock sagged into the river beyond. Lights from the city sparkled on the far shore, such an odd and startling bit of beauty resting beside this dreary place.

The building looked empty from the outside, but around the side of it, almost hidden from sight, the shiny hood of a dark SUV reflected a bit of moonlight.

NuPet.

Deep inside me, something stirred. They were here. I could feel their presence buzzing through my body. I could picture them inside, so much clearer than those grainy pictures.

"Now what?" I asked.

"I didn't have time to find blueprints for the building," Jane said, "so we're going to have to improvise."

Ian grabbed his bag off the floor. "I think we need to treat this like our first mission. The execution was flawed, but that was because we were sold out. It wasn't because our plan was bad. That plan would have worked."

"But there are only three of us," I said.

"And three's plenty," he said. "We split up inside. That will give us a greater chance of finding them without getting caught. Whoever gets to the girls first will cut their chains and lead them back out to the truck. If you come across a guard…subdue them."

If the guards here were any bit as large as the men I'd just fought off at the church, I wasn't sure how easily any of us would be able to subdue them.

"What if there are too many of them?"

Ian sighed. "We've got one last canister of gas. If something goes wrong, I'll detonate it. But let's hope we don't need to."

It wasn't much of a plan, but I was willing to try.

Together, we circled to the side of the building that paralleled the train tracks. A long ramp lined with metal fencing sloped up to a pair of large, arched wooden doors. This must have been the way the cows had been led inside years ago. I wondered if they had felt it, the terror of being led to their death.

The three of us crouched next to the entryway. A rusted chain and padlock that must have been holding the doors shut for the past thirty years lay on the ground beside them. The wood was warped, making it impossible for the doors to close all the way.

I stared through the gap. The room inside was huge, a cavernous space with an arched ceiling and empty dirt floors broken up only by more metal fencing, sectioning the room into small holding areas.

"Do you see them?" Jane whispered.

Of course it wouldn't be that easy. I shook my head. "It's empty."

The door groaned as I pushed it open just enough to slide inside. I stayed close to the wall and pressed my body against the brick, hoping I would disappear into the shadows. The room was dark, but there wasn't anything to hide behind. If the congressman had eyes in here, we'd be spotted far too easily. Jane and Ian knew it, too. I could sense their discomfort, the itch in all of us to find somewhere safe.

Besides the door we'd just come through, there was only one other exit, if I could even call it that. On the far side of the room, fencing funneled into a narrow cement hallway leading to another part of the building.

"How are we supposed to split up?" I asked.

"You two follow that path," Ian said, pointing to the cement hallway. "I'll find another way in."

We might not have had blueprints or tools or night-vision goggles, but Ian's calm composure already made him a better leader than Markus had ever been. Jane and

I gave him a quick nod, slipping farther into the room while he crept back out into the night.

We dashed across the floor, the fine dirt beneath our feet puffing up and completely covering our legs by the time we reached the cement tunnel. The opening turned out to be only a little taller than me.

Jane ducked into the tunnel behind me, and the dim light of the holding room died away, enveloping us in blackness, a dark so pure it felt thick, like it had weight.

"I can't see anything," I whispered back to Jane. I couldn't even make out my own hand in front of my face.

"Don't worry. I'm right behind you." Her hand found a place on my upper back, and my breath steadied a bit.

My fingers dragged along the rough concrete. The wall curved slightly, and I followed it, one cautious step at a time. Without Jane so close, I might've drowned in all the darkness.

The wall twisted again, opening to a gray glow at the end of the hall. I picked up my pace, trotting forward until I was standing at an opening to another room. This one was quite a bit smaller than the last, but any similarity to a farm had disappeared. There weren't any fences. Soft dirt became cold cement. Down the middle of the floor, an old, rusted metal grate covered a shallow trench. Above that, a long row of huge metal hooks hung from a pulley system that traveled the whole length of the room, disappearing around the corner.

I shuddered, knowing without a doubt, that this room had seen more death and carnage than I could ever imagine. How many rivers of blood had flowed through the drain below my feet? And those hooks… I shuddered.

I didn't want to think about them. If I did, all I'd see were bodies hanging limp and lifeless.

The bodies of all the girls I'd been too late to save.

Jane crouched behind me, peering over my shoulder into the room. "This place is straight out of a nightmare."

Was she picturing the same horrible image? "There still isn't any sign of them."

"That's not necessarily a bad thing," Jane said. Her gaze traveled up to the hooks running along the ceiling. "Honestly, this is the last place I'd want to find them."

We crept out of the tunnel and into the room. Jane grabbed my arm. "Did you hear that?"

I held perfectly still. "No."

"Up here," she said, pulling me along with her.

We wound our way quietly through the room, careful to avoid the bits of warped grates sticking up from the drain. Even though my mind screamed at me not to look, my gaze rose to the track holding the large steel hooks. Not too far ahead, it rounded the corner into the next room.

"There," Jane said, poking me again. "Do you hear it?"

And then I did. It wasn't much sound, really just a low scraping, like metal being dragged against the floor. I strained to hear more, but that was all there was. No low murmuring of girls' voices like they'd used to fool us at the warehouse.

"I'm going to go look," I whispered. "You stay here."

I pressed my body tight to the wall and peered around the corner. The next room wasn't large, either. Just long and narrow with an old conveyor belt running along one wall, and tall, tiled basins running along the other side. I studied the area, searching for the source of that sound, and then my eyes landed on it—a big metal box, at least ten feet tall and twice as wide—in the center of the room. At one time, it might have been a huge refrigerator, but I was pretty sure it had a new use.

A cage.

And I knew what was inside.

A thick chain had been wrapped multiple times around the refrigerator and latched with a heavy lock that rested on the floor. It was the chain rubbing against the side of the refrigerator that was making the noise Jane had heard.

The door to the refrigerator was open a few inches, just enough for an arm to reach through. Such a bold move. The girls inside that box wouldn't know whether a guard was near, but they were obviously desperate. The hand that had snaked its way through the crack was fumbling for a better grasp on the chain. Slowly, the heavy lock was dragging across the metal toward the opening.

"They're in there," I whispered to Jane, pulling her forward so she could see the box, too.

"We've got to hurry," Jane said. "They're going to draw attention if they keep making that noise." She dug into her bag and pulled out the heavy metal cutters, handing them to me. "Do you think you can cut through that chain?"

"I'll do it," I said. If I needed to, I'd find a way to break through those shackles with my bare hands.

"They're going to be scared," she said. "I'm afraid they might be hard to control once we get that box open, but

I'm hoping they'll listen to you better than me. Do you think you can handle that?"

I nodded, but the truth was, I didn't know.

As if she knew what I was thinking, Jane squeezed my shoulders, looking me straight in the eye. "It's extremely important you keep them calm, Ella. We can't have a mad rush or the guards will come running. Okay?"

I nodded again. She was right. This whole time I'd spent all my energy thinking about getting to the girls, and hadn't really considered how we were going to sneak all those people out of the building without being heard. I looked back over my shoulder at the dark tunnel. There wasn't much room. They'd have to go through one by one.

"Are you ready?" Jane asked.

My fingers tightened around the handle of the metal cutter. "Ready."

"Okay. I'll cover that door on the other side. Luckily, we know the rooms we came in through are clear…or they were." She frowned, then shook her head. "You just focus on getting the girls out, and let me take care of the rest."

She hitched her bag up on her shoulder and pulled a stun gun from her waistband, took a deep breath, and jogged forward. I followed close behind, my eyes trained on that metal door and the thick chain straining across it. I couldn't think of anything else. Only that metal. Only the cutter in my hand.

I couldn't let my mind go to the girls inside that dark cage or the guards who hovered somewhere nearby. If I thought about them, I might freeze.

I slid up to the refrigerator, a bit of dirt and crumbled

concrete grinding beneath my feet. The girl's arm snaking through the door retreated into the dark, and there was an audible gasp.

*Let them believe I'm a guard*, I thought. At least that might keep them quiet.

Without speaking, I clamped the cutters around the chain and strained down, imagining the way the restraints would fall away, slipping to the ground like the broken body of a serpent. But they didn't budge. I readjusted the blades, squeezing as hard as I could with both my hands.

Frustration buzzed through my body. Where was Ian? And why did Jane think I'd be strong enough to do this on my own?

I let go, looking down at the chain. Had I even made a dent? In the dim light, the chain looked exactly the same as it had before.

My hands trembled. If I wasn't strong enough to cut through this chain, I'd have to find another way.

*Think*, I told myself, breathing in slowly. *Focus*. I cleared my head, letting the eerie surroundings of the slaughterhouse disappear.

I readjusted my grip on the handles of the metal cutter. I could do this. I just needed traction if I was going to cut through something so thick. I needed to use the refrigerator's solid side to my advantage. If I put one of the handles against the metal wall, then I'd be able to push down against it with my whole body.

The only problem was that with the door open, the chain was pulled too tight to be able to fit the blades of the metal cutter between the wall of the fridge and the chain.

If the door was closed, it just might loosen the chain enough.

I pushed against it, but it barely moved before dozens of hands strained from the other side to keep it open. A panicked buzz echoed inside.

I pressed my face to the opening. It was too dark inside to make out any faces. "Let me close it," I said. "It will only be for a minute. I promise. I'm going to get you out of here."

"Who is that? Who's there? What's happening?"

The hum of voices rose from inside the metal box, resonating, amplifying.

"I need you to be quiet," I said into the dark. "Please!"

There was a dull *thump* near the doorway, and I looked up. Two huge bodies appeared on the threshold. Where was Jane?

"What's their deal?" one of the guards asked.

"I told you we should have sedated them first," the other said. "They've got to know what's coming."

They stalked through the doorway, the two hulking men. I couldn't fight them off by myself. But maybe, just maybe, if I could get the door open in time…with enough people, we could subdue them.

I heaved my body against the door and this time the hands didn't push back. The door glided shut with a *whoosh,* and the chain loosened.

My heart thudded desperately in my chest. I wiggled the metal cutters between the wall of the fridge and the chain and clamped down, throwing my weight against the handles. My arms shook. Strained. I didn't breathe, didn't blink. Every ounce of force I had was directed at that chain. The metal creaked and groaned and the handles pressed ever closer together.

I could do this.

Hands shaking, I squeezed as hard as I could…

The cutters clattered to the ground.

The guards whipped around. "Hey!"

I grabbed the cutters, a whimper escaping my lips, and locked the blades back in place.

"Go get Debow," one of the guards growled. "I'll take care of this one."

I heaved once more, tears pricking at the corners of my eyes, and the chain snapped…

Just as the guard's hand tightened around my arm.

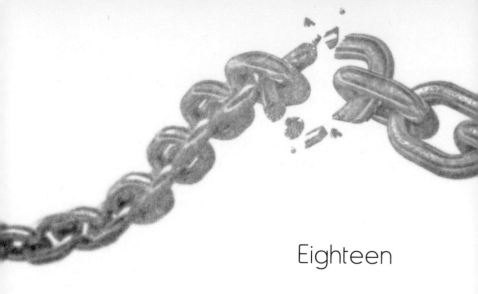

# Eighteen

*T*he chain fell with a crash to the ground, and the
air inside the refrigerator swirled with noise. Thumping.
Rumbling. Guttural and wild, the girls churned like a
storm inside their small cell.

I tried to jerk out of the guard's grasp, but he held
tight, his hand a vise on my arm, squeezing so hard I was
sure the bone would snap. His breath was hot in my ear.
"Not so fast—"

His eyes opened wide, and his body shook. I stumbled
as his weight shifted, but then he drooped to the ground
at my feet, his body as slack as the chain he lay on top of.

Jane stood behind him, wielding the stun gun with
two shaking hands. "I'm sorry," she said. "I should have
gotten to them sooner."

Behind her, the feet of the other guard stuck out from
the hallway.

"We need to move fast," she said. "Help me move him."

The guard had toppled in front of the door to the refrigerator when he'd fallen. I grabbed one burly arm, she grabbed the other, and we tugged. He was huge, over two hundred pounds of meat and bone. If Jane hadn't been there, he would have broken me like a twig.

We moved him just enough to slide open the door and I poked my head inside. It was hot and humid from the breath and bodies of so many girls. In the dark, I couldn't make out how many there were, but I could feel the mass of them. Their fears and their hopes choked the air. A bit of light shone through the opening, glinting off the eyes staring out at me.

"I need you to come with me," I said.

"There's more of them," the girl who was closest to me said. "They'll be coming to check on us."

I stepped back from the doorway. "Then we don't have much time. This is what I need you to do. Follow Jane. There's an exit through the room back there, but you're going to have to file out one at a time."

"Don't worry. We'll hurry," she said, moving forward into the light.

Her long blond hair was a tangle around her face, which was smudged with a bit of dark grease along her chin. The white smock she was dressed in was filthy, too. It probably hadn't been washed since the girls had been taken. Still, she was lovely. Perfect, even. Just like all of them were in their own ways.

She brushed past me, followed quickly by the other girls. And it hit me...there was rebelliousness in all of us. They hadn't bred it out. It only took the flick of a switch and it glowed in each and every one of us.

My heart swelled for her. For all of them.

I searched their faces, knowing with each one that passed, Missy wasn't among them. She wouldn't have been caged with the others, but she had to be here. She *had* to be. I couldn't come all this way and leave without her.

The last one filed out of the metal box. Thankfully, the two men still lay passed out on the floor, motionless except for the slightest rise and fall of their chests. As vile as they were, a part of me was grateful the stun gun hadn't killed them. They were huge and terrifying and cruel, but they were just hired help. It was the congressman who deserved my true revenge.

The last girl disappeared around the corner at the end of the room, and I hurried after her, wishing I could join them. I wanted to be pulled along in their current instead of feeling this responsibility for them. But things had changed.

*I* had changed.

Yes, I was a pet. I was a Greenwich Girl created by NuPet, cultivated and sold. I always would be. But I was more. I was an accumulation of every touch, every stolen moment, every ache and kiss and bruise and scrape. NuPet may have created the vessel, but I had filled it. I was a rebel. I was a lover. I was a thief, a learner, a friend. I was a human, complex and complete.

I caught up to the group as they slipped out of the tunnel and into the open room with the dirt floor. Jane waited at the entrance, quietly signaling them through and into the cool, dark night. Standing next to her, Ian nursed a bloody nose.

"Missy isn't with them," I said. "I have to go back."

"We don't have time," Jane said. "We need to get them out of here."

"I took down a pair of guards inside the main office," Ian said, "but there are more, too many for us to take by ourselves. It would be insane to go back in."

"He's right," Jane said. "It isn't going to take them long to figure out we were here."

Behind them, the girls streamed across the darkened lot. Their white smocks caught the air, billowing out behind them like wings that glowed in the moonlight. The sight of them knocked the breath from my lungs. They were magical, soaring and taking flight like the birds inside the church.

I wished they could fly free on their own, but I knew Jane could get them to safety, with or without me.

"You take them," I said.

Jane frowned. "And just leave you?"

"Yes. I'm okay. I'll figure out where Missy is."

Jane looked to Ian like she was searching for an answer. "Tell her it's not worth it."

Ian looked me in the eye, but he didn't speak.

"*Tell* her," Jane demanded.

Ian shook his head. "She knows what she's doing," he said, not looking away from me.

"You'll get them out of here, won't you?" I said.

He nodded.

Jane's mouth dropped open. "You're not seriously considering letting her stay here by herself, are you?"

"What other choice do we have?" Ian asked.

"Make her come!"

"No." He smiled sadly. "This is her life. It's what we've fought for. Choice. I won't tell her what to do."

I wrapped him in a tight hug. His body was supple and strong, solid and independent. He was just as human as I was, just as whole, no matter what had happened to him before. My eyes stung. Sometimes I forgot how well Ian understood me. Our stories weren't identical, but we both knew what it was like to be used, what it was like to have our choices stripped away until even the decision of whether we would be allowed to live or die belonged to someone else.

"Finish this," he whispered, his lips moving against the top of my head like a kiss.

He pulled away, and I squeezed my eyes shut tight.

The crunch of his footsteps disappeared as he ran to the truck. I couldn't watch him go—I'd watched enough people I'd grown to love leave.

I turned back to the slaughterhouse just as a cloud cloaked the moon, casting the building in shadow.

"Well, if you're going back in, I am, too," Jane said.

"You don't have to," I told her.

She stared back at the building, swallowing. "I know."

The inky blackness pooled in the windows as if the entire structure were filling up with something thick and oily. I could almost taste it in my throat, feel it choking me with bitter sludge. I wrapped my arms around myself as we sneaked quietly back around to the other side.

"Ian said they've got a makeshift office set up inside," Jane said.

"Maybe that's where they've got her."

We rounded the corner, and my hand tightened

around my stun gun. The black SUV I'd spotted earlier still sat close to the building, but in front of it, another vehicle was parked. It must have pulled up while we were inside.

But this one didn't belong to NuPet's fleet.

"The van." Jane gasped.

There was nothing special about it, no logos or identifying markers, but we both knew immediately it was ours.

Just then, the moon broke free from the clouds, illuminating the inside of the vehicles enough that we could finally see the dark form of a person sitting in the driver's seat.

Dave.

Jane gasped, and her eyes narrowed. She didn't wait for the go-ahead from me—she sprang forward, sprinting toward the van with an intensity I'd never seen in her before.

"Jane, wait!" I called, sprinting after her.

He hadn't spotted us yet. There was still the chance we could sneak past without being seen, but it was obvious Jane's priorities had changed. The *mission* had changed. If Missy had ever been at the forefront of Jane's mind, she'd been replaced now.

"You bastard," she growled, throwing open the front door of the van.

She moved clumsily, overtaken with anger. She didn't reach for the stun gun still strapped to her side. Instead, her hands flew wildly around his face, smacking and scratching as if she were trying to claw the skin from his skull.

Dave reeled back, but his face quickly cleared with

recognition. His body stiffened, and he struck back, throwing his elbow into her side. She stumbled away from the open door.

"Don't be stupid, Jane." He climbed out of the van and grabbed her by the arm.

"You *bastard*," Jane spat. She yanked her arm away from him, finally reaching for the stun gun. She raised it with shaking hands, pointing it at his chest. "You're a coward and a liar, and I hope you rot in hell."

Dave's eyes darted briefly to me. Perhaps he was remembering what it felt like to be hit with the blast of electrical current from that gun. "Listen. I know what I did was wrong. But I didn't do it to hurt you. I promise, Janie."

She snorted, shaking her head as if she could erase the way he'd said her name. "It's not going to work," she said. "You can't sweet-talk me. I don't give a damn about you anymore. You're a monster. I see that now."

"I'm not a monster." Dave sniffed pathetically. "I didn't want to hurt anybody. I *had* to do it. They didn't give me a choice."

"Who?"

"The people at NuPet."

She gasped. "You've been working for them the whole time?"

"No. Not at the beginning."

"Not until they bought out your soul, you mean?"

"You think I want all these girls to die?" Dave asked. His eyes were wide, desperate. "I don't, but they've got me raked over the coals. These people are no joke. They need those girls gone, and they'll destroy anyone that gets in their way."

"But isn't that a reason to stop them?" I asked, disgusted. "Someone has to stand up to them."

Dave shook his head frantically. "No. I can't. They'll wreck me. They can do it. They hacked into my life. Froze all my assets."

"Your *assets*?" Jane spat. "Do you hear yourself? You shot your friend tonight. You remember that, right? If he ever was your friend. If any of us were. So don't whine to me about your assets. I couldn't care less about them!"

Dave wiped a shaking hand across his forehead. "You don't get it," he said. "You don't understand the pressure. They'll kill me if I mess this up. They'll kill Vanessa."

A smile cracked across Jane's face. "Well, you're a bit late to the game, sweetie. Those girls are long gone."

Dave whipped his head toward the building as if he should be able to tell whether the girls were there or not simply by looking at it.

"You're lying."

"No. You've got the market cornered on that, I'm afraid."

Dave's lips curled, and in a flash, he leaped for me. He snaked one of his hands around to the waist of his jeans, pulling out the weapon he had tucked into his shirt. I'd assumed the gun I'd stolen from him at the church had been his only one, but that had been a huge mistake. I should have known better. The cold muzzle pressed against the base of my neck.

Dave twisted my arm behind my back, squeezing with such force my fingers went numb and my stun gun fell to the ground, useless.

"You've got to bring them back," he ordered. "Call Ian.

Call him and tell him to bring them back."

Jane snorted.

"I'll shoot her," he threatened.

The gun dug deeper into my neck, and I gasped from the pain of the metal pressing into the sensitive skin at the base of my skull.

"And I'll make sure she doesn't die when I do it," he went on. "The congressman wants her alive. That's all he cares about. I'll make sure she's still breathing when I deliver her."

"He'll still be mad…about the others." I gasped.

"He'll be upset, sure, but you're the one he really wants. He didn't even care about Missy. This whole time, she was just collateral for you."

At the sound of Missy's name, I bucked against him. "Where is she?"

"Oh, that's cute." Dave laughed, squeezing me so tight the air pressed from my lungs. "You thought she was here, didn't you?"

"Where is she?" Jane demanded.

Dave chuckled. "You think he would leave her here? She's every bit as valuable to him as the stuff on that server."

Jane's eyes met mine, and she gave the smallest nod. Dave might not have realized what he'd just done, but she and I knew. It wasn't much of a hint, but it was enough.

Jane's face softened. It was amazing she could control her expression like that when I knew what she must be feeling inside. "Just tell me this one thing… Vanessa, she's not your sister, is she?"

He chuckled uncomfortably. "Is it that obvious?"

"She's what? Your girlfriend?" Jane asked, unable to

hide the disgust in her voice. "Your wife?"

He shifted, unaware of the way the muscles in his body responded to her words, but she was ready, and so was I. While his mind still lingered on the thought of Vanessa, I leaned forward, jerking away from his pistol as Jane lunged at him. She pulled the trigger of her gun, and the jolt of electricity struck Dave on his upper shoulder.

His hand released its grip on my arm, and he fell away from me, his body slamming against the front of the van with a *thud*.

"Go!" Jane shouted.

I hesitated, staring down at Dave. Jane's shot hadn't hit him directly in the chest. He sat partially upright against the tire, still clutching the gun in his hand, stunned but not knocked out.

"Hurry!"

The driver's side door to the van was still open, and I clambered inside, slamming it closed behind me. Luckily, Jane had startled Dave enough earlier that he hadn't taken the keys out of the ignition when he'd gotten out. They still dangled in place, waiting for me.

Outside, Jane took another step toward Dave, once again raising her stun gun. I couldn't see where he sat slumped against the tire, but I hoped his gun wasn't raised, too.

I twisted the keys and the engine hummed.

*Hold on, Missy*, I thought, twisting the wheel as I pressed on the pedal.

*I'm coming.*

I'm coming.

# Nineteen

*T*he index card with Penn's mom's carefully drawn directions was still sitting in the glove box on top of the map Jane had printed. It had started out crisply folded in half, but by the time I pulled the van onto the long dirt driveway leading to the congressman's cabin, it was crumpled and bent from the way I'd clutched it against the steering wheel while I drove.

The yellow beams of the van's headlights bounced across the tall trees. Up the road, the massive building squatted in front of me like a fortress. Still, I sped on. There was no point in parking a mile away like we had before. This wasn't a covert mission. It didn't matter if I sneaked up on the congressman this time. In fact, I preferred that he saw me coming. It was time for *him* to be afraid of *me*. I was tired of hiding from him, tired of letting him control me.

The van skidded to a stop in front of the tall, metal gate, and I carefully moved the shifter to P. Above me, a sensor light flicked on, shining a white spotlight down onto the road in front of me. Without hesitating, I leaned against the wheel, pressing on it with both hands.

The horn wailed.

It didn't take long for the floodlights lining the top of the cinder block wall to flash on, blinding me in their harsh white light.

The gate began to slide. It cracked open three feet, not enough to allow a car through, and a man dressed in a dark suit—and clearly armed—emerged. He held a long flashlight and directed the beam into the front seat of the van, even though the other lights were bright enough to make it feel like day.

He gestured to the van and then drew a finger across his throat. "Cut it!"

I continued to press on the horn.

"Remove your hands from the wheel and shut off the vehicle!" He stopped a yard from the car, leveling his gun at me. "You're on private property."

Calmly, I lifted a hand in surrender and with the other I rolled down the window. "Let me in."

"I'm sorry, miss. Private property."

"I need to talk to John." It felt weird calling him by his first name, but it also seemed to make him smaller, less intimidating.

He eyed me suspiciously. "You've got the wrong location."

"Tell him Ella is here," I said.

The man shifted on his feet, but he didn't lower the

gun. "I think you're mistaken," he said. "You need to turn your vehicle around and leave."

"I know this place belongs to John Kimball," I said, "and I know he's here. Now let me in, or find someone who can."

"Like I said," the man repeated. "I think you're mistaken. This is a ranger station. State owned. There's no John here."

*Liar.* "I'm not leaving," I said. "Either tell him I'm here, or I plow through that gate." My foot dropped to the gas pedal, and the engine revved wildly.

The man stepped back, shaking his head. "Threatening me isn't going to do any good," he said. "And that gate could keep out a tank. I'm sure it will hold up against this."

"Why does the state need to keep a tank out of a ranger station?" I asked.

The man rolled his eyes. A remote radio buzzed at his side, and he pushed a button on it, lifting his hand to a small microphone connected to his ear. "What would you like me to do, sir?" he asked.

The slight mumble of a voice hummed in the earpiece.

"So, should I send her away?" He listened. "No offense, sir, but how big of a threat can one of them be?"

The voice on the other side of the radio rose, and the man jerked his head. "I'm sorry," he apologized. "I understand."

A moment later, the gate churned to life, slowly opening. The man with the gun stepped away from the car and signaled me through with the wave of his hand.

I sat up straighter, scooting closer to the edge of

the seat, and put the car back in gear before I inched it forward. My stomach constricted, and even though my body trembled, I was ready for a fight. My muscles clenched, so tense my jaw ached. I clamped my fingers tighter around the wheel.

The van slipped past the gate, and the courtyard opened up in front of me. On this side of the wall, the concrete building looked just as fortresslike as it had before. There was nothing soft about it, not even any plants to break up the harsh lines of the building.

Behind me, the gate slid shut, trapping me inside the compound. Now that I was in, I wondered if coming had been a mistake. Had every move I'd made been orchestrated by the congressman to bring me here, to his outstretched arms? My hand drifted to my pocket. If it had, at least I had a few surprises up my sleeve.

The door opened, and the congressman stepped out onto the wide slab of concrete running along the front of the building like a porch. The lights that shone on the driveway had been bright, almost blinding, but the door was only lit by a single bulb. It shone down on his head, casting sharp shadows across his face, making the peculiar scowl he wore even more terrifying.

Unlike the others, he wasn't dressed in a dark suit. A silk smoking robe was draped across his shoulders and tied at the waist. I couldn't tell what he wore underneath, but I imagined he was wearing a pair of fine cotton pajamas like he had each night when I lived at his house.

Seeing that I'd caught him off guard in his night-clothes should have been encouraging—maybe this was proof he hadn't been expecting me?—but seeing that familiar robe didn't soothe my nerves. It only distracted me.

Even though I sat safely inside the van, my world turned hazy around the edges. The memory of being inside the congressman's study pushed in on the fringes of my vision, like the realm he owned, the one he'd controlled, was materializing beneath my feet. I could feel the thick carpet against my soles, could smell the wood oil and old books.

He approached the car, and I fumbled for my stun gun. It wasn't anything compared to the guns his body-guards wore strapped to their sides, but it might get me inside to Missy.

The congressman stopped a few feet from the car. His fingers twitched at his side, clenching into a fist. Now that the floodlights lit his face, I could see the shock written there. He *hadn't* been expecting me.

"I hardly recognize you with that haircut," he said too calmly. Maybe he could contain the astonishment in his voice, but I'd seen it on his face. "It's surprisingly becoming. Not my cup of tea, really, but it suits you."

"Is that supposed to be a compliment?" I sneered.

He didn't smile. "Oh, I'm through complimenting you, Ella."

"I never asked for your compliments."

"Didn't you?" he asked, coolly, leaning one arm casually against my rolled-down window. "Weren't you just dying for my approval? For my affection?"

I shuddered, thinking of the way his hand felt against my cheek.

"Don't make me out to be the bad guy, love." His hand twitched. I knew what he wanted to do, to reach out and stroke me, to tuck my hair behind my ear. But he didn't. "I gave you a splendid life, and you stole from me. You got greedy, didn't you?"

I picked at the steering wheel. I wouldn't meet his eyes. "You're twisting things."

"Am I? You saw the life we'd worked so hard for, and you wanted it for yourself. You thought it was owed to you, just for being alive. And maybe I underestimated you. Your duplicity. Your self-indulgence," he said, spitting out the words like they were bitter in his mouth. "I did it once. I don't really feel like doing it again."

I shook my head, trying to focus. This was what he was good at, wasn't it? He knew how to use words to distract people.

"That's not why I'm here," I said. My voice sounded too high. Too weak.

"No? I thought you'd want a chance to rehash your grievances," he said, cocking his head coyly. "If that's not why you're here, what *do* you want?"

I lifted my chin. "You've got her."

"So it's the girl you want?" he asked. "How short-sighted of you."

I raised the gun, pointing the muzzle at his chest. His eyes traveled down to the weapon, and he chuckled, stepping away from the car. "You're making this too easy," he said. "Really! I'd expected more from you. After all the trouble you've given me."

"Take me to her."

He sighed as though he was disappointed. "And if I don't?"

"I'll shoot."

"It *will* hurt," he said. "I'll give you that much. But you're not going to kill me with that. It only stuns. If you want to kill me, you're going to have to get your hands dirty. Are you up for that?"

I fought to keep the fury from distorting my face. "I don't want to kill you."

"You don't want to, but you might have to." He laughed softly. "That's what I'm asking you. How far are you willing to go? Why would I just give you what you want if you're not even willing to play my game, love? I hear you've become quite adept at murder. There was that woman—what was her name? Miss Gellner? And that fellow from the district attorney's office."

"You're sick," I said, unable to keep the heat from rising into my cheeks. Was he really bringing this up right now? "What sort of person frames his own son for murder? How can you live with yourself?"

"Oh no, you don't get to blame me for that," he said, wagging a finger at me. "Penn's problems sit squarely on your shoulders, not mine."

I cringed at the sound of Penn's name on his lips. He knew just what he was doing. I hadn't even made it inside and he was beating me, not with force, not with weapons, simply with his words. They were sharper than any dagger, more painful than the shock of electricity inside my gun.

"Take me to her," I said, shaking his words from my head. I swung the door open, closing the distance between us in one bound. I pressed the stun gun against his sternum, pushing him back toward the building. "Take me to Missy now or I'll pull this trigger."

The congressman raised his hands, but his eyes traveled to the men standing behind us with their weapons trained on me. "It's okay," he told them matter-of-factly, as if this was just a simple game that the two of us were playing. "You can put your guns down. She's not going to shoot, are you, Ella? We're just going to go inside for a bit. Take care of some past due business." He looked down at me. This close, I could see the small wrinkles surrounding his eyes. "If you put that thing down, I can take you in."

Slowly, I moved the stun gun to my side.

"Good." He smiled. "Now we can act like civilized people." He gestured to the building.

I followed, but hesitated at the door. My eyes had grown used to the bright floodlights, and I blinked, trying to adjust to the dim overhead bulbs.

Clearly impatient, the congressman ushered me into a wide-open sitting room, almost as stark and severe as the outside of the compound. The concrete floor was polished to a shine, and a few steps led down into a large seating area. It wasn't plush and comfortable like the house in Connecticut, but there was no denying it was expensive.

On the far wall, a gigantic fireplace crackled with a dying fire. In the center of the room, two huge black leather sofas faced each other, separated by a gigantic lacquered tree trunk that served as the coffee table. It was bare except for a tray of liquor bottles. A glass still partially full of honey-brown liquid and ice sat sweating on the shiny surface.

"Come in. Sit. I was just having a nightcap when you arrived."

I scanned the room, but it was empty. No sign of Missy or Ruby.

"Where is she?"

The congressman sat down on the sofa and picked up his glass. The ice clinked as he brought it to his lips. It was such a small sound, delicate, intimate. He took a small sip and smiled. "Have you forgotten your manners?" he asked. "All those years of training, and you lose it so easily. What a shame."

I scowled. "I'm not here to socialize."

"No." He frowned. "Not even a little bit? Come on. Let me fix you a drink."

He leaned forward, plucking the lid from a small silver bucket. With a delicate pair of tongs, he reached in and picked out a large square ice cube, then dropped it into an empty glass. The ice rang against the bottom of the glass, and he repeated the process. He moved slowly, purposefully. I'd seen all of this before. It was like a dance, although he had never performed it for me before. This was the choreography he performed for the men who visited him.

He popped the lid from a crystal decanter, pouring a splash of the same honey-colored liquid on top of the ice.

"Sit," he said, and slid the glass across the table toward me.

I kept my feet planted, unmoving.

"*Sit*," he said again. This time there was no mistaking that it was an order. I lowered myself to the edge of the sofa, tucking the stun gun back into the waistband of my pants.

He watched me carefully. I knew how I must look:

like a pet dressed up as a rebel; a child playing make-believe. He was right. Those years of training still lived deep inside of me. They ran through me like a spine, holding me in place, rigid, obeying. Even now, I could feel it taking over, controlling me; the way my hands folded in my lap, the way my legs crossed delicately at the ankle. The arch of my neck. The tilt of my head. How could I fight it and fight him at the same time?

He nudged the drink closer to me, and I picked it up, trying to still my shaking hands. I took a small sip. The liquid scalded my throat, and I sputtered, coughing into my hand.

"Scotch," he said. "It's an acquired taste. Some people might call it poison, but I think it's magic. Liquid warmth."

I took another small sip. This time I didn't cough, and he smiled.

"Scotch can only be made in Scotland," he said. "Really, this is just whisky. If you asked for a whisky in Scotland, this is what they'd give you." He held up his glass and studied his drink, twisting his cup this way and that. "You could make it here, in the U.S., but they wouldn't allow you to call it scotch, even if you used all the same ingredients. It might as well be illegal."

I stared at him. If he wanted to talk, I'd let him talk.

"It sounds silly, I know," he said. "Why make such a fuss out of it, right? It's just a drink. Mash up some grains and distill them. Why worry about what they're called?"

I set my drink down on the edge of the table. The tiny bit of it I'd sipped still burned in my throat, making its way down to my belly.

"But there are others who want things to be special.

You know what I'm talking about. You're the scotch, after
all, and instead of realizing what you are—how prized,
how valued—you want to make yourself common. Don't
you realize that?"

His voice had risen. His face had grown flushed.

"I am what I am," I said. "I don't need to be prized to
know my value."

He tipped back his drink, swallowing the rest of it in
one gulp before he slammed the glass down on the table.
"Did you come up with that one on your own, or did you
read it on a motivational calendar?" He rolled his eyes.
"You spout that drivel, and all the morons of the world eat
it up. Which goes to show why our country needs men of
foresight running it. Men who can look at the big picture."

"Enough," I said, standing. "I'm done talking. Take me
to Missy."

He leaned against the couch, draping one arm up
over the back and studied me. "Are you sure, love? We're
having such a nice conversation."

His gaze darted over me playfully. This was entertain-
ing him! He wasn't trying to stall me so he could figure
out a plan. He was simply enjoying watching me squirm.
There'd been a stray cat that lived at the congressman's
house that I'd seen do this very thing with a mouse. It
would catch one in the orchard and bring it up to the ga-
zebo where it would play with it for an hour, batting it
and flipping it into the air, not to kill it.

The killing came later, after it had tired of it.

I stood up abruptly. "If you won't take me to her, I'll
find her myself."

"Fine, fine, fine," he grumbled, getting to his feet.

I'd disappointed him. The thought sent a ripple of energy through my limbs. He was used to things going his way, and maybe that worked with most people, but I was fine being the one to defy his expectations.

I followed him out of the living room and down a long hallway running the length of the building. All of the doors were shut tight, but a row of huge black-and-white paintings lined the walls. They towered above me, reaching almost to the ceiling, canvasses full of big brushstrokes of inky paint that dripped down the surfaces like hidden messages waiting to be decoded.

At the end of the hall, the congressman unlocked a large wooden door, just as massive and impenetrable looking as the one we'd come through from outside. I followed him down a few steps into what looked like a small mudroom. Inside, the temperature dropped, like all that unpolished cement was winning out.

This place wasn't putting on a show like the rest of the house. This was here for a purpose.

We rounded the corner, and the room opened back up. Sitting in the center, locked inside a massive steel cage, was a tall bank of computer equipment, reaching up well above my head. Thin white-and-blue wires ran between the machines like veins. They buzzed and hummed softly, alive and alight with blinking red and yellow lights.

It was clear this was the congressman's other pet, one he was just as scared of losing.

The server. The digital vault for all the congressman's evil.

My gaze darted over the mess of wires, and my hands clenched at my sides. If that cage weren't in the way, I would tear those cables and cords from every inch of those machines. I would rip the life from inside of them. I would crush them. Smash them to dust.

The machines couldn't feel pain, but the misery the congressman felt would be real.

I wanted him to feel it.

I wanted him to pay for what he'd done.

To me. To Penn. To Elise. To Miss Gellner and Mr. Vasquez. To...

I looked past the huge machine in the middle of the room to another small cage sitting against the wall, and my mind stuttered to a halt.

Inside the bars, slumped on a lone wooden chair sat Missy.

Her eyes blinked open, her gaze settling on my face.

Then she screamed.

## Twenty

*I*t wasn't a scream of terror, or pain, or fear.

It was a scream of rage.

Missy jumped to her feet with what looked like the last of her strength, her fists flailing against the thick metal jailing her inside. "You bastard," she wailed, her voice breaking. "Let her go! Let her go right now!"

My hand flew to my mouth. She was in much worse shape than the last time I'd seen her. Her hair, tangled before, was now matted in a thick clump on one side of her head. Her skin was grimy and smudged with dirt, smeared in tracks where the tears had run down her face. She would have been mortified to know her pain was written so clearly on her face that the congressman would be able to see vulnerability every time he looked at her.

The wound I'd seen the congressman's henchman cut along her cheek at the warehouse didn't look like it had even been cleaned. Dried blood, black and crusted, coated the inside of the cut, but the outside edges were truly agonizing to look at. The hot, angry red must have pulsed with pain every time she spoke.

I took a step back. "How— How could you *leave* her like this?"

"I'll kill you!" Missy continued to scream. Her voice was reedy and thin, hardly carrying the force I knew she hoped it would, but her eyes were fierce. "You let her go, or I'll peel the skin off your face! I'll break every bone in your body!"

The congressman chuckled. "Oh, believe me, she's done this to herself. I'd gladly take her out, let her bathe, change into something more comfortable... She could even stay in one of the guest bedrooms if she didn't put up such a fuss." He gestured to Missy. "Calm down!" he said to her. "I didn't bring her here. She came here herself."

Her mouth dropped open, and her fists fell to her side. "You didn't," she whispered.

"I came for *you*," I said defiantly.

The disappointment in her eyes swirled back into rage. "You idiot. You know he'll never let us go. You know him. You shouldn't have come."

The congressman smiled as if she'd paid him the most extraordinary compliment. "I'm flattered you think so highly of me."

"I think you're a *monster*."

"A monster?" He nodded, considering. "I guess that depends of what sort of monster. I've always fancied myself a—"

"Daddy?"

We turned toward the small voice behind us. Ruby stood at the edge of the room, groggy-eyed and in her pajamas. Her hair stood up in a wild halo around her head, a mane as curly and uncontainable as her personality. I wanted to run to her, to scoop her in my arms and lay my face against her head, to breathe her in.

"Ruby?" the congressman said. His face blanched, and he tried to step in front of me. From where Ruby stood, the machines would block her view of Missy, but there was no overlooking me. "Go back to bed now. You know you're not allowed back here. I've been very clear about that."

She rubbed her eyes. "The door was cracked open," she said. "I thought I heard someone yelling and I..." Her voice trailed off, and her eyes landed on me.

She swallowed, seeming to assess the situation. It wasn't the reaction of a child. It was the cool, calculated look of a girl who had been forced to grow up too fast. A few short weeks ago, she would have squealed in delight at seeing me standing in front of her, but things had changed. The cruel reality of the adult world must have wormed its way into her innocent mind, because she looked at me with such sadness and regret that my heart split open.

"Why is she here?" she finally asked.

"This doesn't involve you, Ruby. Now please go back to bed."

She shifted on her feet, taking the smallest step away from him.

"Now," he ordered.

She didn't move. "You lied to me," Ruby said. "You lied. You said you didn't know where she was. You said she and Penn were doing bad things. You said they hurt people." Her face contorted.

"We can talk about this later," the congressman said. "Go back to bed."

"No!" Ruby yelled. "I don't believe you. Ella wouldn't hurt anyone. Neither would Penn. You lied about that, too!"

"Don't speak to me that way," he said, clamping a hand on her shoulder. "You're a child. You don't know the half of it."

"Get your hands off of her!" I flew at him, trying to tear his evil hands from her.

The congressman let go, swatting me away. His gaze flew between us, and for the first time since I'd arrived, I saw real fear in his eyes.

"She shouldn't be here," I said to him.

"You think I don't know that?" he snapped.

"Make her leave. But don't you dare touch her again."

He narrowed his eyes. "I already *asked* her to leave, remember? And when I tried to physically remove her, you lashed out. I'm afraid I can't win with you."

Ruby's eyes widened. "No! Ella...don't make me go!" She wiggled past her dad, flinging her arms around my chest so my arms were pinned to my sides. I wasn't much bigger than she was, but she felt so small pressed against me, just a little girl. "I wrote to you. Every day." Her body shuddered against me. "I wrote you letters and stories and poems that you could read, because I knew you'd come back. I knew. I *knew*."

My throat tightened. How could I break her heart

again? How could I tear her away from me once more?

I wasn't strong enough to finish this. I wasn't strong enough to stand up to the congressman. I was stupid to think I could outsmart him. Ever since I'd walked through the door, he'd shown me that.

"You can't stay here," the congressman said, prying her arms from my body.

She took a quivering breath and raised her red eyes to meet his. "No!" she yelled. "I'm done listening to you, Dad. You can't keep doing terrible things and expecting me to go along with it. I know you're the reason I'm not staying with Mom anymore. You say it's lawyers or whatever, but I know better. And you don't want me here. That's the worst part. It's not like you even pay any attention to me. You just don't want me to be with Mom. And now you're trying to hide *Ella* from me?"

Her eyes were wild and bright. Any bit of grogginess had melted away. But then her hands, which had been flapping at her sides while she spoke, quieted and she looked around, frowning as if seeing the room for the first time.

"What is this place?"

"Ruby," the congressman said slowly. "I'm. Losing. My. Patience." He towered above her, his teeth clenched, eyes bulging.

She didn't know to be terrified of him, but I did. Her father wasn't the man she thought he was. He wasn't even the man he used to be a few months ago. He'd changed. The blackmail, the lies, the greed—it had been there before, simmering. But his hatred for me had truly transformed him.

"Tell me!" Ruby shrieked. Her face reddened, the flush drowning out her freckles so she looked like a girl possessed.

The congressman reached for her again, but she was too quick. She bounded to the left, skidding past him farther into the room. Her gaze flicked over the machines and landed on Missy.

"Why is there...?" Her mouth opened in horror. "Dad? Why is there another girl here? Is that Jayne's pet, Missy?"

The congressman didn't answer.

"Why is she here?" Ruby screamed. "Tell me! Why is there a girl inside a cage?"

She ran to me again, dropping to the floor in front of me and wrapping her arms around my legs as if I could tether her here. Her body shook, her little eyes filled with all the pain in the world. She'd seen snippets of evil, but only from the safety of her books. This was different.

"Tommy!" the congressman yelled. "Get in here!"

Ruby's breath caught in quick, ragged little puffs, and she shook her head, her eyes wide. "You did this, didn't you?" She gasped. "You can't... You can't put people in cages. You can't do this to them."

Behind us, one of the congressman's thugs appeared. "Boss?"

"Get her out of here," he said, pointing to Ruby.

The man raised an eyebrow. "What am I supposed to do with her?"

"I don't care," the congressman snapped. "Just get her out. One of your men was supposed to be watching her, and now I'm dealing with *this*!" He gestured at his daughter as if she were a malfunctioning machine.

"You want me to put her in her room?"

"No!" the congressman yelled. "I said get her out of here! Out! I don't want her in this house. Take her for a drive. Take her back to Connecticut for all I care."

The man nodded.

"Please, take her to her mom," I said, kneeling down to hold Ruby.

He looked down at me with disgust before he pushed me aside, prying her from me. "I've got my orders," he said.

I didn't want his hands on her. She needed to be with someone who loved her, not this stupid brute, but it would be worse if she stayed. I knew it. This house was the last place I wanted Ruby to be. Before the night was out, some terrible things were going to happen here. I could see it in the congressman's eyes—what he was planning to do to Missy. To me.

The man scooped Ruby up in his arms. She flailed and kicked, trying to scratch his face, but he only held her tighter.

"Noooooo!" Ruby moaned. "Let them go, Daddy! *Please…*"

Her father twisted away, as if he was trying to avoid a distasteful sight. When the door shut behind them, he slowly turned around to look at me.

All the humor had drained from his face. Where there had once been the thrill of the game, there was only anger.

"You did that," he said.

I shook my head.

"Yes." He kept eye contact with me, his voice a steady drone. "You made her see that. That's your fault. Remember that. You caused her that pain. She was innocent before you barged in tonight."

"You can't blame that on me."

"Oh yes, I can," he said. "I protected that child. I shielded her. But you waltzed in and changed the way she'll forever view me; my own child, my flesh and blood. You *ruined* that. And now you're going to have to pay for it."

He glared at me with eyes that hardly seemed human.

"Don't listen to him," Missy said. "Those are lies, Ella, and you know it."

"If you can't figure out how to shut up all by yourself," the congressman said slowly, "I'll be happy to do it for you."

Missy's eyes narrowed, and she spat on the floor in front of him. "Bring it on."

The congressman froze, slowly lowering his gaze to the wet spot near his shoe. He didn't speak. Instead, he crossed the room to a metal case on the wall and spun the lock, unlatching it.

The air in the room changed, became electric, like all those wires running to all those computers had stretched their tentacles out for us, trying to warn us that something very bad was about to happen.

I reached for my stun gun. "We're done talking," I said. "Let Missy out. Now!"

The lock clicked, and the metal case swung open. My finger hovered over the trigger, and I steeled myself, ready to fire. I could pull it now—I wanted to—but Missy was still locked in that cage, and from the looks of it, there was no way I was going to break in without a key. I needed him to open it for me.

"I'm afraid we have different agendas," he said, reaching inside the box. "You see, dear, letting either one of you go isn't really how I see the night unfolding."

He turned back to face me, smiling as he stroked his finger over the barrel of a gun.

# Twenty-One

"*I* know you aren't going to shoot," he said, nodding to my weapon.

"I will."

"No." He sounded almost disappointed. "You won't. Do you want to know how I'm so sure?" He didn't wait for me to respond. "Because of her. You have no way to get her out of there without me. You've figured that much out, haven't you, love?"

"Fire the goddamn gun, Ella!" Missy yelled.

My hands shook.

"Oh, you're a good girl, aren't you? Even now that sweet little brain of yours is chugging away, trying to figure out how to solve this riddle. You can't leave without her. Or maybe I should say, you won't. Even though that's the smart thing to do. Your friend knows it, too. She would shoot me. But maybe she's smarter than you are." He shook his head sadly. "Oh, you poor, little simple thing… You can't bring yourself to do it."

I raised my gun higher. "I'll do it if I need to."

He chuckled.

"I…I…" It wasn't that I wouldn't do it, but he was right—it wouldn't do me any good to fire now. "I know what this is, all this equipment. I know what this server is holding," I said. It had nothing to do with Missy, but I didn't know how else to distract him.

His eyes narrowed. "That wasn't very smart of you, was it?"

"And I know you've been blackmailing people."

"I certainly can't let you go now."

"I'm not the only one who knows," I said. "There are others."

"You mean your little Liberationist friends?" he asked. "Or should I say friend. Is that what we're down to? One? Although…" He looked at his watch. "By now you might be the only one left."

"You can't keep doing this," I said. "Someone is going to find out and stop you."

His eyes lit up. "Like your friend Mr. Vasquez? I'm not too worried."

I lifted my chin. "There are other people."

"Oh?"

He took a step closer to me, and I cringed, backing up until my shoulders pressed against the cold metal cage that surrounded his buzzing and whirring tangle of power and greed.

"In case you haven't noticed, I call the shots," he said. "I'm the one in control."

"It can't last forever."

"Actually…it can," he said, smiling. "That's the beauty of it. People get so worried about one man holding too much power, but they make it so easy to happen. So easy! They think as long as we get a new president every couple of terms, things balance themselves out. As if the president has any real power. That's where the fools focus. But I have different ambitions."

He took another step, so close to me now the barrel of his gun nudged into my belly.

"Do you know what the term limits are for a congressman?" he asked, leaning in to whisper the hot words in my ear.

I squirmed away from him.

"You don't, do you? That's because there aren't any. As long as people feel like electing me, I can have this job forever. Why else do you think I'd do it? You think I really care about serving the people in my district?" He laughed. "Their problems are shortsighted. They only care about their own little circles, their own little lives. They get up in arms about zoning and jobs. But I have bigger plans. You've seen it. I don't care if anyone knows who's pulling the strings as long as I'm the one doing it."

"But NuPet is going to get tired of you," I said. "They'll find out about your blackmail and they'll decide you're too big of a risk. They won't want to be associated with you."

"NuPet?" he bellowed, throwing his head back with laughter. "Oh, love, if you think NuPet is the one making decisions, you really are as clueless as you look. They're just another one of my pet projects." He stopped, smiling as if he was pleased with the pun he'd made. "When you said you knew about all this, I thought you might be telling the truth. You actually had me a little worried there."

I swallowed. What had I done? I should have stayed quiet, let him think I had more power over him than I really did. But it was slipping away. I thought I could wield a gun and a little information and take back all the power he'd stolen from me, but I'd overestimated myself. With each passing second, I grew weaker and weaker. I could feel it sliding through my fingers like sand.

He sighed, staring down at me. "I'm growing tired of this, my little pet," he said. The gun pressed farther into my gut. "Now we just need to decide—do you want to be first or should I start with your friend?"

I tried to swallow, but my throat was dry.

"I've been imagining this moment for a long time," he said, lifting the gun up so its cold muzzle touched my temple. He ran it slowly down across my cheek to my neck. "No one ever tells you that a revenge fantasy can be even more titillating than a sexual fantasy, but it is. I've spent hours dreaming up the ways I'd kill you. And each one is as delightful and satisfying as the last."

Missy banged her fist against the cage, and the congressman's words wormed their way across everything.

"Hmm. All that time I spent imagining… I don't want to waste it," the congressman said. "I feel like a kid at Christmas, waiting to unwrap the biggest gift, so I think you'll understand why I can't start with you. Besides, I really think I'd like you to watch some of the things I've been imagining," he said, turning his gun on Missy.

I glanced frantically around the room.

There had to be something I could use to overpower him, but all that stared back at me were blank cement walls and the black faces of his machines.

*It's over*, I thought. *Over.*

My vision tunneled, growing dark around the edges, until all I could see was the cold metal machine in front of me, and a single red light blinking. Blinking. Blinking.

A red button. A red button.

"Stop," I said, dropping the stun gun.

It clattered against the cement, landing near the congressman's feet. He glanced down and tapped it with the tip of his house slipper. With a little kick, he sent it skidding across the floor.

"It's a lovely gesture," he said. "Just a tad late."

"I mean it!" I yelled, reaching into my pocket. "Drop your gun!" I clamped my fingers around the small box with its perfect red button.

The congressman's brow crinkled, not scared or annoyed, just confused. His gaze traveled to the hand I'd pulled from my pocket.

"Put down the gun and let her go, or I'll press it."

He stared at my hand for a long beat, understanding finally dawning across his features. His look of smug satisfaction faded.

"You asked me if I was ready for things to get messy," I said, backing away from him. "Does this answer your question? If you don't let us go, I'm going to blow this house up with everything in it."

"And how do I know that's not just a trick? That could

be the control to a video game for all I know."

"I guess you'll just have to take my word for it," I said. "But believe me, there's a bomb connected to this. You can appreciate a good bomb, can't you, John?"

"Don't antagonize me," he growled.

"I'm simply explaining, so you can make an educated decision," I went on. "This thing is called a remote detonator. All I have to do is press this red button and you'll lose everything: your fancy computer, all your precious blackmail. This whole building will go up in flames. And if you happen to live...well, what are you going to be without all this? Anything? For a man with so much power, it sure seems like most of it doesn't actually belong to you."

"Press that button and you'll kill yourself, too."

My eyes clouded, but I raised my chin defiantly. "I'm not afraid to die."

He studied my face for, what—weakness? Fear? For any hint I was lying? I wasn't. And the realization actually surprised me as much as I hoped it would him. I would do it. I would press this button.

I would end it all.

My throat constricted, the ache of loss pressing in on me with such force I thought I might suffocate. I didn't want to say goodbye to this life, but I would if it meant stopping him. Cold resolve washed over me, hardening on my face like ice.

His face morphed, surprise and fear creasing his brow, making him look so much older than he really was. He pointed at Missy. "You'll sentence her to death, too."

Behind him, a wicked grin bloomed across her face.

She wasn't afraid to die, either. "Do it," she urged. "Press the button."

The congressman's mouth dropped open, and his gaze flicked between us. Was he realizing, for the first time in his charmed life, he'd lost control of the situation? If only I could read his mind. His lips twitched, curling back into a snarl.

"This is what it feels like to have your power taken away," Missy said sweetly. "How do you like it?"

A growl rumbled up through the congressman's chest. His eyes bulged. His face reddened. The veins on his forehead pulsed with each beat of his heart, and right in front of us, he morphed from a handsome, successful politician into someone hideous.

"No one threatens me. I *own* you."

He lifted his gun and fired into Missy's cage.

The shot rang in my ears, and the bullet struck, hitting Missy in the stomach. She bent over, cradling the wound. Slowly, red trickled between her fingers.

I opened my mouth to scream her name, but there was no air in my lungs.

"You'll never...own us," she said, her gaze holding mine. "We've got...more power in our pinkie fingers... than you have in your whole body."

She smiled wickedly, and then crumpled to the ground.

Rage flared through me. This was it. It all came down to him and me. The congressman and the pet he never really owned.

He stalked toward me, and in a flash, as if I were watching a film playing inside the congressman's mind,

I imagined what he would do to me: the way he would strike me across the face, knocking the detonator from my hand before I had a chance to press it. I saw the way he would kick me, cracking my ribs again and again before he finally stood over me and pulled the trigger, watching with a smile as this one precious life bled out of me.

"No," I whispered, backing away.

My hands trembled, raising the small plastic case on the detonator with a flick of my thumb. And then my finger found it—the red button.

I shut my eyes. I wouldn't let the congressman's deranged face be the last thing I saw. There was beauty I wanted to remember. Like a gift my consciousness was giving me, one last beautiful hurrah, a perfect image of Penn appeared in my mind. His face hovered above mine, so close I could see the specks of gold, like tiny universes, floating in his eyes. His lips parted as if he was about to speak, or maybe lean down to kiss me.

I didn't know what came after death. Maybe only blackness. Maybe a beautiful blinding light. Or, if I was lucky, this…this image of Penn could be my eternity.

I took one final breath and pressed the button. "Goodbye, Penn," I whispered.

His name left my lips just as the bomb blew.

Far away, glass shattered, high-pitched and piercing.

*Goodbye, Penn.*

Around me, cement crashed in from all sides.

*Goodbye, Penn.*

*Goodbye…*

# Twenty-Two

So this was it. Blackness.

The image of Penn was gone, replaced by a throbbing pain somewhere deep inside my head. Or maybe it was only the memory of pain. Maybe death was memory. If so, there were worse things it could be.

My head ached. It felt so real, this memory. Like my body remained. If I concentrated I could almost feel it there...my chest, my belly, my arms. They felt so heavy. My legs, too. Like they were weighted with steel instead of flesh and bone.

*Ella.*

My name sounded like a whisper. It came from some-place far away, reminding me who I used to be. Ella.

*Ella.*

I was a girl, wasn't I? Or I had been. A girl who started out small and grew into something powerful, a fairy-tale creature, a dragon. Someone who couldn't be contained by small ideas or small men. I had been a human. I had been my own.

"Ella."

I was so close to something. So close.

"Ella."

It pulled me. My name. It pulled me from someplace deep.

My eyelids strained, and I blinked. Light flooded back inside me, like golden water filling me up, and I gasped.

"There she is."

I opened my eyes, turning my head ever so slightly. The pain was real. It all was. Real, like the bed beneath me, lined with crisp white sheets. Like the sun-drenched room, machines clicking and beeping softly next to the bed. Like the chair beside me where Elise leaned forward, her face so close to mine.

"I knew you were in there," she said. "Welcome back."

I opened my mouth to speak, but my tongue felt too big.

"Don't try to talk," Elise said, stroking my forehead. Her hand felt like a song against my skin. So soft. Perfection. How had I never realized what a treasure touch was? "You just rest. You've been through a lot."

I breathed in and let the darkness take me again. But this time I knew it wasn't for good.

When I opened my eyes again, the room had darkened. Elise still sat beside the bed, curled in the chair with a blanket draped across her shoulders. She sat up when I stirred.

The darkness that had shrouded my memory pulled back a little, and the last few days came rushing back to me.

"Where's Missy?" I mumbled, trying to form the words through what felt like a mouth full of cotton and dust. I struggled to sit up, but my arms refused to lift me.

"Try not to move too much," Elise said, placing her hand softly on my shoulder and easing me back down into the pillows. "You have a concussion, bruised ribs, and a lot of contusions. When they found you, there was a piece of pipe lodged in your cheek. It barely missed your eye."

I lifted my fingers to my cheek where a thick patch of gauze was taped below my eye.

"The doctors want you to try to rest."

"Is Missy…?" I squeaked, unable to form the rest of the words.

"You're a very lucky girl," Elise said, ignoring my question. "It's amazing you made it. The way your body landed when the explosion went off… They think it saved your life. The bomb threw you against that cage and it folded over you when the roof fell. It made a perfect little shield." She shook her head and chuckled sadly. "It looks like for once in your life, being small was a good thing."

She stroked the hair back from my eyes.

"You need to know something else," she went on. She swallowed. "John's alive. He's in bad shape, but he's alive. Which might be a good thing for you. At least, that's what our lawyers are saying."

"But… What about…"

She lifted her finger to her lips, silencing me. Holding my gaze, she reached for my hand. "She didn't make it, Ella. I'm sorry."

I closed my eyes. There wasn't any energy left in me to mourn. I'd lost Missy. She was gone. Forever. I wanted to scream, to cry, but my body refused. It was too tired. Too weak. Instead, I lay paralyzed as the sadness welled up inside me like water filling up a pitcher. It rose up my legs, through my belly, over my ears until my whole self was submerged. And finally, when I couldn't hold any more, it spilled from my eyes, falling onto the pillow underneath my head.

How could I live in a world where the congressman survived and Missy didn't? Was it possible to lose anything else? My body was broken, Missy was dead. The Liberationists had failed. And Penn sat somewhere far away in a cell that might hold him for the rest of his life.

I wasn't strong enough to face it. Drowning, I sank back into darkness, wishing it would keep me for good.

*B*ut it didn't keep me. My spirit was broken, but my body wanted to live. It didn't care about heartbreaks and betrayals. It didn't care whether good won out in the end. It only wanted to exist. It wanted food and oxygen and, if it was lucky, a soft place to rest its head.

When I opened my eyes again the pillow was dry. My tears had evaporated in the night, and even though my head ached, it felt clearer than it had the day before.

The chair next to my bed was empty, and I scooted up a little bit, turning slowly to take in the rest of the hospital room.

"Hello, sunshine."

In the bed next to mine, Markus sat sipping water out of a bendy straw. He wore a pale-blue hospital gown, and his head and shoulder were wrapped in white bandages.

"But I thought…"

"You thought Elise would at least spring for a private room?" He gave me a lopsided grin. "Sorry. I guess she thought we should be together."

"You're alive!" I croaked. My voice sounded ridiculous, rusty and unused, but I didn't care. I wanted to leap out of bed and hug him.

"Disappointed?" He chuckled. "It looks like you and I are harder to get rid of than some people would like to think."

"I thought Dave shot you," I said. "I thought I saw…" I gasped. "I left you… I'm so sorry—"

"Ella, stop. You did the right thing," he said. "Dave, that little worm, is a different story. Lucky for me, he's a lousy shot. The bullet took off a chunk of bone," he said, tenderly raising a hand to his shoulder. "But that can be fixed. And believe me, when I'm better, that guy's going to have hell to pay. He'll think he got off easy with Jane."

"Oh my God! Jane!" I gasped. "And Ian. Are they okay?"

He nodded. "Worried about you and me, but yeah, they're okay. Dave's in custody, so they're both happy about that. Vindicated. You know, he confessed to setting

Penn up for the bomb that killed that attorney."

There was a rap at the door, and a moment later Elise poked her head in.

"I go away for a second, and she wakes up. There's someone here that wants to see you."

She opened the door a little wider, and Ruby's curly head peeped in. "Ella!" she squealed, running into the room and scrambling up onto the bed.

"Be gentle with her," Elise cut in.

Ruby set the bouquet of flowers she'd been holding onto the blanket and carefully wrapped her arms around me, burying her head into the curve of my neck.

I squeezed her closer to me, wincing at the pain in my ribs and my cheek, but I hardly cared. My chest swelled with warmth at knowing, whatever happened, this little girl would love me unconditionally.

"Is it true?" I asked, stroking Ruby's curls as I looked at Elise. "Dave confessed?"

She smiled, sitting down on the edge of my bed. "Yes, to everything," she said. "The explosion at the training center and at the pizza place where…" Her voice trailed off.

I knew she was thinking of her friend. Who knows what they could have meant to each other if things had gone differently. But her eyes only kept their dreamy look for a moment before she shook her head.

"I thought we might have some problems with the police. John had his friends there, if you want to call them that. But with him incapacitated, I was able to get into his vault back home. I found everything I need to help clear Penn. Diagrams, old emails… He should be released by the end of the week."

I leaned back against the soft pillow and let the sunlight that shone through the window warm my cheek. At my side, Ruby wriggled in tighter, making a nest in the blankets. She plucked a flower from the bouquet and tucked it behind my ear.

"Don't get too comfortable," Markus said. "Just because that server has been destroyed doesn't mean we can be complacent. There's still a war to be waged."

"The two of you almost died," Elise said. "I think you can take it easy for a couple of days."

"Not if your husband is still breathing," he said.

Elise cringed at the word "husband." "John almost died, too. Believe me, he isn't going to come back from this easily," she said. "It'll take him years to climb out of this mess."

"Well, the congressman isn't NuPet," Markus said. "He's just one man. We can't let our focus waver."

I thought back to what the congressman had said about being the man that pulled the strings. "But if he was the one orchestrating everything, scaring people into helping him, maybe things will fall apart without him there."

"We can't count on that," Markus said. "We can't assume things will change. You think those people the congressman was blackmailing will suddenly grow a conscience just because he's been hurt?"

"They might…"

"Get your head out of the clouds." He scoffed. "People are horrible. People can't be trusted. They're rats. Traitors. All of them."

"Will you two stop?" Elise said.

Markus cringed, cupping his shoulder. I could see

he wanted to keep going. Dave's betrayal had only sharpened the intensity of his desire for revenge. He'd always been passionate, but there was a different light in his eyes, a force that frightened me.

"I didn't want to give this to you yet, but if it'll get you to shut up..." She dug into her coat pocket and pulled out a small thumb drive. "When I was going through John's things, I found this," she said. "I don't know if it has everything that was on that server, but it has most of it."

Markus's face lit up. "That's the blackmail?"

Elise nodded, pressing the stick of plastic into my palm. "It's yours now, Ella. You can do with it what you'd like. Use it to take the power John used to have. Whoever has this information is in control. It's as simple as that. And this is the last of it. John would die for the material on this thing."

I cupped the thumb drive in my palm. It was hard to believe this tiny thing could control so many lives, could ruin them...could ruin mine.

"Elise," I said. "Do you think you could do one more thing for me? Do you think you could arrange to have a press conference?"

"That"—she paused, smiling—"is something I think I can handle."

*I* walked out of the front door of the hospital dressed in real clothes instead of the pale-blue hospital gown I'd been wearing for the past week. My ribs were still bound tightly beneath my blouse, which made me descend the stairs in stiff, robotic steps. I hoped all the people watching wouldn't think this rigidity made me look less personable. The last thing I needed right now was to seem distant and unfriendly.

There was still a bandage on my cheek, although they'd changed it out for a smaller one. The wound had been deep and wide and even though they'd done their best to stitch me up, I'd probably have a jagged mark a few inches long that would mar my face for the rest of my life. They said this as if a scar would upset me. As if this imperfection, this bright-pink gash, would change everything.

Now, as I stepped in front of the microphones the press had lined up in front of the crowd, I reached up to touch the bandage. Elise had said not to worry about it. The bandage showed what I'd been through. It made me vulnerable, but I wondered if it actually made me look strong. I'd survived an explosion, and here I was, still standing.

At the edge of the crowd, Elise and my small group of friends smiled back at me. She gave me a nod, and I leaned down to the microphones.

"Thank you for coming," I said, surprised by the way my voice echoed back at me from the speakers placed at the base of the steps. "The last few weeks have been ugly, as you know. You've seen the news. There have been riots and bombings and murders."

I looked out into the sea of faces before me. There were hordes of reporters standing stony-faced before me, ready to fire questions the moment I stopped talking.

And beyond them, a crowd of onlookers stared angrily up at me. I had no idea what they must have seen. Was I another waste of their tax money? Was I a corporation's malfunction or was I a person like them, hurt and hoping for more?

"I only ever wanted to have a chance to live my life," I said. "Just like all of you. I never wanted trouble or violence. I never wanted attention."

I thought back to those quiet moments I'd spent with Penn. They felt like ages ago, a lifetime. I could hardly remember what it was like to think my worries only existed within my own small sphere. How naive we'd been, thinking the two of us were the only things that mattered.

"Liar!" someone shouted from the crowd. "You're not like us!"

"This is the thing you need to know," I said. "I didn't choose any of this. There are men, powerful men, who make these choices for the rest of us. They decide what they think is best. Not in our interests, but in their own."

"Were you a member of the Liberationists?" a reporter shouted from the front row. "Is your group taking responsibility for the recent string of bombings?"

"Let her talk," someone else shouted.

The energy in the crowd was shifting. In another minute, I'd lose them all. I'd lose this chance.

I raised my voice. "For years, Congressman John Kimball has been blackmailing people." I held up the thumb drive I'd been clutching in my hand. "All the information is right here. Hundreds of people were involved: police officers, lawyers, politicians, business owners. He used this power to get whatever he wanted. He's used it to ruin people's lives, to hold them captive the way I've been held captive."

A hush fell over the crowd.

"It has to end!" I yelled. "People can't be controlled anymore. They can't be owned. One man can't own another. It isn't right. I believe people are good. I do! I've seen it. In the black markets, I saw girls without any hope still finding the strength to lift one another up. I saw people who had nothing to gain from helping me risk their lives for a cause they believed in. I know that sort of goodness."

The reporters' pencils had stilled, no longer scratching against their notepads. Instead, they stared up at me, wide-eyed.

"I know love is at the root of humanity," I said. "It's how I know I'm human. Because I've felt it. And yes, I know humans can be greedy, and selfish, and cruel. I know they can hurt one another, but I think, if given the chance, goodness will win out."

I stared straight into the camera, imagining the men and women whose secrets I held in the palm of my hand. I could expose them, I could ruin them, use them…or I could try something different.

"That's why I've decided to set these people free. To all of you out there who have been imprisoned by Congressman Kimball's blackmail, I'm giving you your life back. Right now. Enough lies. Enough secrets. Enough pain."

I threw the thumb drive down on the steps by my feet.

"No!" Markus yelled. He lurched forward, trying to

push his way over to me.

"It's *over*."

I brought my foot down hard, crushing the plastic under my heel. Again and again I stomped on it, until it was a mess of crumbled plastic and metal.

"He doesn't own you anymore!" I shouted. "No one does! Now use your freedom to do something good. It's yours, this life. You might not even realize what you've been given, but it's there. Go out and do something beautiful with it."

I choked on my words, hoping they were enough, that I hadn't made a huge mistake.

My gaze shifted to the edge of the crowd. There, pushing his way to the base of the steps, was Penn. My Penn, exactly the way I'd imagined him so many times. His smiled up at me, that beautiful grin lighting his face, sparking something inside me that I thought had been lost.

Around me, the crowd disappeared. I didn't feel the ground beneath my feet. The space closed between Penn and me, and then I was in his arms, like a dream I'd had again and again. It came back to me. Present. Past. Future. It all existed at once. A galaxy. A universe. The fleck of gold inside his eye. A blazing sun. Eternity.

This broken body didn't even matter. I flung my arms around him, kissing his cheeks, his eyes, his mouth, his chin. I wanted to touch every inch of him, simply to remind myself he was real and finally we were together.

My throat tightened, thinking of Missy. Even in this moment, I couldn't forget her. It wasn't fair I was standing here, alive, so close to the person I loved, so close I could almost hear the thoughts in his head as if they were my own.

Would this feeling follow me for the rest of my life: happiness and sorrow intertwined so tightly inside me they could never exist without each other? Maybe it would. Maybe this was what it meant to truly be alive, to own a life, not just to exist inside it.

Perfection wasn't the state humans were meant to live in. We were built for pain as well as pleasure. We were meant to be broken again and again so we could remember what it was to heal.

I smiled, focusing on the bittersweet agony. I would take it. Every heartbeat. Every glorious, painful, beautiful breath. Because it was mine. All mine.

# Epilogue

*T*he flagstones were cold beneath our backs as we stared up into the dark sky above the pond. The stars seemed brighter now that winter was almost upon us, as if the cold sharpened them, made them crisper. But I was warm in the crook of Penn's arm.

It was the first time we'd been back to the garden. We could have come weeks ago. Penn's mom had invited us as soon as she moved back into the house. Now that the divorce was final, his dad would never come here again. The restraining order she'd filed against him assured that, even if he wasn't going straight to jail. There had been plenty of other charges brought against him over the past few weeks. Once he finally left the hospital, he'd be lucky to see the outside of a cell before he turned one hundred.

"Are you comfortable enough?" Penn asked, pulling me closer to him.

Ever since I'd gotten out of the hospital, he'd been constantly at my side. But even though my body had been broken in so many ways, I'd never felt stronger, more powerful, more in control of my life.

And I wasn't the only one that was healing. So were the rest of the pets, who'd finally been placed in real rehabilitation centers and programs.

The breeders, like NuPet, were still fighting to over-turn the rulings, which had once again made it illegal for them to operate. But now that the congressman had lost all control over the other legislators, there wasn't any real traction for them. Especially not now that the public was finally paying attention. It was pretty obvious they'd be bankrupt by the beginning of the year.

"Just think," Penn said, softly stroking the top of my head, "this time next week we'll be in Ithaca."

It was dark, but I was certain he could hear the smile blooming across my face, as clearly as if it had its own music.

I still couldn't believe it. Elise had worked her magic, calling in every favor she could imagine, and not only had she gotten Penn enrolled in her alma mater, but me, too. Granted, I wouldn't be an official college student. I was going to be enrolled in the new program Cornell was funding to educate former pets. The other girls and I would live in dorms on campus, every bit of our education paid for. And when we finished that coursework, there would be a full scholarship waiting for us.

This was it. This warm glowing in my chest was the feeling of the world opening up to me. For the first time ever, I believed that the things I dreamed might actually be within reach.

At first, Ruby had been devastated that Penn and I wouldn't be living at home with her. But once she realized that we'd only be a few hours away, and that we'd come visit almost every weekend, she couldn't contain her excitement.

She still considered herself my first real teacher, and honestly, I did, too. It was an honor she was proud of, and she'd taken it upon herself to make sure I read all her favorite books, handing me stack after stack each time she saw me, so I'd need my own small library when I finally moved into my new place.

"I love you, you know," Penn whispered, pulling me even closer to his chest.

"I know," I said. There was something I'd been wanting to ask him. "Penn, I need to talk to you about something."

He pulled back a little, studying my face in the bluish light of the moon, and his brow crinkled. "What is it?"

"I... I don't know really how to say this." I swallowed.

A concerned look flashed across his face. "What?"

"When we get to Cornell, I was thinking..." I paused. It felt like such a weird thing to ask. "Will you... I was hoping you'd go on a date with me? A real one."

Relief flooded Penn's features, and he tipped his head back, laughing. "Oh my God! You freaked me out. I thought you wanted to break up with me or something."

"No, no!" I sat up, placing a steadying hand on his wide chest. "I want to be with you. It's all I want. We've been through so much—so much horror, so much pain. I just want a regular life full of—" I stopped short.

"Full of what?"

"That's it." I laughed. "I don't even know. What do people even do on dates?"

"Let's just keep it simple and start with dinner and a movie," Penn said.

I smiled. "Perfect. As long as I'm with you."

"I can't think of anything better." He reached out and cupped my face. "Is it weird that I think this makes you more beautiful?" he asked, tracing the scar on my cheek.

It was healing nicely. The skin had grown back together, reminding me how magical a body was. The cut, which had once been bright red, was now softening to pink.

"It *is* beautiful, isn't it?" I asked, touching my cheek.

I'd never been proud of my looks, but I was proud of that scar. It was a part of myself I'd earned. My eyes, my nose, my lips—they were part of my breeding, but this scar was my own.

I hoped the rest of the pets could find beauty in their own scars, whatever they were. Someday soon they would be real citizens, and then maybe they'd be able to truly believe in themselves, the way I did.

Until then, I'd keep blazing a trail for all of us, my one small, powerful, perfectly imperfect body leading the way.

# BONUS
## *content*
### Keep reading for exclusive scenes from Penn's point of view!

# SKYSCRAPERS

$\mathcal{I}$ woke up like a guy rising from the dead. Seriously. I gulped down air like one of those zombies in the movies that sits up in the grave and gasps like they've been stiff and gone for weeks.

After what Ella and I had been through, it felt like I'd died and risen from the grave ten times over.

My gaze darted around the dark room, trying to orient myself. It seemed like I was always waking up in strange places lately. Every time I woke up, for the first thirty seconds or so, I literally couldn't remember where I was.

My hand fumbled under the blanket beside me, and my palm found Ella's thigh. I let my fingers spread across her soft skin, grounding me in her smoothness. As long as she was next to me, I was where I needed to be. That was all I really needed to know.

She moaned softly, shifting, and pressed her body closer to me.

In front of me, a little light filtered in through the slatted blinds. Now that I was more awake, I could make out the faraway sounds of sirens and horns outside.

The last couple of days came back to me in a rush, like the floodgates of my memory had opened and they were all spilling over me with the force of a tidal wave. I remembered it all: running from those creeps at NuPet, Markus finding us, training with the Liberationists at their headquarters, the rescue mission that got totally botched, those pictures they had of my mom.

As if there wasn't enough to worry about, now I had to stress about my mom and Ruby. It's not like I'd forgotten about them when Ella and I left, but I'd just assumed they'd be fine. They weren't wrapped up in this mess. It was between Ella and my dad and me.

But now I wasn't so sure.

Ella shifted again. "Are you okay?" she asked.

"Yeah, I just can't sleep," I whispered, tracing circles over her skin with my fingertip. "I'll be fine."

She sat up. Her dark hair spread like a wild halo around her lovely face. She looked like an angel in a rock video. Or maybe an untamed Madonna in one of Michelangelo's paintings.

"Come here," she said, getting groggily to her feet and stretching out her hand for me.

I took it in mine, letting her lead me out of the guest room. Our bare feet padded across the carpet, and the sound of Jane's and Dave's sleeping breaths faded.

In the living room, Markus and Ian lay sprawled across the couch, snoring. But on the other side of the floor-to-ceiling windows, the city lights sparkled. We stopped near the glass, staring out at the universe of lights below us.

It wasn't enough.

I smoothed a hand down Ella's back. "Follow me."

We tiptoed past the sleeping guys, me hoping the floor wouldn't squeak and wake them, and into the small library near the kitchen. I closed the door behind us.

The room wasn't big, but it was private, just enough space for a shiny desk and the leather armchair tucked beneath it. The bookshelves were lined with vases and picture frames and a couple of books.

"It doesn't look like Vanessa does a lot of reading," Ella whispered.

"I don't plan to do a lot of reading, either," I said, pulling her to me.

She looked up at me, and I stroked a few wild pieces of hair away from her face.

She closed her eyes and breathed deeply. "Are you worried? About tomorrow? About what's going to happen if we find your mom?"

"I don't want to think about that yet," I said. "Right now, I just want this."

She opened her eyes, and I stared into their shiny depths. They reminded me of the ocean at night. I could get lost in there. I let my hands trail down to the edge of the white shirt she was wearing for pajamas, so thin that I could make out the outline of her whole body. I rubbed the edge of the fabric between my fingers.

"You can take it off," she whispered.

I turned my head toward the door, thinking of the others sleeping so close.

"We'll be quiet," she said, and in one clean swoop, she drew the shirt over her head.

The beauty of her body always stopped my breath, and I froze, staring, dumbstruck. I must have looked like a complete fool because a wicked little smile cracked the corners of her mouth. Was she happy about the power she had over me?

"Are you just going to stand there?" she asked, stepping closer to me.

A crowd of desires filled my head, ping-ponging from side to side. It was too much. How could I handle it without exploding?

I wanted it all.

I wanted to draw her to me, to feel the press of my lips against her skin. I wanted to drag her back into the shower and love her the way we had our first night in the apartment.

I wanted to touch her more than I wanted to breathe.

And at the same time, I wanted to step back. I didn't want to take my eyes off her, not even for the second it'd take for me to reach for her. I wanted to let my gaze travel slowly from head to toe, memorizing every curve so that by the time I finally did touch her, my hands would know every inch, strumming her as perfectly as a song I'd memorized.

Clearly she didn't want to wait for me to make up my mind. She placed her hand on my chest and pushed me down into the chair, bending to kiss me gently on the mouth.

That was all it took. I reached out and dragged her onto my lap.

Why couldn't time just stop here?

Ella was fierce and vulnerable and stunningly beautiful all at once. I could write music about her, about moments like this. A thousand number one songs.

I just had to figure out how to keep Ella alive long enough that I'd get that chance.

# LOCKED UP

"Can't you hook me up to a lie detector or something? I mean, come on, you've got to believe me. We didn't do this!" I slapped my palm against the table and pain shot up through my arm.

I knew it was stupid the moment I did it. I needed to keep my head together. I needed to be calm. Collected. They probably had guys standing behind some fake mirror watching my every move. They were probably all scribbling in their notebooks. *He's gone off his rocker. Clearly deranged. No self-control.* They'd think I was just the sort of privileged white kid who goes crazy and kills a bunch of people in a pizza joint.

Only I wasn't.

This was another setup, and I was the pawn in this messed-up game.

*Checkmate, Penn. You're screwed. Royally!*

And what about Ella? I couldn't stand to think of her

in a room like this. Alone. Confused. Was she hurt?

My ears still didn't feel right. There was a ringing in the back of my head that wouldn't go away, and I wasn't totally sure, but I kind of thought I'd lost some hearing on my left side. When the asshole police officer Agent Foster was pacing circles around me instead of yelling at my face, it sounded like he'd entered a tunnel every time he looped around to my left.

I scanned the room, looking for anything that could get me out. But this wasn't some action-adventure movie... and I was no leading man. There was no way in hell I was going to subdue these guys, break out, and rescue Ella. Even if I knew martial arts. Even if I were a computer genius or hypnotist. As much as I wanted to be her hero, it wasn't going to happen. And that realization felt like another bomb going off inside me.

I rubbed a hand over my face, trying to get the image of my mom's friend Mr. Vasquez out of my mind. But I couldn't stop seeing him. His body. Limp. Lifeless.

I wiped my fingers across my jeans for the hundredth time. When they sat me down in this room more than an hour ago, there'd been a bit of dried blood on my thumb and I'd wiped it away, knowing it was his. When I'd felt for his pulse it must have gotten on me. Literally, I had someone's blood on my hands.

It was crazy. Surreal. One minute you're talking to a guy, remembering this really cool disappearing card trick he did for you when you were a kid. And your mind is racing and you're wondering if maybe he and your mom are an item now. And you want to ask. You want to ask if he's *always* been in love with her. You want to ask if he's kissed her. But then again, you totally don't want to know, either, because it's so gross, and besides, there are more important things to worry about. Like your dad blackmailing people.

And then you blink, and *bam*! Explosion.

*Bam!* He's dead.

It seemed weird to be so freaked out by death, but I couldn't help it. I was. It wasn't like the video games. It wasn't like the movies where the camera pans over it and you know, deep down, that it's just an actor pretending. This was real. And even though I'd been to my grandpa's funeral a few years ago and peered into the casket and even given him a kiss on his cheek, this felt completely different. I knew life was fragile. I knew we were just mortal beings who could be snuffed out at any moment, but this was the first time I'd seen it. And I never wanted to see it again. Ever.

What if the next time was Ella?

Her beautiful face flashed before my eyes, and I imagined that it was her body there, lying broken on the ground in front of me. Gone. The thought felt like poison in my veins, searing, painful.

What if I couldn't protect her?

Agent Foster snapped his fingers in front of my eyes, bringing me out of my reverie. "Did you hear me? How long have you been playing the guitar, Penn?"

I shook my head, confused. What was this guy talking about?

"Guitar? Why?"

"Just answer the question!"

I thought about my first guitar. It was a reddish

Fender…electric, which I had no right to think I could play for my very first ax. It was so beautiful, sleek and shiny, with its own matching amp. My mom had finally relented and gotten it for my birthday when I was twelve (after I'd clearly shown that I would never end up playing the piano or the flute the way she'd dreamed I would). I'd been obsessed with it from the get-go. During our sixth grade talent show, I'd gotten up and played the worst rendition of "Stairway to Heaven" that anyone had ever heard. But I was hooked.

I shrugged. "Six years, I guess."

He smiled smugly and pulled a chair up next to me, dragging it with a screech over the concrete floor.

"Acoustic?"

I nodded. "Yeah."

"And do you play electric?"

WTF? Was this suddenly the dating game or something? I scowled at him. "Yeah. Electric, too. Do you want a private show?"

"Watch it," he said, narrowing his eyes. "I'm not the person you want to be pissing off right now."

I clenched my jaw, but I kept my mouth shut. Years ago I could have dropped my dad's name and all this would have disappeared. Not now.

"And this…" he said, sliding a photograph across the table. "Does it look familiar?"

I glanced down at the glossy picture, trying to make sense of what I was seeing. It looked like a blob of burned plastic and twisted metal sitting in the middle of a pile of debris.

"What is it?"

He reached into a manila file and pulled out another photograph. This one was the same as the first, but it was zoomed in on that hunk of melted plastic. And then I saw it: one little knob in the twisted mess that hadn't melted, and next to it, the slight curve of a silver letter *F*. The rest of the word was obliterated, but I knew what it had said.

*Fender.*

My heart sped up, thudding out a heavy-metal beat inside my chest.

He didn't have to say it out loud. I knew what was happening. That was *my* amp. The one from my first guitar. And things had just gotten a whole lot worse.

*I'm sorry, Ella.*

# FIRST DATE

"Are you ready?" Ella asked, rocking up onto her toes and down again, like the question made her taller, just by asking it.

It was a cute little gesture, and I couldn't help but smile.

She giggled, noticing my dopey grin. "What?"

"Nothing. I'm just excited."

She stood at the front door of our little apartment wearing jeans and a chunky sweater. It was the same sort of outfit that all the other girls on campus were wearing, and she looked completely normal in it. I mean, not normal in a bad way, like some girls would find offensive. But normal in the way that Ella dreamed of being. Sure, she'd always be beautiful, but she finally fit into her surroundings. Over the past couple of weeks, it was like she'd found a new place in her own body. Almost like she was comfortable in her skin for the first time. It was kind of magical to watch.

Then again, Ella had always been a bit magical.

"Shall we?" She offered me her hand.

I pulled her in to me, burying my face in the top of her head. Her hair, which she'd dyed back to its natural color, smelled fresh like shampoo and a hint of coldness, as if the chill in the air had its own crisp scent. It was one of those fall nights where winter seemed like it was hiding around the corner, just waiting to pounce. But this year I wasn't even dreading it. I was looking forward to warm nights inside with Ella.

A lot.

Actually…a warm night with her was all I wanted right now. The thought sent a zing down my spine, and I lifted her face to mine, kissing those soft lips. Slowly, and my hands dipped beneath her sweater, running along the smooth skin above her jeans.

"It's time for dinner," she said with a laugh, pulling away.

"Just one more kiss?" I begged.

She pecked my cheek, giggling. "There! Now come on. It's our first real date. We've been waiting forever!"

"Fine." I sighed. "It's cold. Are you sure you want to walk?"

She tugged me down the front steps and onto the sidewalk. "I'm sure." She seemed extra excited tonight, like something was bubbling just below the surface, sparkling and fizzy.

Ella was crazy about campus. When she wasn't reading book after book or playing one of the pianos in the music department, she was walking the pathways that wound through the old buildings. She already knew every shortcut, every alleyway, every hidden gem. She said there was something about Cornell that reminded her of the garden back home. And I guess I could see what she meant. A few of the brick buildings had thick vines growing up the side that could have been hiding just about anything: sculptures or secret gardens.

"I have some exciting news," she said after a minute.

"More exciting than a first real date?"

She laughed. "Well…almost!"

She'd been talking about this date since we got here, but things had been so busy that it had taken weeks to find the time. Not that she hadn't had a zillion other firsts since then: first classes, first new friends, first time hard-boiling an egg, first sip of coffee. It was all new.

Sometimes I worried that she'd realize I wasn't actually special.

"Are you going to tell me?" I asked.

She let go of my hand and skipped ahead down the empty sidewalk before she did a little spin and turned to face me. Up above her, one of the lampposts shone down, making it seem like her whole body glowed.

"The head of the music department called me into his office today," she said.

My stomach did a little flip. Maybe it was anticipation. Maybe it was fear. I still couldn't believe that I was here studying music. Maybe it was because my dad had told me my whole life that it was a waste of time and that I should focus on real things, important things. I was still so worried that someone was going to pull me aside and tell me that I wasn't actually talented enough to be here. That maybe I needed to get real and think about finding something else to study.

"He heard about us," Ella said, "what we've gone through with everything this past year. And he said he wants us to put on a concert. You and me. He's been listening to both of us play, and he thinks it would be a great way to get our names out there. He thinks maybe our music could be a way to educate people about what pets have gone through. You know, put a real face to things."

My mouth dropped open. "Really?"

"Yes. He wants us to meet with him tomorrow," she said, walking back to me and taking my hand in hers again.

We walked on in silence for a bit. The place our hands touched seemed alive with electricity. It reminded me of the fizzle of energy that poured out of my guitar amps when I plugged them in. Like music was about to be made.

Every once in a while we passed another couple. Some of them looked like they were on a first date, too. They would laugh uncomfortably, glancing at each other like they were trying to get a hidden look at who the other person was, and I was so relieved that I didn't have to do that with Ella. I knew her. Better than I'd ever known anyone.

"Do you think this date can handle another first?" I asked.

"Um, I think so…"

"Good!" I smiled. "Because I think it's about time you had your first hamburger."

Up ahead the lights to the Ale House glowed invitingly.

"It's just a big lump of ground meat!" Ella said, throwing her hands up playfully. "What's so exciting about that?"

*A*half an hour later she stared down at a towering burger with so much bacon and cheese and meat that it could probably give a healthy man a coronary. Her huge eyes blinked, terrified, like she was staring down a wild animal.

"I think it's bigger than my head," she moaned. "How am I even supposed to put it in my mouth?"

I stifled a laugh as my cheeks grew hot.

Her fingers hovered over her fork and knife.

"Don't even think about it," I said, shaking the totally inappropriate thoughts from my brain. Barely. "I will never be able to take you seriously if you eat a burger with utensils."

"Fine." She sighed, carefully gripping the bun. She lifted it to her mouth and closed her eyes before she took a bite. Slowly, she chewed, and I watched her face expectantly, waiting for her expression to change.

And then her eyes blinked open. "Oh!" she said, mouth still full. "Oh, Penn! Why have you been keeping this from me?"

She grinned madly and took another bite, bigger this time, and I couldn't help but laugh. How had I gotten so lucky?

Because that was what it felt like. Luck, being with Ella.

For the millionth time, my stomach twisted.

"What is it?" Ella asked, studying me.

I shook my head. "Nothing."

"Is it something I did?"

I leaned forward, taking her hand in mine. "No! Of course not. It's just…"

How could I tell her how extraordinary she was? Being with Ella was like seeing the world like it was new. For so long that world had been a terrifying place for her, but things had changed. And I didn't want to hold her back.

Opening my mouth might turn out to be the stupidest thing I'd ever done, but I had to make sure she knew where I stood.

I took a deep breath. "I just want you to know that I'll be here for you. Always. Whatever you end up doing. And I'd never be upset with you if you felt like you needed to go try new things. You know? If you needed to go explore the world…without me."

She frowned, staring at me like I was crazy. But then a huge grin broke out across her face.

"Are you crazy?" she said. "Do you know how happy you make me? There's no one in the whole world I'd rather discover new things with than you, Penn Kimball!"

Relief and joy washed over me, and I leaned across the table, kissing her hard on the mouth. Sure, we were in front of everyone, but let them stare.

Ella was mine. Not my pet. Not something to own. She was mine to love. And I didn't care who knew it.

# Acknowledgments

It seems my thanks must always begin at the place where my stories are born: the coffee shop. So, thank you to all the wonderful people at Sugar House Coffee for making me cups full of iced coffee and plates full of hummus and vegetables so that I could fill these pages with words.

Thank you to Dan Beecher, writing partner extraordinaire. Could I even write a book without you anymore? Thank you for brainstorming with me, for pressing me to find the most interesting version of this story, and for letting all the other projects get pushed to the back burner so this book could come to life.

Thank you to my agent, Kerry Sparks, for your continued support and dedication.

To all the people at Entangled: Curtis Svehlak and Fiona Jayde, thank you for helping me bring Ella's story to completion and for giving me a beautiful cover to house it in. And, of course, the fabulous Liz Pelletier for giving me a home at Entangled!

To Heather Howland, my most brilliant editor, thank you for knowing how to cut through all my mess to find the true story inside. Your persistence, your vision, and your direction have been invaluable. Thank you for caring about Ella's story from the very beginning. Thank you for seeing the badass inside us both this whole time. I guess it takes one to know one.

Thank you to my mom, my original, powerful female lead, for embodying feminism. Because of you, it never even occurred to me that a woman couldn't be anything she wanted.

Most of all, thank you to my family. Thank you to Morgan, Noah, and Rebecca for growing up to be remarkable people (despite my mothering). You all give me hope for the future.

And finally, thank you to my Bry Guy. You've been a cheerleader, a masseur, a chef, a housekeeper (I could go on and on), and all with a positive attitude and a smile, and I appreciate every bit of it. Thank you for being the rock that anchors me. I couldn't do this without you.

*Check out these exciting reads from Entangled Teen!*

# FREQUENCY
## BY CHRISTOPHER KROVATIN

Five years ago, Fiona was just a kid. But everything changed the night the Pit Viper came to town. Sure, he rid the quiet, idyllic suburb of Hamm of its darkest problems. But Fiona witnessed something much, much worse from Hamm's adults when they drove him away.

And now, the Pit Viper is back.

Fiona's not just a kid anymore. She can handle the darkness she sees in the Pit Viper, a DJ whose wicked tattoos, quiet anger, and hypnotic music seem to speak to every teen in town…except her. She can handle watching as each of her friends seems to be overcome, nearly possessed by the music. She can even handle her unnerving suspicion that the DJ is hell-bent on revenge.

But she's not sure she can handle falling in love with him.

# ZOMBIE ABBEY
## BY LAUREN BARATZ-LOGSTED

1920, England

And the three teenage Clarke sisters thought what they'd wear to dinner was their biggest problem…

Lady Kate, the entitled eldest.

Lady Grace, lost in the middle and wishing she were braver.

Lady Lizzy, so endlessly sunny, it's easy to underestimate her.

Then there's Will Harvey, the proud, to-die-for—and possibly die with!—stable boy; Daniel Murray, the resourceful second footman with a secret; Raymond Allen, the unfortunate-looking young duke; and Fanny Rogers, the unsinkable kitchen maid.

Upstairs! Downstairs! Toss in some farmers and villagers!

None of them ever expected to work together for any reason.

But none of them had ever seen anything like this.

# True Storm
## by L.E. Sterling

Lucy's twin sister, Margot, may be safely back with her—but all is not well in Plague-ravaged Dominion City. The Watchers have come out of hiding, spreading chaos and death throughout the city, and suddenly Lucy finds herself torn between three men with secrets of their own.

Betrayal is a cruel lesson, and the Fox sisters can hardly believe who is behind the plot against them. To survive this deadly game of politics, Lucy is manipulated to agree to a marriage of convenience. But DNA isn't the only thing they want from Lucy...or her sister.

As they say in Dominion, rogue genes can never have a happy ending...

# Alpha
## by Jus Accardo

Sera is the obsession of a killer chasing a ghost.

G is a soldier with too much blood on his hands.

Dylan lost the only person he ever loved—and will stop at nothing to get her back.

In a whirlwind chase that takes them back to where it all started, Sera, G, and Dylan will have to confront their demons—both physical and mental—and each other, in order to win their freedom.

# 27 Hours
## by Tristina Wright

Rumor Mora fears two things: hellhounds too strong for him to kill, and failure. Jude Welton has two dreams: for humans to stop killing monsters, and for his strange abilities to vanish.

But in no reality should a boy raised to love monsters fall for a boy raised to kill them.

During one twenty-seven-hour night, if they can't stop the war between the colonies and the monsters from becoming a war of extinction, the things they wish for will never come true, and the things they fear will be all that's left.

# Lies that Bind
## by Diana Rodriguez Wallach

What do you do when you learn your entire childhood was a lie?

Reeling from the truths uncovered while searching for her sister in Italy, Anastasia Phoenix is ready to call it quits with spies. The only way to stop being a pawn in their game is to remove herself from the board. But before she can leave her parents' crimes behind her, tragedy strikes. No one is safe, not while Department D still exists.

Now, with help from her friends, Anastasia embarks on a dangerous plan to bring down an entire criminal empire. From a fire-filled festival in England to a lavish wedding in Rio de Janeiro, Anastasia is determined to confront the enemies who want to destroy her family. But even Marcus, the handsome bad boy who's been there for her at every step, is connected to the deadly spy network. And the more she learns about Department D, the more she realizes the true danger might be coming from someone closer than she expects…

an imprint of Entangled Publishing LLC